The Rage of Reading

Book Three of Rage MC

Elizabeth N. Harris

*Congratulations Emma,
all the best
Elizabeth
x*

ISBN: 9781653692613

This is a work of fiction. Names, characters, businesses, places, events, and incidents are either the product of the authors' imagination or used in a fictitious manner. Any resemblance to actual persons, living or dead, or actual events is purely coincidental.

This book was written, produced and edited in England, the United Kingdom, where some spelling, grammar and word usage will vary from US English.

Elizabeth N Harris
The Rage of Reading.
Book Three of Rage MC.

© 2020 Elizabeth N. Harris

Elizabethnharris74@outlook.com

ALL RIGHTS RESERVED. This book contains material protected under International and Federal Copyright Laws and Treaties. Any unauthorized reprint or use of this material is prohibited. No part of this book may be reproduced or transmitted in any form or by any means, electronic or mechanical, including photocopying, recording, or by any informational storage and retrieval system without express written permission from the author/publisher.

Cover courtesy of Wix.com

Books by Elizabeth N. Harris

Rage MC series.

Rage of the Phoenix.
The Hunters Rage.
The Rage of Reading.

Love Beyond Death series.

Oakwood Manor.
Courtenay House.

The Rage of Reading

She was everything people avoided. Shy, socially awkward, terrified of her own shadow and far too happy in her own company. Grieving and heartbroken, she struggles to create a new life for herself. One that didn't include looking for love.

He was a prospect, not a full brother, but he was interested and in more than one night. Then another brother tells him to lay claim or he will. If a brother lays claim to her it's done and dusted, finished. He didn't have the full rights of a brother. She was skittish and so beautiful, it hurt him. How does he lock her down, when a brother also wants her? Will she let him into that place she cherishes and keeps behind walls?

Then fate blows everything wide open, and suddenly he has a past he didn't know about. Would the woman he loves, stay by his side, or will it finally be too much for her? Has he bound her tight enough to him or will she leave and find love elsewhere?

Chapters

DEDICATION. 6

AUTHORS FOREWORD. 7

PROLOGUE. 8

CHAPTER ONE 12

CHAPTER TWO 35

CHAPTER THREE 54

CHAPTER FOUR. 81

CHAPTER FIVE. 105

CHAPTER SIX 131

CHAPTER SEVEN. 158

CHAPTER EIGHT. 179

CHAPTER NINE. 208

CHAPTER TEN. 230

EPILOGUE. 247

THE RAGE OF READING CHARACTERS. 254

BYWORD. 263

Dedication.

To

Michael, Jordie, Connor, Jack and Alex.

Love Mum.

Shaun, who was there when the night was the darkest. To the Readers who love to live in a different world for a while.

Love Elizabeth.

Elizabethnharris.net
Elizabethnharris74@outlook.com

Authors Foreword.

The Elizabethan era has always been a favourite of mine. The dresses, the court characters, the impact on history made for a stunning time period. The characters in this book from the Elizabethan court didn't exist and were figments of my imagination. The only historical figure mentioned is obviously the famous Queen Elizabeth herself!

The Hellfire Club, the Order of the Knights of St Francis did exist! Many serious breaches of society rules were linked to these rich and powerful figures. The Hellfire Club was connected with devil worship, drunkenness, orgies and many other infamous scandals. No one really knows for sure who the members were, we just know they were the wealthy aristocracy. While some names are most certainly members, many were shrouded in mystery.

Lord Montague is a character made up for the Rage of Reading, and the character is not a real person. Nor is there evidence that there was a hierarchy to the Hellfire Club.

Elizabeth.

Prologue.

"Amos Montgomery died," Phoe said, walking up to Drake and wrapping her arms around him.

"Who baby?" Drake rumbled looking confused.

"Amos Montgomery. Amos ran the old bookshop down the road."

"Monty, you mean?"

"Yeah, he's not even that old, Drake. Only fifty-five."

"Christ, how he die?" Drake sounded shocked.

"Heart attack from what Marsha heard. Amos was too young, his son is coming to organise the funeral and will probably to sell the shop."

"Shame that, some stuck-up fucker will probably buy it," Drake frowned, he liked their area as it was. There'd been a couple of high-class shops move in, and their owners stuck their noses up in the air. One, a designer clothes store managed to upset Drake's wife.

Phoe had entered the shop wearing a Harley tee, and jeans. The owner looked down her snotty nose at her and snobbily suggested Phoe shop at the Rage Store or Target. Phoe had been struck dumb and then introduced herself. Phoe told the stuck-up bitch, she and her entire team at HQ would boycott the clothing store. The store remained still there four months on but judging by the number of 'reduced now' sales she was holding, the business struggled.

"We'll see," Phoe mumbled.

I stood looking at the people who'd gathered around Dad's grave, amazed at how many turned out to pay their respects. A tear trickled down my cheek, and I wiped it away, it was too hard to believe Dad was gone. He was only fifty-five!

The priest droned on, and I glanced in his direction. The priest was entirely in his element, even though he hadn't known my father. With a struggle to contain my sobs, I looked away and glanced at the crowd, none of them familiar. These were other shop owners and strangely an MC, and ten to twenty further strangers.

Some of those present were customers, others I guessed acquaintances, none were our family. Dad and I cut our family off years ago, and I'd no idea where any of them were. A few of the people here were honestly distressed, which surprised me considering Dad kept to himself.

In keeping with tradition, I'd organised a wake at Dad's local bar Hell's Rage. The shop would have been too small. The shop was now mine, Dad signed it over a year ago, knowing his heart had begun to fail. Worried, I'd organised book-keeping for Dad and an assistant, made it so Dad could stay in his beloved store without stress.

With a shaking hand, I wiped away another tear. Dad lived an extra ten years despite being told he only had a couple of years. The diagnosis had been poor and had shaken my teenaged world. I had been just thirteen when Dad was diagnosed, doctors gave Dad two years, he fought and won ten. Without Dad, I was lost, he'd insisted that I live my life instead of staying home and looking after him.

I'd gone to college at thirteen, a few months after the prognosis, a child prodigy. I graduated early from High School and then graduated from college early and gone to university. At fifteen which I'd attended Oxford in England. Four years later, at the tender age of nineteen when my schooling ended, I'd earned my qualifications.

Hard work meant I'd a Bachelor of Arts in Literature, Classics and Heritage Studies, I'd also received a BA in Business Management, Finance Management and Computer Processing. Working hard-gained me three Master Degrees' in Literacy, Ancient History and the Classics. Finally, I'd PhDs' in Ancient Art, PhD in Fine Art and a final PhD in Archaeology.

So yeah, Dad had let me live the life I wanted and encouraged me to stay at college and university. The hardest thing I'd ever done was leaving him to go to England, but Dad had studied at Oxford, and I'd wanted to honour him. Oxford had been incredible, and I'd fallen in love with England but hurried home as soon as I graduated to be near Dad.

Except Dad had not let me move home but presented me with an apartment in Pierre a couple of hours away. Luckily, my qualifications allowed me to find a job working in a museum, happily researching and working in the archives, and the responsibility for authenticating items. Being shy and prone to avoiding crowds, the job became a lifeline I excelled at. So while I was happy people had come for Dad, I was worried about how to interact with them.

Dad and I were close, but he kept his private life private. And I'd not met any of the people here, I was surprised to see an MC paying their respects, to say the least. I looked down at my hands aware I'd been twisting them frantically and saw I'd shredded the handkerchief I'd been holding. Luckily the white rose I'd brought Dad remained intact.

The priest finally stopped droning on, and people began passing me, not realising I was his daughter and throwing handfuls of dirt on the box. I walked past them and stood looking down at the coffin that held my world. Heartbroken, I bit back a sob and crouched. Gently, I threw the rose on it and then straightened in my heels and walked back to the car. At twenty-two and an orphan, I was alone.

Chapter One.

March 2015.

In college and university, I'd not been one to party or drink, and I'd never visited a bar. Dad frequented Hell's Rage after he shut the shop and had his daily tipple there, he often spoke about the place, its owners, and crazy women folk. Dad liked the bikers a bunch load even though I imagined that Dad kept his usual distance from people, I'd learnt that from him.

I stared at the bar and twisted my hands again, I'd organised the wake to be here, but I'd prefer to be in the bookshop. That couldn't happen, it didn't have the room for so many people, I was obligated to show my face in Hells Rage. Reluctantly getting out of my car, I noticed the sign that said closed for a wake and pushed open the door. The bar wasn't what I expected, bare bricks walls with neon signs and lots of pictures, a few posters and a large stained mirror. Wooden chairs surrounded round and square tables and the wooden floor scuffed, but it was spotless.

Two walls contained booths, and a wooden carved bar (two men and a girl behind it serving) took up the opposite side. In front of the enormous glass window sat a long table full of food. Many people sat or stood around with plates of food. Unsure who to approach, I walked to the bar and ordered a diet coke. A tall guy fetched my order, wearing a leather waistcoat with badges on it.

The badges said prospect above his left breast, under that, a second patch saying 'Jett' and on the right was what I assumed to be the club's patch. Shamefully, I was ignorant around MCs' even though I'd loved Sons of Anarchy, but I imagined most of that was rubbish. Jett as I assumed the guy's name was, turned his back to me. And I saw in a beautiful script the words, 'Rage MC' at the top and a far bigger design of the patch. At the bottom of the patch were words, 'Live to Ride.' At the bottom of the waistcoat is said Rapid City, it was super cool.

Deliberately avoiding eye contact, I picked up the drink and wandered in the direction of the food. After I filled a plate with sandwiches and nibbles, I looked for an empty table, spying one in the middle, I walked over to it. A few women stopped and smiled warmly as I passed them, I returned a small smile and sat down on my own.

Half-heartedly I picked at the plate listening to conversations around me. Most spoke of memories of my dad, and I listened intently. Others were just random various tales of Dad helping them with books or research and some of him drinking in this very bar. An annoyed rumble made my head in its direction.

A tall, good-looking man with black hair beginning to grey at the temples spoke to a stunning woman, and he looked annoyed. He wore a waistcoat similar to the one Jett had, but his patch said, President.

"It's fuckin' rude babe," the biker growled.

"Drake," she shushed.

"Nah babe, it's fuckin' rude and wrong. Monty's son organises the funeral and wake and then don't turn up? Fucker wants an ass-kicking." I looked puzzled. Monty son? Monty meaning my dad no doubt, but what son?

"Something might have happened," the woman whispered.

"And no call? Drake's right, it's fuckin' out of line. Not to turn up for your own father's funeral," a Native American guy said just as irately. Not turn up? But I was here, except I wasn't a son! I coughed and pushed the plate to one side and stood up. The next words stopped me in my stead.

"It's disgustin'. Kid's never visited his father, no one even guessed Monty had a kid. Poor fucker went to his grave alone." A flush started at my cheeks. That little spark of anger I often held back, lit inside of me.

"Excuse me, I don't think you knew Monty well enough to pass judgement. Certainly not on either of us," I snapped at them and received surprised looks.

Not bothering to wait for a reply, I stormed past another surprised man, this one, the one from the bar. Nearly in tears, I pulled Dad's keys from my pocket and headed down the street to the shop. Blearily inserting the key and unlocking the store, I turned the handle and let myself into the shop.

Quietly I entered the alarm code and shut the door. Taking a deep breath, I drew in the scent that remained my father's legacy. Musty books and caffeine, the smell was so familiar. Dad's mug sat on the wooden counter, and I ran my fingers down it, making a trail in the light covering of dust.

Tears welled up, and I blinked them back as I saw Dad's grey cardigan hanging on a wooden stool behind the counter. I walked around the counter and picked the cardigan up and held it to my nose, my nostrils filled with the scent of Old Spice. Tears fell freely now and walking to a battered leather armchair, I curled up, holding Dad's cardigan and crying freely.

I was so upset I didn't hear the door open and close, nor did I hear booted footsteps come towards me. Someone picked me up, and I stiffened in shock and opened my eyes and peeked over the top of the cardigan. It was the guy from the bar, Jett. He sat his ass in the chair and pulled me into his lap, and one hand gently pulled my head towards his shoulder.

"Let it out," Jett whispered, I lifted Dad's cardigan and pulled it back to my face and sobbed.

Deep down I'd been burying the pain of Dad's death, arranging stuff and organising the funeral and wake and not dealing with the fact Dad finally died. That, I was alone in the world. Jett sat there and let me cry, one hand wrapped around my waist, holding me tight and the other gently stroking my hair.

Finally, I sniffed and took a deep breath and looked up. Jett was gorgeous, I noted vaguely, I wiped my eyes and sniffed again, calm dark brown eyes looked down at me.

"Sorry."

"You knew Monty well."

"Of course I did, he's my dad," I told Jett indignantly. Jett looked surprised.

"Heard he'd a son but not a daughter, where's your brother?" Jett asked.

"I don't have a brother, it's just Dad and me." Jett's eyes blinked as he struggled with something.

"Monty has a son sweetheart," Jett mumbled as if he didn't want to upset me further. "Called Sinclair." For the first time today and possibly since Dad's death, I gave a giggle.

"I'm Sin."

"Not gonna deny sweetheart you certainly look like sin, but you've a brother called Sinclair." I shook my head at Jett.

"No, I'm Sinclair Montgomery. Sinclair was Mom's maiden name, and she was determined boy or girl that I'd be called Sinclair. Most people call me Sin." Jett looked surprised again, and his eyes studied me.

"No, wonder you were pissed at the bar," Jett murmured, and I nodded.

"I'd never miss Dad's funeral, and we were close, we saw each other twice a week, phoned every day. Dad came to Pierre or I came to his house here, Dad enjoyed keeping things separate. He hated socialising with people, I didn't get to meet the other shop owners, with whom Dad shared a row of shops. In truth, we didn't mix too well with people." I felt the need to explain, defend myself.

"Don't need to explain," Jett rumbled.

"Clearly, I do. Everyone back there thinks I deserted Dad, I'd never do that, not even when Dad sent me to England to study. I didn't want to go, but Dad attended Oxford and wanted me to follow in his footsteps.

When I came back, Dad insisted he wanted me to be independent, but I wanted to come home. He bought an apartment in Pierre for me, as a compromise, I really wanted to come home," Sadness coloured my voice.

Jett's arms tightened around me, and tears choked me again.

"I know why Dad didn't want me to come home, home. Dad understood he didn't have long, they told him two years, and he outlasted the estimate by eight more years. Dad wanted me to build a circle, a network of support around me, but I couldn't. People can't relate to me, they think I am standoffish, rude and priggish, but I'm not," I broke off, and Jett stared at me. I was rambling, I knew it, but I was so nervous I couldn't stop.

"I'm shy, and get nervous easily, being a child prodigy, I missed most of the nuances of social niceties that came with growing up. Most of the time, I spent studying with my nose in a book. I'd never been to a bar until today, I was uncertain how to act." Tears fell down my face as I told this handsome guy all my shit.

"Sin," Jett whispered.

"I didn't know anyone at Dad's wake, I tried to be friendly but wasn't sure how. And then that man Drake said nasty stuff, and it wasn't true and…" A sob escaped me. Jett's arm tightened again. "I miss my dad," I wailed. Jett tucked my head back into his shoulder as I wept again. Jett held me tight as I sobbed for a full ten minutes.

Finally, I stopped with a huge breath and rubbed my fists into my eyes. Jett's brown eyes studied me, and he gave me a half-smile which made my eyes widen.

"Oh god, what must you think of me?" I exclaimed. "I don't even know your name, and I'm dumping everything on your lap."

"Alexander Cutter. The MC calls me Jett."

"I like that. Jett, it's cool, MC'ish," Jett grinned at me full on this time, and I was mesmerised.

"Thanks, sweetheart."

"What does prospect mean? I watched Sons of Anarchy." Yeah, the rambling continued, I was so far out of my comfort zone, it wasn't funny.

"Prospect means I'm a brother in trainin' basically. Get the shit jobs until I make full brother."

"Shit jobs? Is the MC like Sons of Anarchy?"

"Shit jobs, cleanin' up the clubhouse, includin' puke, doing food runs, doing runs other brothers don't want to do. Lookin' out for old ladies, they're a handful."

"Drugs? Guns?" I asked thinking back to Sons of Anarchy. Jett shook his head.

"Don't touch the club. Drake keeps Rage clean, keep the streets around here, clean and safe." In my muddled mind, I didn't pick up on what Jett said, which basically admitted they were vigilantes.

"You'd best be getting back. They'll wonder where you are." I wouldn't lie, I'd no idea what to do in this situation, and it grew uncomfortable. The door opened, and then booted feet clanked on the wooden floor. I lifted my tear-stained face and saw Drake and the Native American standing in front of me.

"Meet Sinclair Montgomery," Jett blurted at the curious looks on the two men's' faces. Drake blanched as his words came back to bite him, and the Native American looked shamefaced.

"Sinclair?" Drake rumbled.

"Yes, I'm Sinclair. As you can see, I attended Dad's funeral," I whispered nestling deeper into Jett. More than a little afraid of the huge men standing in front of me.

"Thought you were a man," Drake said.

"Guessed that." I nodded, and another tear fell down my cheek. Drake's gaze took in my tear-stained red face, the death grip on Dad's cardigan and how I was snuggled up in Jett's arms.

"Apologies. Assumed Sinclair meant a son, didn't know to look for a daughter," the Native American said.

"Yeah, I guessed that too," I mumbled my nose buried in dad's cardigan.

"We've not seen you around," Drake said pointedly.

"Nope. Dad kept things separate, he understood I don't do well in social circles. We spoke to each other on the phone every day, and twice a week, Dad visited my apartment for dinner. We liked things separate," I repeated what I'd told Jett again feeling the need to explain, to not be judged.

"You anti-social?" Drake asked.

"Not so much anti-social but shy and nervous, and I lack social niceties and subtleties. Dad understood I preferred it to be just us," I explained again. Stop explaining! I owed Rage nothing! Drake's eyes narrowed in sympathy.

"Didn't know Monty well. Decent fella from what I saw, he'll be missed, Sinclair."

"Want to come back to the bar? Can introduce you to people," Jett asked me. I shook my head.

"No, I want to be alone with Dad," I said. The Native Americans eyes now also narrowed on me.

"No one should be alone to grieve," he said kindly. I didn't know how to refuse the kindness and insist on being alone. Luckily, Jett sensed my difficulties.

"Apache. Sin wants to be alone," Jett said firmly. Apache looked at Jett and gave a curt nod.

"Leave you be," Drake said and tilted his head at Jett. Jett shifted me in his arms and then with a heave, lifted me and himself out of the chair. He gently placed me on my feet and cupped my face.

"We'll give you alone time Sin. If you need us, you can find us down at the bar, or in the clubhouse or Rage garage. Don't hesitate, if you don't see us just ask anyone behind the bar or on the forecourt for one of us. We'll come, I promise," Jett said, gently looking into my eyes.

I gave Jett a nod still clutching Dad's cardigan, and the three men left the shop. I scurried behind them, locked the door and returned to the armchair and began crying all over again.

Two days later, I sat in the shop's darkness and away from the dingy window in a corner where no one could see me. I'd been going through the shop books that the accountant had dropped off, they weren't dire, but definitely not great. Most of Dad's money came from selling manuscripts and rare books.

The actual book sales were down, which was to be expected in today's era. Online reading replaced the paperback at such a fast rate it was scary. I sat back with a sigh. Long ago I'd had an idea that would have upped sales and kept the bookshop well into the black, but Dad rejected it.

There were two choices open to me, I could sell off the stock and sell the shop. The rare books in stock would make a small fortune at auction. The Reading Nook had no loan or mortgage, I owned the shop outright. The other option was the one I'd floated to Dad when I returned from England and make that work. Yes, I'd choices but no idea what to do, I looked at Dad's cardigan, which lay folded up on the table next to me.

Dad loved this shop, he'd owned it thirty years. He'd bought it with a small inheritance from my grandfather and then made it into a roaring business. Dad met Mom here, and I'd been born in this very shop. Mom being ornery, went into labour right in this shop.

The idea of selling the Reading Nook made me sick, but things had to change to make it more lucrative. Dad's contacts for rare books were reliable, and I'd my own from England and the museum. I could keep up the rare book trade with ease. Although Dad and I had eschewed social contact, we were well known in our fields.

So yes, the rare book business could easily be kept going, the bookstore was a different matter. I frowned at a knock on the door, and I glanced up, and to my amazement, I saw Reid standing there. Flying to the door, I opened it and jumped into Reid's arms, they folded around me with familiar comfort, and Reid tucked me close to his leanly muscled body.

"Oh god babe, I came as soon as I heard," Reid muttered, dropping his chin to the top of my head. My arms snaked around him, and I burrowed into his body.

"Reid," I whispered tears beginning to fall.

"Christ babe. Why didn't you call me?" Reid whispered his arms tightening.

"It was too far, you were in England, and your job…"

"Fuck the job. Museum fired me the minute I said I needed emergency leave to come here," Reid grunted.

"Oh no, Reid," I exclaimed in horror, "I'm so sorry, you shouldn't have come!"

"Of course, I'd come, you're all I have. Just took a few days to pack my shit up and have it shipped here. Your phone's been off baby girl, how many times do I need to remind you to charge it?" Reid muttered. I clung to him, crying now for Dad and for him. To say I was sick of crying was an understatement, I'd never been one for tears, Dad's death had rocked my foundation. Touched that Reid's loyalty had no bounds, I couldn't control the tears.

"Can't believe that the museum fired you," I sobbed.

"They were assholes to work for baby, have no doubt I'd begun looking for another job. Let's take this inside Sin, we're making a scene," Reid's English accent clipped. I raised my head and saw several feet away Drake standing with a woman and Jett. I allowed Reid to shove me gently into the store. He kicked the door shut and held me while I cried in his arms.

"So babe, what we going to do here and with this?" Reid asked twenty minutes later after I'd stopped crying and told him about the finances.

"Huh?" I asked, surprised.

"I'm all you have left, I'm not leaving, I've dual citizenship, so no barriers to me staying. So we'll turn Dad's business around baby," Reid grinned.

"You will stay?"

"Did you miss the part where I said it took a few days to pack my shit up and have it shipped?" Reid asked a teasing note in his voice.

"Yeah, I thought I was alone," I replied softly. Reid shook his head at me.

"You'll never be freaking alone," Reid cursed.

"You're giving up everything to come here."

"Don't be daft, you know I'm going to stay. So stop moping and put a plan together for us to make a living," Reid said firmly.

"I sort of got a plan."

"Talk to me, sweet girl."

"I spoke to Dad about buying the store next door and knocking the walls down between them. Then putting in a coffee counter and a pastry and sandwich counter in, possibly serving hot snacks, chilli, jacket potatoes. Upstairs can be changed around, creating study booths with computer desks."

"You can't make this an internet café," Reid denied shaking his head. "That will ruin the atmosphere here."

"No, not an internet café. Upstairs has wooden panels same as here, it's just been left empty, I thought about creating a library atmosphere. Kids in local colleges and universities often struggle for books. If we convert the upstairs to a library atmosphere and include books the students struggle to get at their college/university libraries, we'll get customers.

If we include several study nooks with computers and some desks like the Bodleian, it can work for us. Shift the bookcases around down here and keep the panelling and set up seating areas amongst the shelves strategically placed, will increase book sales. Keep the upper level of the new store as a storeroom."

Reid grabbed my hand and dragged me out of the shop and dragged me to look next door. Together we peered through the dirty glass, and Reid gave a sharp nod.

"The shop is one and a half times bigger than the Reading Nook. I can buy this Sin, and we can do it together," Reid put a hand up in my face. "If not, you buy this, and I'll work for you as a manager or something," Reid snapped his mouth shut. I looked at him.

"You're all I have left Reid. I believed I was alone in the world as you were in England," I said in a small, sad voice. Anger crossed Reid's face as I repeated my words and he reaffirmed the point he'd made earlier.

"The only thing that stopped me moving out here sooner was the fact Dad was here, and I was selling my house anyway this year. I'll never, ever let you be alone sweet girl," Reid growled. I reached up and touched his face gently and then carried on with my plan, not knowing what to say, considering Reid's raw emotion. Emotion always made me awkward.

"We can expand the rare book and manuscript sales, maybe you can take the lead in that. Both of us have experience and outstanding reputations. We need to hire a shop manager and staff, devise a layout plan and get an architect." I bit my lip suddenly overwhelmed at what lay in front of us.

"Got to learn to lean on me Sin, I leant on you enough. Years ago, I told you, you're stuck with me, I meant it," Reid swore holding my hand, I clenched his tight.

"This is a massive undertaking."

"Yeah but together we can do it. The question is Sin, do you want my buy-in or my working for you? I'm happy either way." My darling Reid, always happy to take a backseat to my needs. I wondered when the last time was that I'd told him I loved him.

"Together, Dad would have liked that." No doubt in my mind Dad would have been overjoyed at Reid and I working together. I'd expected to be alone here, never expected Reid to drop everything and come. Reid's job had been demanding, working at a well-known Museum in London. Drop everything, he had, and at the cost of his career, I was deeply touched.

We'd met at Oxford, both of us studying much the same courses except Reid had also gone into archaeology. We'd studied together, two lost souls although Reid was four years older than me. I'd seen Reid through relationship drama after relationship drama, good times and bad and he'd been there for the shy, reserved girl I'd been. Friendship became family.

Reid had a tragic family life, his parents, content to be blue-collar workers, hadn't understood the brilliance of their son. Reid's brothers followed their father into working in construction, so a son wanting to go to university and study archaeology caused upset. The family cut Reid off and out of their lives.

Reid had several papers published, and he'd been working on a book the last time we'd spoken. I'd given Reid all the pent-up love and encouragement I'd buried within me. Dad approved of the young English man who was out of his depth and spent a lot of time with Reid.

Dad loved Reid like a son and always made time to speak to Reid once a week through Skype. Reid had taken to Dad like a trooper, he'd loved Dad, so I knew Reid was dealing with his own grief. Reid's face looked slightly ravaged, and his skin had a slight pallor to it. I knew he too, was grief-stricken, but nothing mattered to Reid but me and the plans.

"Need to make some calls," Reid said finally into the silence that fell between us. I nodded. "I've got money, I'll buy that shop, we'll work this together, I have more diverse contacts in England, and you have them here."

"Yeah, we'll get things started, an architect first. Then builders," I nodded in agreement.

"Estate agent first! I need to buy myself a shop," Reid laughed, and I poked him with my finger. Reid snapped his teeth at me, and for the first time since Dad's death, I felt better, not alone, not lost. I had someone, and I'd plans. What Reid had done, leaving England and everything behind meant the world to me, I just had to show him.

Three months later, Reid and I stood in the newly refurbished and finished Reading Nook. We'd kept the name of the shop, to honour Dad. I looked towards the front of the store, the original part, in the window the lead gleamed darkly against the bright bevelled glass. Dad had a whimsical side and had a bay window installed many years ago with the leaded glass windows often seen in Victorian England. The window resembled something from a Dickens scene.

The window took up three-quarters of the original shop front, the door had been removed, and Reid and I had a second narrow bevelled window installed. Our builder had put in a third sizeable bevelled window in the new part of the shop. A lot more light now streamed into the shop, which was fantastic as I was aiming for a well-lit cosy atmosphere.

In front of the original bay window was a large muddy brown leather sofa that could seat three with a matching sofa opposite. There were two cream leather reclining armchairs at either end of the sofas boxing in an ornate iron and glass coffee table. Behind the other sofa was a large wooden bookcase with romance books. Against the far wall was a further bookcase filled with thrillers.

The layout had changed completely. Knocking down the wall between the two shops had given us an extensive floor area. The free-standing bookcases had been saved, and we moved them around and done as I suggested, designed little seating areas hidden amongst them. The bookshelves had been restored, and their wood shone brightly in the lights of the stop.

Two-thirds of the new shop had been given over to books. The remainder formed the café idea for the shop, it also held the new entrance to the Reading Nook. Dad's wooden counter was a few feet from the new door, with a modern cash register, although it was styled old fashioned. Reid found it online and fallen in love with the damn thing, it was hard to use! Next to that, hidden discreetly behind a panel was a laptop with an updated registry of the books the Reading Nook stocked.

Behind that, near the wall was a pastry counter and a serving refrigerator. Reid hired a lady who loved to bake and cook. Penny was a gem and helped design the kitchen to be what she needed. There was plenty of room to cook things like chilli and soups and bake pastries and cakes. Penny planned to make snack items, pork pies, sausage rolls, burritos, and so on.

Ten small round wooden tables which seated two or four people were in front of the counters and backed onto a half wall full of books. A customer could gaze into the main bookshop without craning their necks.

Next to the chilled refrigerator was a second counter, this one for hot goods. There were four hotplates and a microwave behind it. The hotplates would hold foods such as soup and chilli. The back of the new shop had been sectioned off into a galley kitchen that as I said, Penny helped design. Penny loved the chance of creating her own workspace and was in heaven

Reid also hired two shop girls and a young man. Andy was a technical wiz and would be on hand for any issues arising with the twenty computers we'd set up. He'd used internet cafes himself and helped us set a reasonable charge for usage. Andy also helped set up advertising for the shop and its new study areas.

To my relief, Andy blocked the naughty sites that could be viewed. He also set up links to the local colleges and universities. This caused me a headache, and so Reid had taken it over.

The two young girls would operate the cash register and fill the shelves and help with customer queries. Obviously, there hadn't been enough free-standing bookcases nor enough bookcases to fill the new walls we'd opened up. Reid hired a carpenter to install new shelves that matched the design of the old.

A secure restoration area had been designed and built-in half of the basement of the store for the rare manuscripts we'd hold and sell. There were display cabinets with alarms attached to them for valuable works of literacy, dotted around the floor. Bookcases lined the walls with books on history, research and so on. The majority of valuable works would be kept in what we called the Vault. There were further seating areas with dimmed lights, but the basement was mainly about the Vault. The Vault was essential to our business.

All in all, modernising but keeping the originality the three levels of Reading Nook boasted, had been hard, sweaty work. The result was fantastic, and I hoped beyond hope that this would work out for Reid and myself. Dedicated to the shop, I'd quit my job two weeks after we'd decided to do what we discussed.

I'd been scouring auctions and sales and store closures for rare works of literacy and been quite successful. In fact, Reid made me stop four weeks ago as I'd been so successful, but our name was out there now. More than it had been and then Reid went on his own spending spree!

Dad bless him left a substantial life insurance policy, and I'd money from Mom, which I'd never touched. Reid's cash from the sale of his house in England and his own savings he'd squirrelled away meant we were in a comfortable position. And we'd no loans or mortgages against the shop. The decision had been made to sell my apartment, and I was amazed at the price it fetched. Reid and I were both living in Dad's house.

Dad had looked after my future, I just hope he approved of what Reid and I were attempting to do. Andy contacted the local colleges and universities and got lists of the books that often had a waiting list and stocked them upstairs.

Upstairs now greatly resembled the Bodleian Library in Oxford, dark plush wood, low lighting, green table lamps, reading nooks, study tables. And of course, more bookshelves. The study tables nestled in between them, giving privacy to the customers. It was a beautiful and relaxing area and gave me no end of nostalgia.

Reid and I spent a fortune on getting our vision right. While it severely dented our available money, we weren't on the breadline. Internet sales kicked off six weeks ago and were building up steadily. Offering a loyalty card and anything from next day delivery to a three-day delivery slot meant our business built up slowly but nicely.

Andy had the website up and running within a week. All of us had taken an inventory of the stores' books and entered them into easily clicked on pages each covering a section. The directory had pages for genres from romance to motor cars, history to fantasy and autobiographies to language. Every subject we could think of was covered, and if we could think of it, we made sure we stocked books in it.

Some I guessed wouldn't sell well, and other genres would sell better. So we'd monitor sales and condense or expand sections as need be. I wandered around the floors with Reid pointing out snags to the builder who'd joined us, there wasn't many thankfully.

Security cameras were installed, although I thought Reid paranoid. Reid purchased thin security strips that covered the barcodes on the books and could be deactivated and peeled off at the cash register.

I'd disagreed with Reid, but he'd insisted on discreet security barriers being installed. Stock in the Vault was valuable and therefore, could be likely to be stolen. I'd let Reid have his own way, and the three women and I, spent two weeks security tagging every single book in the store. It had taken ages but had been worth it when Reid tested several times the anti-theft device.

Reid remained looking for a manager, we hadn't found one that fitted with the Reading Nook. Several had been interviewed, but I'd refused them on a variety of reasons. The rudest was a guy who'd asked when the refurbishment was planned to start. Clearly, he wasn't a fit. Another began telling us how to run our business, and while we wanted someone for that, we didn't need her to challenge every decision. So yeah, we were still searching.

The new, improved Reading Nook was due to open within a week, and I was antsy. Reid being the public face of the store, happily meant I was left to do what I did best. Find old stuff and value it and then buy or sell as I determined. I'd found real bargains, a set of first edition Dickens books, a first edition of Jane Eyre rarely signed by Charlotte Bronte. A well-kept first edition of Yeats and several other items.

These had been entered onto the website but not yet published to the public. Reid and I'd discussed holding rare book auctions, and he was looking into that field. He had to check if we needed further legislation or licences, I was excited at the thought of it.

Reid bought several manuscripts from England that come up for sale and been undervalued. He knew instantly they'd sell for a higher figure and he'd gone Kung Ho and bought them. I trusted him, Reid knew as much as I did, he'd had several exceedingly rare finds and was lucky in their pricing.

A knock at the shop door echoed, as we came down the spiral wooden staircase with its iron bannister. I glanced over to the door and saw the figure standing outside, hurrying over to it, I unlocked the door and faced Jett. He gave me a slight smile.

"Oh hi Jett, I'm sorry we aren't open yet," I told him softly, growing awkward. I hadn't spoken to Jett since my collapse in his lap and the floods of tears I'd shed.

"Not lookin' to buy honey, just wondered how you are. Not seen much of you around and saw you and your boyfriend come in earlier and thought I'd catch you," Jett said in his husky rumbly voice.

"Boyfriend?" I asked, sounding confused.

"The English guy," Jett replied frowning.

"Reid? Oh no, he's not my boyfriend!" I said, looking horrified. I heard a noise to the side of me and saw Reid doubled over pointing his finger at me and laughing hysterically.

"Jeez Sin, the look on your face." I blushed and began stuttering.

"I didn't mean it like that Reid," I began twisting my hands, noting Jett looking at us curiously. Reid stopped laughing long enough to step forward and put his hand out. Jett caught it in a firm grip, and they shook hands.

"Reid Hershley, I attended Oxford with Sin. We're like brother and sister hence her horrified look," Reid explained with a curious grin at the biker standing on our doorstep.

"Jett, a prospect in Rage MC. Mechanic and engine designer," Jett replied, letting go of Reid's hand. "Glad Sin has someone with her, said she was alone in the world." Now it was Reid's turn to look horrified. Reid turned to me with a frown.

"Alone in the world? Sin, you knew you had me," Reid snapped with a bite in his tone.

"You were in England when I said that, I didn't expect you to drop everything and come running Reid, I wouldn't ask that of you." The frown deepened at my explanation.

"You'd piss me off, sweet girl, if I didn't understand that you hate to put on people. Sin, you only had to pick up the phone, and I'd have come. Luckily I came anyway."

"You got fired over that," I reminded Reid gently.

"From a job I hated and getting fired was no loss. Sin, look around, the Reading Nook is getting a second life," Reid said pointedly. He sniffed at me in annoyance and turned back to Jett who watched the byplay expressionless.

"Good to meet you," Jett said.

"Ditto, Sin's not alone although she hates leaning on people. I'm Sin's honouree older brother, I watch out for her, and I moved here a couple of months ago," Reid said making a point. Jett grinned suddenly, and my breath caught in my throat. Wow, Jett was gorgeous.

"Good to hear. So can I be nosey or you gonna keep me on the doorstep?" Jett asked.

"Come on in," Reid said and shoved me out of Jett's way. I aimed a punch at his arm and bounced ineffectively off him. Reid looked down at me, "you hit like a girl, Sin."

"I am a girl," I muttered.

"Thank god for that," Jett muttered back, and I looked up at him from under my lashes and saw Jett studying me intently. Reid gave that sharp, knowing grin of his and began taking Jett around the shop pointing out new things we'd done and so on. I stuck my head in a box of books that just arrived and watched them surreptitiously.

Celine's mouth dropped open as she gazed from one man to the next. Reid was stunning, chiselled features, shaggy blond hair, round glasses perched on his nose. Reid's body was lean and rangy, and he worked out at a gym, so I knew he'd well-defined muscles.

Jett next to him was darkness, black hair, dark brown eyes, high cheekbones, a square jawline and firm, soft lips. He was slightly taller than Reid and broader, but Jett was lean hipped, long-legged and as tightly muscled as Reid.

Oh yeah, I could understand why Celine's mouth had dropped open. It was panty-dropping, hot flushing, and sweaty sex appeal from both men. Together, the result was devastating. Reid was often unaware of his impact on women, and I got the impression Jett was the same. Both men took a stance with hands-on-hips as they looked at the restored mural on the ceiling, a scene from Dantc's Inferno and Celine dropped her box.

I couldn't blame Celine at all. I shoved my nose back in my box as both men's gazes glanced over me and then Reid continued his show and tell tour. Reid liked Jett, I could tell. And Reid was asking his own questions, curiosity in his gaze and an inquiry as to Jett's relationship to me.

I heard Jett ask something and Reid rumble a reply and then both men's gazes came to me. My skin burned as I kept my head down, and then they both went upstairs. I breathed a sigh of relief.

I was on the phone when they came down so had a perfect excuse not to speak to Jett, whose gaze lingered on me. And then my eyes shot to Reid who invited Jett to pop in any time he wanted. Jett said he'd take Reid up on that and then with a hot stare at me Jett left the store.

Reid turned to me, and I pointed a finger at him, and the slashed my throat in warning. Reid laughed!

Chapter Two.

I wandered around the shop, straightening stands and making sure everything was perfect. The Reading Nook was due our grand opening in an hour, and I was as nervous as a kitten. Penny was finishing up stuff in the kitchen which smelled terrific, and Celine was putting away a book delivery which had arrived late. Andy was upstairs in the mock Bodleian and Reid was in the Vault putting out last additions in the display cabinets. Which left me to pace nervously.

My mouth twitched as Zoe rushed past dressed as a witch, the costume was exceedingly authentic. Zoe was carrying two trays over to one of the coffee tables on which we had placed nibbles. Today was Halloween hence the costumes, Reid had insisted on us all dressing up to my chagrin. Andy was dressed as Frankenstein, Reid wore a headless horseman costume, Zoe was a witch. Penny's face painted as a mask from the Mexican holiday Day of the Dead but dressed in bloodstained English serving wench clothes.

Celine dressed as a bad Tinkerbell and looked fantastic. Reid had nagged me to dress up, and I'd refused several times. But this morning I discovered a highway man's costume waiting and dressed reluctantly.

I wore knee-high brown low-heeled boots with a black band around the top of them and a waist-length black cape. Skin-tight light brown breeches tucked into the boots and a mid-thigh white chiffon shirt that had a thick black belt around my waist and a pair of pistols attached. Topped off with a black masquerade mask, and although Reid would never get me to admit it, it was sexy.

Reid had done several interviews over the last week drawing attention to the shop and the grand opening. Together, Reid and Andy had posters made and adverts in local newspapers and organised a leaflet drop with several promotions advertised. Colleges and Universities had allowed us to advertise offering a ten percent student discount on production of a student identification card.

Reid had done a radio interview and a local tv station interview. Everything possible to get our name out there had been done, and now we were going to excel or crash. Quietly I was terrified. A quick glance at the clock told me it was eight am, half an hour to go, we were opening the shop later today. The usual time would be seven-thirty to catch the breakfast crowd. A loud knock on the door startled me, I stared over and saw a crowd, Celine hurried over and opened the door. Astonishingly, a small group of strangers pushed through.

"The shops not open yet!" Celine cried out as I recognised three of the men in front. Jett gave me a shit-eating grin.

"It's okay Celine," I said, walking forward. Jett's eyes lit up.

"Hi, we thought we'd come and support you. It looks good when one sees a business with a crowd of people. We've set up shifts for the next few days to help support and keep sales going. I'm Phoenix, Drake's wife." It was the lady from Dad's funeral, Phoenix stepped forward and put out a hand, I grasped it and shook and let go.

"That's neighbourly of you," Reid called loudly from behind us, coming forward to shake hands with people.

"Rage and HQ enjoy being neighbourly," Phoenix said with a grin. "This place looks amazing, not going to lie, I've peeked when you've gone home at night. And seeing this for real, I got to say the shop looks fantastic."

"You're English," Reid queried, I stepped away and let him take over as I was wont to do so.

"Yes from London and then I lived in Devon before moving my family here. Where are you from?" Phoenix asked curiously.

"London via Oxford and Devon," Reid laughed, Phoenix grinned back.

"Wow, small world. This is my husband Drake, his VP Ace, Ace's father, Apache. This is my assistant Emily, and Director of Fund-Raising, Stefan. That's Jett who you know, and they're Mac and Slick, Slick booked the day off work as he loves reading.

To be honest, Slick's usually encased in my library at home, so Drake's cursing you as Drake knows he won't get much work out of Slick today. At the same time, Drake's celebrating as Slick won't be invading our home as much." Phoenix shot Slick a grin, and the man grinned back.

"This is Silvie, one of the old ladies at the club, and Silvie loves historical stuff. Oh, that's my Director of Public Relations, North. North enjoys reading too, so I agreed to give him the morning off as North was ready to pull a sick day to attend," Phoenix continued. I blinked at all the information whereas Reid took it in stride.

"I'm Reid one of the co-owners, that's Sinclair, who's

hiding," Reid said, tossing a grin over his shoulder at me. I glared before scurrying away, conversation drifted around the shop, and coffee orders were placed. Easily, I disappeared into the autobiography section, which was at the back of the shop and bemoaned the fact I'd left my chocolate latte on the counter.

I sat down on one of the snuggly armchairs that we'd dotted around and drew my knee's up to my chest. I was fooling myself, I couldn't do this, I didn't know how to interact with people. Even the friendly Phoenix had made me feel gauche and uncomfortable.

A shadow fell across me, forcing me to glance up, Jett stood there with a quizzical expression on his face. He leaned against the bookshelf and crossed his arms across his chest, making his biceps bulge. Long legs were crossed at the ankles, and my mouth went dry.

"Okay?" Jett asked, concerned, I shook my head, unable to talk. Jett dropped his gaze of concern and frowned.

"Sin?" Jett asked, unfolding his legs and Jett crouched down in front of me.

"I can't do this," I whispered. Jett propped his elbows on his knees and laid his hands on my legs.

"Do what, honey?" Jett asked softly.

"Deal with people. Reid was wrong, I can't be in public, I need to be downstairs in the Vault, I'll be happier there. The Vaults are where I'm needed," panic lit my voice. Jett rubbed a hand up and down my leg soothingly.

"Honey you're havin' a bit of a panic attack. Need to calm down, you're rightfully nervous, anyone would be."

"I'm a coward, scared of saying or doing the wrong thing," tears welled in my eyes.

"Hey, don't do that, I can't handle tears. Yeah, you may say the wrong thing, who cares?"

"The person I say the wrong thing too will care. What if I can't answer a question? I'll look stupid." Jett's face changed then, and I blinked.

"No one can ever call you yellow honey, you quit a good-paying job to start this with Reid. From what Reid's said, your old job let you hide in an office away from people. To suddenly quit that safety and continue with your father's shop and work with the public is brave, really brave.

A coward would have sold the shop and remained hiding in the underground office away from everyone. A coward never would have undertaken the extent of the rebuild you did and designed a fuckin' awesome place. You're no coward honey," Jett said firmly and touched my leg again. Forcefully, I blinked away the tears.

"I'm not?" I asked wobblily.

"No, you're not."

"Okay, but what if I say the wrong thing?" I whispered, it was my worse worry.

"So what if you do? Call for Reid or someone else if they ask you somethin' you don't know. And if they take offence fuck 'em, I'd be damned amazed if you meant to cause offence, so any offence perceived is on their heads, got me?" I nodded and took a couple of deep breaths.

"Those assholes Sin met at school and college messed with her head, made Sin feel inadequate and awkward for being a prodigy. Screw them Sin, revel in what you've accomplished in Dad's memory. Told you I won't leave you alone, Sin, I meant it," Reid said from the bookshelves. "I'll leave her in your hands, you got Sin handled." I watched as Reid walked away and bit my lip and looked back to Jett and saw his gaze on my mouth.

"Honey, let's go get some customers. How about I tell

Drake I'm spending the day here today and be by your side?"

"You'd do that?" I asked Jett with hope in my voice. I don't know what it was about Jett, he was as sexy as hell, and I wanted to lick him head to toe. But I felt safe, comfortable around him despite Jett's innate sexiness.

"Sure. Will be fun, bein' your bodyguard," Jett grinned and hauled me to my feet. Okay then, I'd gained a huge, muscle-bound bodyguard!

Thanks to Jett and Reid the morning didn't go as bad as I'd initially expected. I didn't panic, nor did I make a fool of myself or say the wrong thing. Jett escorted me back out of the bookshelves, and I found the people from Rage standing around drinking coffee and eating Penny's goods.

"Are you okay?" a gentle voice asked. I looked at a pretty blond woman, I thought her name was Silvie.

"Yes, minor meltdown, I don't do well in situations like this," I said with a smile.

"Meltdowns are not fun! If you need me, I'll be in the historical romance section," Silvie said with a cheeky grin. Jett gave a low groan, I guessed romance wasn't high on his reading lists.

"There's a queue," Zoe yelped excitedly dashing past me to peer out of the Charles Dicken window. Phoenix dashed up to peer out with her.

"Zoe!" I hissed as Reid and Jett chuckled, she flung a smug look over her shoulder.

"There are loads of people queueing outside. Oh, wow, look!" I rolled my eyes at Reid, silently telling him to deal with the over-excited salesgirl.

"Zoe, my dove, come here," Reid said. Zoe's eyes grew huge, and she stopped peering out of the window and looked at him.

"Yes, Reid?" Zoe stammered.

"Sweet dove, go and see if Penny has enough food to feed everyone, those people look hungry."

"Penny has been cooking since five am this morning. Of course, Penny has a load of food!" Zoe said grumpily. Drake chuckled, and Zoe looked at him, and her jaw dropped open.

"Oh, boy," I muttered. "Everywhere that girl looks is a hot guy, she's in heaven." Jett snorted next to me as his gaze shifted to Zoe.

"Like wow," Zoe grinned at Drake. I stared at Reid, silently telling him to do something.

"Hey girl, that door will be open in five minutes, you sure you're ready for the stampede that will come through here?" Jett said. Finally, someone stepped in and saved my sanity.

"I'll check!" Zoe chirped, turning large blue eyes on Jett. I could swear I saw her drool, then it was my turn to drool when Jett turned that devastating smile at me. Jett's grin grew bigger as I stared at his mouth. Okay! Enough of that.

"Love your outfit," Jett murmured leaning towards me, making me blush, "I'd deliver anythin' you demanded." Damn Jett, I grew even redder, I heard a snicker and saw Phoenix and Silvie looking in my direction. Both old ladies had knowing looks on their faces.

"Ready?" Reid called in a loud voice, giving me an out. I hurried towards the kitchen intending to hide when I was hauled firmly against a man's side, and Jett's arm pinned me there. I wondered whether to sulk or gloat as I looked up at Jett and he grinned again and whatever I was planning to say disappeared in the face of that grin.

Reid unlocked the door and stepped back as the first customers entered. Within half an hour, the shop was rammed, and Slick was handling the doors, (which was really kind) letting new customers in as happy customers left. Celine had a queue at her register, as people were buying books, lots of books! Zoe had been sent to operate Penny's register as Penny was in the kitchen baking more stuff.

Andy had taken root upstairs, showing a heck of a lot of students what the Reading Nook could offer them. Reid disappeared downstairs in the basement with several potential buyers showing what we had in the Vault. I appeared to have been given the main floor, with Jett firmly attached to my side.

Jett kept his word, he'd informed Drake that he was spending the day here and after a sharp stare, Drake had agreed. There was a mention of patrol tonight, and they both gave each other chin lifts. Every time someone asked where something was, Jett followed me to the correct shelving with the customer. Thanks to Jett, my confidence grew.

Reid shook hands with an older man carrying a wrapped parcel and escorted the customer out. Reid gave me a cheeky grin and a thumbs up and disappeared back down to the Vault. I hoped that meant he'd made a sale, the Vault had its own register, so I didn't know. Penny was in and out a lot re-filling the counters and monitoring what sold well.

Today Penny had prepared chicken and vegetable soups, chilli and pulled pork. She'd made jacket potatoes, a rice dish and burritos. The chilled snacks were flying, the sausage rolls and pork pies had gone down well as a specialised English dish. The demand for sandwiches, subs and a chicken and bacon salad kept Penny busy in the kitchen.

To my surprise, she'd prepared snacks that I didn't think would sell but had flown out of the door. Penny made meat and chicken samosas and duck spring rolls, from scratch and the cakes were flying off the counter, she seemed happy enough. I was keeping a careful eye on what was selling, and I had to admit to my surprise, everything was. Penny had chosen correctly, to her credit.

I caught Jett with a sheepish look on his face as he ate his fifth sausage roll with crumbly flakes around his mouth. Jett did have the grace to look ashamed at his greediness.

"They s'good," Jett mumbled around a mouthful, I nodded knowingly.

"Staple of students all over England," I grinned at him. Jett nudged Rock who had been introduced to me half an hour earlier, who was biting into what I thought was his third samosa.

"Tell me," I mused with a shy grin, "Are all of Rage getting their lunch and dinner here?" Rock looked at me, and I blanched thinking I'd said the wrong thing. Rock suddenly grinned, and I blinked in the light of it.

"Sweetheart serve these every day, I'll be here buying' them," Rock mumbled, swallowed and wandered back over to the counter. I rolled my eyes as Rock bought two more and sat his ass down in an armchair.

Jett sat down in an armchair opposite Rock and patted the arm. I hesitated before sauntering over and gingerly sitting on it. Jett's arm shot out and wrapped itself around my waist as he relaxed back and took a massive bite out of the samosa Rock offered him. I groaned at Jett who winked.

"I need to handle the register so Zoe can get lunch," I told Jett. He looked over his shoulder and then dragged the armchair over to a space to he could keep an eye on me and the register. I didn't say a word as Rock followed suit and re-arranged my carefully thought out seating arrangements. Zoe went on her hour, and Reid came up and offered to cover Celine.

I looked around the shop, it was still busy, but I didn't like the Vault being left unwatched. The Vault and mock Bodleian had camera coverage which I could see on a hidden monitor at the counter, but I didn't like the Vault not being covered. Silvie saved us, she came back over and offered to help, which freed Reid up to watch the Vault. Penny refused to take a break, happy to sit in the small dining area we'd created around the counters. She grabbed herself a cup of coffee and a salad.

Thanks to Silvie, we managed the lunch rush, and I realised that we'd need to stagger the girl's lunches to just before and just after the rush hour. Either that or I needed two-part timers which I thought maybe pushing it a little. Yeah, the shop was doing well today, but I needed to see the sales for at least three months before we hired anyone else.

Zoe was scheduled to work Monday to Friday and Celine would work Tuesday to Saturday. Penny got Tuesday as her day off, and we'd serve up stock that Penny would prepare on Monday. Andy got Wednesday as his day off. Reid and I would be present every day and shut the shop on Sunday.

By the time the doors shut at six o'clock, I was worn out. Reid was buzzing, and the girls seemed to be as well, Andy was his usual stoic self and said goodnight. Reid had to push the girls out of the shop, and I collapsed back against the counter. Finally, I'd silence. I peered around and realised Reid and the girls had straightened the shop for the morning.

Reid, Jett and I, were the last three standing. Reid had a huge grin on his face as he turned towards me, phone in hand. I raised an eyebrow as I recognised that grin.

"Who is she?" I sighed, and Reid's grin widened.

"She was into craft books," Reid replied. I stepped away from the counter and opened the door.

"Go on get out of here," Reid bounced towards the door and then stopped. I saw indecision cross his face. "Go, Reid, I'm okay, I'll lock up and pick up food on the way home." Reid dropped a kiss on my forehead and strolled out.

"He's so going to get laid," I muttered, forgetting that Jett was still with me. Jett snickered, and I turned in surprise.

"Yup," Jett agreed.

"Thanks for today Jett, it meant a hell of a lot, giving me a confidence boost. Free lunches for a week? Suppose I better let you go too," I said, re-opening the door. Jett walked over and placed his hand on the frame and shut the door.

"Let's go eat," Jett suggested.

"You're still hungry?" I blurted at him, Jett hadn't stopped eating all day. Jett laughed, and I liked that, the laughter sent a tingle through me. Jett had probably funded half the food sales alone! Mind you, so had Rock and another Rage brother, Gunner.

"I can always eat," Jett said with a double entendre in his voice. I bit my lip and gave him a shake of my head.

"I'm not comfortable in restaurants."

"Can pick up take-out honey, give me your address." I

thought it over and began to shake my head again when Jett placed a finger under my chin. "Give me your address," Jett said more firmly, and I blurted it out.

"Pick up Chinese," Jett suggested, I didn't want Chinese, and I wasn't sure how to tell him. "Fried chicken?" Jett asked seeing my face, I lit up, I could really eat that about now.

"Please," I said.

"Be at yours in an hour," Jett smiled. Gently he moved me to one side and went through the door. I locked it after him and wondered how the hell I ended up agreeing to eat with Jett. I checked my watch, did a final walk around the shop before setting the alarm and closing up.

I drove home carefully as I usually did, Reid called it granny driving and drove up the dark drive at the house. It was nothing special, a simple detached house with a big front and back yard and a white picket fence. Reid kept threatening to paint it black as a thumbs up to the cliché. The house had a wide drive at the side which easily held four cars. I got out of my car and walked to the front door.

Unlocking the door, I nearly tripped over Mr Snuggles, Dad's Persian cat. Why on earth Dad had called the egotistical cat Mr Snuggles, was a joke only my father had known. The cat wrapped around my ankles, and I bent down and picked him up. Mr Snuggles purred at me and then batted my nose with a pad.

"Hungry Ramses?" I asked. The little nose furrowed and I got the dirtiest stare the cat had in his repertoire. Okay, so Mr Snuggles wasn't taking to Ramses. But I was damned if I was going to yell for Mr Snuggles at the back door, when he needed to come home. I carried the cat into the kitchen and put him on the floor, keeping my balance as he wrapped around my ankles again.

Quickly I fed him and gave Mr Snuggles fresh water and then checked around the kitchen, it was a decent size with an open dining area attached. Thank god it was clean and tidy. I stuck my head into the study and closed the door on it, yeah Jett didn't need to see that mess. Time was passing when I checked the lounge and was thankful it was spotless.

Running upstairs, I quickly dumped the costume and dragged on a pair of black loose yoga pants and a tee. I pulled on a pair of fluffy socks and dragged a brush through my hair. I paused, wondering whether to put on something sexier and decided I was too worn out. Tonight I needed comfort, Jett would have to lump it.

The doorbell rang, and I hurried to answer it. Jett leaned against my cream painted porch juggling a colossal bucket of chicken and a crate of beers. He grinned and strolled towards me.

"Bought a large, didn't see you eat much. What the fuck is that?" Jett asked, peeking behind me. I knew without checking that Mr Snuggles had followed me to the door. I bit my lip and wondered how to introduce the cat.

"Don't judge me," I told Jett, and his left eyebrow rose. "This is Mr Snuggles, he was Dad's, I'm trying to get him to answer to Ramses," I blurted, and Jett's mouth quirked in amusement.

"What type of cat is he?"

"Blue Persian. Ramses is okay with me but doesn't like men," I trailed off as Ramses threaded his way between Jett's ankles.

"Yup, Mr Snuggles hates me," Jett chuckled, looking behind me at my open door.

"Oh hell, sorry, come in," I stammered shooting a glare

at Ramses.

"Your father called his cat Mr Snuggles?" Jett asked, amused still.

"Yeah. Dad said Ramses looked like a snuggly ball of fluff when he got him and Dad didn't enjoy picking names, and so he stuck with Mr Snuggles. Dad, for his love of reading, didn't have much imagination," I said over my shoulder as I led Jett into the kitchen.

Jett placed the bucket of chicken down and picked up Ramses who was attempting to haul himself up Jett's jeans. The minute Ramses found himself in Jett's arms, Ramses laid himself flat showing his extremely fat fluffy belly and expecting a rub. Jett obliged.

"Yeah, Mr Snuggles really hates men," Jett grinned as a loud purr erupted through the kitchen.

"Ramses," I snapped mock glaring. Jett grinned again.

"For most cats, I'd agree with Ramses, Mr Snuggles is just emasculating, but it suits him." I dropped the mock glare and just glared.

"Ramses," I insisted looking at the cat whose legs were splayed wide open and his head laid back in the crook of Jett's elbow. "Ramses is a whore, you're a whore," I said, pointing at Ramses nose. The cat shot me an evil stare and then continued his cat romance with Jett. I turned my back and pulled out two plates.

"Cutlery?" I questioned, happy to eat with my fingers, it was the proper way to eat chicken, after all. Jett shrugged and put Ramses down on the floor and washed his hands as I put the chicken on the plates. He cracked a beer open and offered it to me, I accepted even though I wasn't a big beer drinker.

"Follow me," I said, carrying the two plates and bucket. With one foot, I kept Ramses out of the lounge as I set the bucket down on my coffee table and sitting down, I handed Jett a plate. Jett lifted the lid of the chicken and my mouth watered. Jett nudged the bucket in my direction as he sat down on my couch, and I took three pieces and a bag of fries.

Sinking my teeth into the chicken, I moaned out loud. I'd have to ask where Jett bought the chicken from, it was so good! The coating was crunchy just as I liked it, and the chicken was cooked through and through. I hated sometimes you got that wishy-washy yukky chicken, this was good stuff.

"Good?" Jett asked as he picked up five pieces for and two bags of fries. He tipped them onto the plate and pulled out a side of coleslaw and another side of corn on the cob. Jett offered me a cob, and I whipped it out of his hand and bit into it. He watched as I licked my lips intently, making me squirm under his stare.

"I'm sorry I'm starving, don't think I ate today, and I love sweetcorn. Cobs with melted butter are one of my most favourite foods ever," I said to explain my greediness. Jett slowly smiled at me, and I melted.

"Noticed you ran on coffee today, which is understandable, you'll eat tomorrow," Jett said. His smile disappeared, and a frown took its place, I blanched at his high-handed tone and bit into my chicken. Shy and socially inept I may be, but I wasn't a pushover, I finished the chicken and looked at my laptop, Jett caught my glance.

"What's up, honey?" Jett asked as I gave an uncomfortable wriggle.

"I wanted to check how the shop did today. Reid and I were going to go over it tonight, but he's run off to get laid," I blushed as I said the last and cursed under my breath.

"Boot the laptop up, I'll help," Jett offered. Um, that wasn't what I was getting at.

"Don't worry okay, I'll check tomorrow," I replied, giving my laptop another yearning glance. Jett laughed, which made me curl my toes up, and I wondered what was wrong with me. A drop-dead gorgeous man was sat on my couch, and all I could think of was my figures!

I sighed, I'd not seriously dated, and so the feeling was new and uncomfortable. Yet another situation in which I didn't understand how to react. Flustered, I shoved the laptop to one side and looked at Jett.

"I don't date, I've not had a date since university, and it was a disaster. What are we doing Jett?" I asked him summoning up blind courage and facing him head-on. Jett didn't give me a chance to think. His head bent to mine, a wicked smile crossed his lips, and his mouth slid across mine. Jett nibbled and teased my mouth open and took over the kiss as it ignited.

Our tongues duelled with each other, and my hands slid up Jett's chest and slid into his hair. I pulled his hair tight, and Jett cupped the back of my head and angled the kiss deeper. I thought my toes had curled before! I moaned into his mouth, and Jett moaned back, pushing me back against the couch and half-covering my body with his heavy solid one.

Trying to get closer, I wriggled around as Jett lifted his mouth from mine and dropped to my neck. I shuddered as Jett slowly kissed his way down, who knew my throat was so sensitive! A heavy leg covered both of mine, and I felt a hard tightly muscled thigh as I slid a hand down and then around as I cupped his ass. Jett ground against me and drifting kisses upwards covered my mouth again.

Hands cupped my face gently, and I drowned in the smell and taste of him. Jett smelt wonderful, man and spice. A hand slid up my thigh to my waist and then slid under my tee. Jett didn't move his hand upwards to my breast as I expected him too. But instead spread it wide, heating my flesh as his thumb drew lazy circles under my ribs.

"Honey," Jett said huskily, "you're still a virgin, aren't you?" I stiffened under his hands and pulled my head away and glanced to the side. Was it that obvious I didn't know what I was doing? A red-hot flush crept up my neck, and I felt tears in my eyes.

"Hey, look at me, Sin," Jett said, forcefully but gently turned my head back to face him.

"I didn't realise my ineptitude showed so much," I whispered ashamed. Jett's eyes flashed in anger, and he bent his head and gave me another panty-melting kiss. Damn Jett, I wanted him to leave so I could curl up in a ball and cry.

"I asked honey 'because I didn't wanna hurt you. If this carried on, I was gonna be inside you, fuckin' you hard within minutes. Gotta slow this down, or you won't be a virgin in five minutes. Drivin' me mad with those little moans and sighs," Jett drawled and nipped my bottom lip. I stared at him with huge eyes, and Jett smiled slightly bitterly and shifted away from me. Hey, I was okay with him being inside me in five minutes!

I felt cold and instantly bereft as his body warmth left me. Jett sank elbows onto his knees and tilted his head into his hands. He seemed to struggle with something, and I straightened my tee and pulled myself into a small ball. Jett lifted his head and looked at me.

"I'm not my brothers." Whatever I was expecting it

wasn't that.

"Okay," I said in puzzlement.

"Some of my brothers were involved in gettin' the club clean. They did shit they don't see a clear path from, it haunts them, keeps them from forming bonds. Ain't got that baggage, got my own baggage but not that.

Couple of my brothers who ain't got an old lady, bang anythin' with a pulse. Not me, I've had women when I've had an itch, but I'm not a man whore as Phoe calls them. Been looking for my own Phoe, my own Marsha, thinking I found her. But you see she's skittish," Jett broke off and reached out and touched my face gently.

"She's beautiful, but she don't know it, she's brave but thinks she's a coward. Girl's smart and shy, and she's fuckin' funny. She don't see this shit, so I gotta go slow and show it to her, show her what a fuckin' miracle she is in my eyes.

Show her, she can have exactly what she wants and not fear reaching for it, 'cause if someone slaps her back, they going to get my fist in their face. I fall, there'll be a brother behind me to take my spot and another and then another, show her what we got to offer her."

"Seems to me you're giving her a lot, what's she giving you?" I asked softly.

"Everything I dreamed of. That's what she going to give me, everythin' I dreamed of and told I wasn't worth. See in her eyes, I've not known her long but she sees me, she sees somethin' in me, I want her to keep seeing."

"Jett, we are talking about me?" I asked, making sure. Jett threw his head back and roared with laughter. Jett's shoulders shook he laughed so hard, he dragged me across and curled me into his side.

"Yeah, honey, we talkin' you. Cute and fuckin' funny,"

Jett said, dropping a kiss on my head when he finally stopped laughing. Well then! I was just making sure.

"What does this mean?" I asked cautiously. I needed Jett to spell it out so there could be no misconstruing anything or me taking something for granted.

"Means I'm going to date you, be interesting as I never dated a woman before."

"Never?" Jett shook his head.

"Never. Clicked my fingers, and they come running. Gotta learn how to date a woman," Jett mused as I scowled at him. That hit a chord, I didn't like the fact Jett clicked his fingers, and they come running, he was mine, or would be, or was for now. Whatever!

"Will you have other women if we date?" I asked softly, I wasn't a fan of sharing him. Jett gave me a ferocious frown.

"What did I say? Claimin' you woman, which means you're claimin' me. No one else for either of us. Especially you, I like the idea of being the only man to be between your legs and make you wet with need."

"Jett!" I exclaimed blushing deep red again, he chuckled and let me go.

"Put a movie on woman. Otherwise, you're going to be flat on your back, and my control is hangin' on by a thread," Jett muttered. He adjusted a rather large erection in his jeans. I picked out one of my favourites, The Pirate Movie and listened to Jett chuckle at the old movie.

Chapter Three.

The next day, I was curled up in the armchair opposite the Dickens window with a huge mug of hot chocolate in front of me. My laptop was balanced precariously on my lap. The shop was open, and while still earlyish, it was only half-past nine, the shop was bouncing. Penny had recruited a friend to man the counters while Penny cooked. Reid had apparently agreed to this without my knowledge.

I was worried about paying another member of staff, but she'd be working part-time, which eased my mind. The girl, I discovered, named Henry, short for Henrietta was a coffee genius. Henry's shifts would cover lunches and Saturdays, and if we opened on Sunday, she agreed to work

Although I'd my laptop open, I was listening carefully to the ooh's, and aah's as people sampled Henry's coffees. Henry had found a blackboard from somewhere and was running specials of her own creation. She'd worked in several coffee shops and had gained more skills than my little shop demanded. But listening to the customers' praise and in some cases, nearly cry over Henry's creations, I thought she'd be worth her weight in gold.

I had ordered a hot caramel chocolate, one of the specials with a secret spice and had almost orgasmed over it! It was my second cup for the day. Shamelessly, listening intently to a couple of office workers from Phoe's HQ raving over the coffee, I decided to try Henry's secret spice latte next.

Reid was down in the Vault, showing a theatre nut a couple of original manuscripts he'd picked up randomly. Adam was in the StudentZone, changing the name from mock Bodleian, his zone as Adam called it. I was down on the main shop floor with Celine operating the register. Zoe had come in on her day off as we'd swapped her days around for this week and Zoe was helping customers get what they needed. Penny was banging and clanging in the kitchen, and wonderful smells drifted out of there.

So I sat in relative comfort in one of the armchairs that were in the window's corner and trying to get work done. I wanted to track yesterday's sales and see how well we'd done. Andy had set an app up, so I was able to monitor the footfall was for each day, and I was looking at yesterday's numbers with wide eyes.

Yes, I was aware we'd been busy, but the numbers were astounding. When I clicked on the sales page and studied the figures there, my eyes nearly popped out of my head. The opening day figures had bypassed projections by a long shot. Andy being Andy, had set apps up so I'd be able to track each genre's sales.

The app was simple, when a book came in, we scanned it into the system and the quantity of the book we stocked. Once scanned in, we entered it into a genre, and it was possible to see how well that genre was selling. Andy set up a top fifty best sellers and a worse fifty sellers, of course, the worse sellers would take a few weeks to kick in with results.

As of yesterday, romance was the best-selling genre. Closely followed by historical romance, thrillers and horror. That was good. When a book sold the system automatically ordered another one. At the end of the business day, the books needing re-ordering would be collated.

Thanks to Andy, because we had multiple suppliers, when we entered the book into the system, we entered in the supplier too. So we didn't have to scrabble around to find them to re-order the books. Made everything far more straightforward. Reid and I had decided it was my job, checking orders at the end of the business day and take off any re-orders that we'd stocked for a while and not sold. That meant that re-ordering the book would be pointless and I'd confirm the order to be sent at the end of the day.

Each book had its own page in the system. Andy had worked hard setting the system up, but each page told who the author was, when the book was first published. Details such as what edition we had in stock, how long we'd had it in stock and who the supplier was. Things included were, how much it sold for, how many we'd sold, how many times we'd re-ordered the book, how many sales it had. Lots of information on hand which was nice, I was admittedly anal.

Sipping my drink, I flicked over to the student's page and was pleased with the numbers I saw that had signed up to our students' scheme. The StudentZone was starting off on a deficit. We'd invested in over thirty laptops which had cost a whack, and we'd our fingers crossed that this part of the business took off. There was a way to go until the StudentZone paid back the deficit and began making money.

Andy had created several packages, knowing how tight money was for students. He'd created a three-tier system. The basic package offered three hours of internet time a day, for a twenty-dollar week payment. And up to the higher level which allowed unlimited access a day, for a fifty dollar a week payment.

I'd baulked at the charges, but Andy assured me as we'd super-fast fibre optic internet, (my speak, Andy explained it in speed and so on and I went blank). Most cafes charged around five bucks upwards an hour for internet, so the students were getting a dirt-cheap bargain. Included in the packages was a ten percent discount card to be used on books and sundries. A five percent discount on food and coffee.

The students could book laptops upstairs, and they could bring in their own laptop or device and use the Wi-Fi free. Andy had liaised with local universities and colleges and set up links to their sites. No-one was allowed to bring food or drink into the shop. A loyalty scheme was offered, when the students spent ten dollars, the programme gave them stamps on a saving card. Which gave them an extra ten percent off a purchase when filled.

The loyalty card was something that was offered to every customer, and we gave senior citizens a discount card of five percent. Curiously, I checked the signs ups for the loyalty card and saw they were slightly under what I'd projected. The savings cards I couldn't track until they were used.

Clicking, I checked the pages that linked to the food counters. There was a page for hot drinks with the sales we'd done yesterday, which exceeded my expectations.

Each type of hot drink we sold was tracked at the till. The food cash register confused me, there were so many buttons, but Penny and Henry had a handle on it. There was a page for food, boring for most people, but each type of food was tracked again to ensure maximum sales. The kitchen had started off the in red too but looking at the profits from the counters they'd soon clear that.

For all of that, the two things that worried me was the book sales which were above excellent for yesterday and the internet usage. I was concerned both wouldn't pay their way despite the incentives offered. For our first day, the Reading Nook had great sales, they'd beaten expectations. In truth, it was the first day of business, the shop was a novelty in the neighbourhood, it would be interesting to view sales in a few months.

Not wanting doubt to run roughshod over my fragile confidence, I beat the worries back and concentrated on the positives. Reid and I had discussed theme weekends to bring in more business, and the first was set for thanksgiving weekend where we'd dress up and run several promotions. Book signings may also help promote the Reading Nook loads.

"Hey, how's it going?" a voice said that I didn't recognise. Long legs set themselves down in the armchair opposite mine, I looked up and saw a man I didn't recognise, but I knew the cut. Jett has explained bikers didn't wear waistcoats, they wore cuts. This guy was from Rage.

"Hey," I said shyly.

"Manny." I looked confused. "My name's Manny," he said with a bigger grin. Oh boy, Manny was sexy cute in the boy next doorway. Tussled long blond hair past his shoulders and light-coloured amber eyes studied me.

"I'm Sin." Manny nodded.

"Guessed that. So business doin' well today."

"Fingers crossed it keeps up that way. I'd hate for Reid to have been fired and then I mess this up."

"You're partners, right?"

"Reid's like my big brother, a grouchy know it all, big brother but yeah we're in this together."

"Family can make anythin' work," Manny agreed and stared at me for a few minutes. It got uncomfortable, and I squirmed in my chair.

"Is there something you want to say?" I finally asked, feeling my cheeks redden. Manny's gaze turned intense.

"Got an ex-husband who's a whack job?" Manny asked, and I blinked in stunned surprise.

"No," I replied with a hint of a question in the word.

"Got over two kids?" Manny asked.

"No kids."

"Got skills that the CIA would die to recruit?" What on earth?

"No."

"Got no qualms taking a fucker down and using a knife to gut him?"

"What on earth, no!" I spluttered.

"So you're not gonna go to war with a crime boss and rain blood down on the city?" Manny kept asking questions.

"Seriously? No!"

"Fuck me, a normal chick," Manny mused. Yes, I was normal, what on earth was Manny talking about?

"Care to explain?" I asked curiously. Manny must have a reason for these weird questions.

"Phoe got her ass kidnapped by a fuckin' whack job of an ex, who beat the shit outta her and the club went after him. Ace got his ass shot to shit saving Phoe. Artemis is a fuckin' badass, not even the terminator would stand against her. She declared war against the club, took out a load of people who fucked her up and took out a crime boss and his shit."

"Um, I'm uncertain where to start with that information. Who is Artemis?" I said my mind buzzing.

"Ace's old lady. Woman is a one army ninja," Manny carried on, staring at me.

"Okay." I felt an intense curiosity around these stories.

"Drake and Phoe got hitched recently because of Ace saving her ass. Ace and Artemis got hitched a few weeks ago. There was a brawl between Ace and Artemis on their wedding day, bitch took him down and made him cry," Manny grinned. I was wondering if I'd met Ace.

"Okay."

"So you're normal? The MC not gotta brace for shit? I don't need to be warnin' my brothers to gear up."

"No, I mean yes, I'm normal and boring," I stuttered. Manny sighed and sent me a look of relief.

"Thank fuck for small miracles," Manny said and took a deep swallow of coffee. I looked at him and pursed my lips. The burning question had to be asked.

"Why does it matter if I'm normal?" Manny sent me an 'are you kidding me look?'

"Jett," Manny said shortly, and his eyes lit up in amusement.

"What about Jett?" I pushed for more information

"You kiddin' me?" Manny growled.

"I don't understand," I told him honestly, his eyes twinkled.

"You will," he promised me. Manny rose to his feet, and I stared up at him. Confidently he gave me a wink and strolled away, I'd no idea what just happened, it was damned odd, I looked up as Reid approached me looking excited.

"Remember the old Marchmont Estate?" Reid asked as he sat down where Manny had been sitting.

"Huh?" I said eloquently.

"The old Marchmont Estate, in Derbyshire," Reid said nearly bouncing in his chair.

"Yes? The old library?" The estate held an extensive and comprehensive library, which I'd once visited and nearly reduced me to tears. I had so wanted it, Reid had dragged me out of there before I moved into the building.

"Yeah, the old Lord Montague died, and the son has taken over the estate. It's a mess," Reid said gleefully.

"Reid, you shouldn't be getting off on someone else's misfortune," I scolded. Reid didn't even have the grace to look ashamed.

"We were at Oxford with the new Lord Montague, Antony Montague, he needs some quick money. He's got trunks filled with old paperwork and letters and shit. Man's offered us the lot for a fair sum." Ah-ha, I narrowed my eyes.

"How much do you call a fair sum?" Reid named a figure that made me flinch.

"Are you for real? What's in those trunks may be worth nothing," I snapped as Reid grinned.

"Montague's selling Bram Stokers Dracula, Mark Twain, The Adventures of Tom Sawyer, Faulkner's Sound and Fury and finally Tolstoy's War and Peace, all first editions. And all included in that price, Montague's selling a few other books as well."

"And all Lord Montague wants is that figure?" I shook my head. "Those books are worth more, and you know it,

Reid."

"Montague said he needs cash now, doesn't have time to go to auction. He wanted a far lower price, I named that price as it was fairer but still way under what we'd get for those books. As a balm, I offered Montague ten percent of the sales, not going to screw a friend over Sin."

"Far happier with that, I don't want to take advantage of a friend in need," I sighed.

"It's because we're friends Montague came to me, I gave him a better deal than most out there would have. Montague will be okay, there's money in the family, but it's tied up. He'll be able to free the money eventually, but time's what Montague doesn't have to save his estate now. And there are death taxes to pay, Montague says they're crippling.

Montague's got several copies of those books, old Lord Montague was an avid collector, so he's not damaging the collection by any means. Montague just needs readies for now."

"Okay, make sure they're in good condition, you know the condition will screw the price. I'm guessing you're flying out soon."

"Tomorrow, I'll get everything packed up and settled. Montague has offered the option to pick which of the copies he has. I'll recommend that if Montague has more than two copies that he gets the rest to auction and set a base rate." I nodded slowly. Reid had been flying across the country for sales the past couple months. I didn't enjoy being alone, but this was an opportunity Reid couldn't afford to miss.

"Okay, we'll be fine, I'll be fine," I replied, biting back sudden fear.

"I know you will, Jett is going to spend tomorrow with

you. He'll take you home after work and stay with you until bedtime." Wow, my mouth dropped open, and my mood changed from mellow to completely pissed off.

"Tell me, you're joking," I snarled, Reid shook his head. My fledgling confidence took a hit Reid, obviously felt I needed watching over like a baby. Did Reid really perceive me as that weak?

"No, I don't think you're weak, you don't enjoy being alone, I'm aware that you hate walking into the house alone. And Jett will be fine with checking the house out. Possibly checking you out too." Reid winked, and I wanted to throttle him.

"Stop reading my mind! I lived alone since I returned from Oxford," I sniped.

"Yes, I know Sin, but you don't like it. Tell me I'm wrong, but you never liked it, and there're a couple of other sales I want to check out. We've invites to several private sales, and there're three more in Scotland, I want to wrangle an invite to," Reid said.

"Don't spend the budget," I warned Reid worried.

"No, it's fine, I've a silent auction ready to go when I return, for some of the material in the Vault. That auction will turn us a profit and put some readies back into the pot. Did you notice the bidding war getting ready to start on the Lady Downing papers?" I shook my head.

Lady Downing had been a notorious Elizabethan noble whom, on being widowed became a popular courtesan at court. She'd had several high-powered lovers at court, and last year my father had stumbled across a box full of love letters from and to her. He'd had the writing verified against several known letters left in museums.

Once they'd been determined genuine, Dad sat on them, I wasn't sure why, but Reid and I had found the letters. These letters were risqué and detailed and showed several of the Tudor Queens high ranking courtiers in a different light. I'd blushed many times reading them.

Reid and I had valued them and got a second valuation. The two figures had matched bar a few hundred dollars. Reid had placed the letters on the new auction site, and we'd had a lot of queries. Unsure whether to sell them per lover, per letter or as a whole, we still had a decision to make. Considering Lady Downing had letters from thirteen lovers, I was happy to sell per lover.

"No," I said finally as Reid lifted an eyebrow waiting for an answer.

"Lot of interest, a few private collectors and a couple of museums. We've had a few offers, substantial ones for the Marshall and Perry letters. Need to sell them per lover, we'll make more money as we're selling a complete set. I've changed the auction page to that already, so it's good to go Friday. And I've put a reserve price on them, I calculated what they'd fetch individually and added it up and made that the reserve price."

"Indeed," I said happily. I was glad Reid had the same mindset as myself.

"Yup. The Jameson ones are causing a heck of a lot of interest, the Kinnock ones aren't doing as well as the others. But we'll see how they sell at auction as they're the more salacious letters," Reid grinned. Salacious was a mild word for it, Lady Downing had written Elizabethan porn and had it returned tenfold. Lady Downing had key and powerful personalities in Elizabeth's court as lovers.

"They most certainly are," I replied, grinning back.

"Still mad?" Reid asked. I turned my grin into a glare, "that's a yes." Oh hell, that was a yes, infuriating bugger.

"I don't need babysitters Reid." Reid's gaze grew

serious, and he sat down on the arm of my armchair.

"Never thought you did, you're shy and retiring and don't enjoy mixing with people because your fantastic brain works at a different level from the plebs. That made you unsure and uncertain of yourself. People couldn't talk to your level not even at Oxford." I snorted.

"Oxford is full of brilliant people."

"But few child prodigies. Not ones who can tear down an idea or alleged fact within minutes. I'll never forget when you challenged our professor of mythology about Atlantis and stated your facts clearly."

"Believing in Atlantis and arguing its existence got me kicked out of his class."

"The professor was an asshole who didn't enjoy being told by a far younger and brilliant student to get his head out of his ass and open his eyes. To be fair, the professor was out of his depth and couldn't refute the arguments you made. You were brilliant, and although you were shy, you shone that day. Never seen something so beautiful.

Fifteen years old and hiding at the back of the hall and telling a professor that just because he couldn't touch Atlantis that didn't mean it didn't exist. Then telling him, he couldn't be a Christian because he couldn't physically touch God, which meant God was a myth. No-one was surprised he kicked you out, you had more knowledge than him." Reid made me smile at the memory.

"I still don't need a babysitter," I informed him snottily. Reid snorted and ruffled my hair, I hated when he did that, and Reid knew it.

"No, because you're one of the strongest people I've met, you don't enjoy social situations, you feel inept and hate feeling like that. Sinclair, you don't enjoy depending on people because Dad taught you not too. From thirteen when you left for college and graduated, you've been independent Sin.

Oxford had no idea what to do with your brilliance, I always believed you should have finished with more qualifications than you did. You and I both know that in the few years you've been back in the states you've built a solid reputation as the appraiser for rare texts.

Obviously, you don't enjoy being alone even though you're used to being alone and Jett likes you Sin, so yeah, I meddled. Deal with it," Reid told me and unfolded his long frame from my chair. Annoyed, I glared at him and kicked his ankle lightly, and Reid ruffled my hair again, causing me to bat my hands at him as he strolled away. I saw a shadow out of the corner of my eye and saw Manny standing there.

"You lied," Manny said accusingly, I bristled.

"Did not," I denied instantly although I wasn't sure what the man thought I'd lied about.

"Did too," Manny said, pointing a finger, "you said you were normal. College at thirteen? Oxford at fifteen? That's not normal. Jett better buckle up, think you're gonna run rings around him."

"I'm not going to run rings around anyone," I shook my head. Manny let out a beautiful smile that stunned me into silence.

"Lady, you're already doing it," Manny said, and the smile broke into a grin. Did Rage have a requirement that all their brothers had to be panty meltingly gorgeous? Manny folded inked up arms and regarded me.

"I am not!" I said, letting ire slip into my voice, he kept grinning.

"Going to be fun, about time we got one who's fun,"

Manny said bizarrely and strolled away. Now I wanted to kick Manny too. Men, they were so confusing.

I looked back at my reports and finally, after ten minutes of reading the same one I put my laptop to one side and took a stroll around the shop. It was as busy as yesterday, which was good, and I kept hearing the sound of the registers being rung up. I'd noticed an influx of people who seemed to know each other and a young purple-haired woman strolled in my direction.

"Hey, I'm Emily, Phoe's P.A, if you need anything here's my card, call me. We're tight around here, try to help each other out, and Phoe likes HQ supporting local shops so we do the best we can. HQ has some avid readers so you can expect our custom," Emily said with a friendly smile. Her right hand held a cup of coffee and her left arm had about eight books balanced there.

"Here, let me help you," I said, taking the books.

"Thanks, I couldn't hold them all, and I want to get the rest of the Feist books before Slick does. Phoe lent me Magician, the other day and I'm hooked, I love Prince Arutha," Emily jabbered at me, I agreed. Prince Arutha held a secret place in my heart too, I preferred him to his brother Liam.

"I got to agree, but Tomas is something special."

"Have you read them?" Emily asked, smiling.

"All of them about ten times, they're one of my absolute favourites. Jimmy the Hand." I winked at the purple-haired pixie. Emily made a humming noise.

"If he was real, oh boy things I'd do to Jimmy the Hand! Do you have any other series' you could recommend?" Emily asked.

"Have you tried the Shannara series by Terry Brookes or Terry Goodkind's books. They're both addictive."

"No, neither," Emily muttered, she looked over her shoulder and back at me.

"Do you have them in stock?"

"Which ones?"

"All of the Feist books, and the two authors you mentioned." I laughed.

"All the Feist books are here, and so are the Shannara ones, and you are in luck because I have the Goodkind books. Let me sort you out, although that is a heck of a lot of books. Wouldn't you rather buy one set for now?" Purple hair flew as Emily shook her head vigorously.

"No, someone else might buy them, namely Slick, who I saw coming over and then I'll have to wait. Can we please get them? Would you please store them, and I'll get the MC to help me carry the books to my car?"

"Okay, I can put the books in boxes for you." Emily looked cheekily at me.

"I've heard mention of the Dragons of Pern series?" she queried, I laughed.

"Yes, I have Anne McCaffrey's books and her son's Todd's. Now that is an amazing pair of authors, I love Master Harper Robinton. I have to tell you this will cost a fortune!" Emily pulled a card out of her pocket.

"Got it covered!" Emily laughed. "Phoe gave me a bonus last week, and I'm blowing it on books. Of course, I could borrow the ones in her library, but Phoe gets pissed if we crease a page. So better to buy my own and I don't have to worry about ruining them." I nodded, smiling. This sale would be huge. A huge man stepped next to the pixie, and I thought I recognised him from the MC, the man called Slick, I thought.

"You have the Ian Randall books in-store, been getting them from the library, I saw the Feist books too." Slick turned a glare into Emily.

"I saw them first Slick, and Sin said I can have the ones she has in stock. Go place an order dude," Emily told him and shoved him, Slick glared down at her. Emily grinned at him.

"Thought you got that other series," Slick growled.

"I'm getting all three. Sin is going to help me get them," Emily purred, batting her eyes. Slick gave me a resigned look.

"I have doubles so don't worry but how about the Cassandra Clare books? The Shadowhunters. That's a great series, I can recommend that," I suggested. Slick nodded his head.

"Hey, get your own personal shopper, I got her first," Emily told Slick who dropped his head and looked down his nose at her.

"Phoe know you're taking an extended lunch?"

"Yup, so find your own shopper," Emily told him and poked her tongue out. I let out a laugh, this slight woman was crazy, Slick was huge.

"When you've finished with this demanding brat if you'd spare a few minutes?" Slick asked, and I nodded and led Emily to where the books were that she wanted and the recommendations I'd made. Emily bought every single one and Slick bought all the Ian Randall and Cassandra Clare books. Between those two, it was possible to keep the book sales going on just them!

By the end of the day, I was tired, and my feet hurt. Reid and I had been busy on the sales floor, and luckily, Emily and Slick had helped me be more approachable to customers. I'd handled them and their queries well, even if I said so myself. I'd let the girls out and discussed hours with Henry who seemed happy enough with the hours and what I'd pay her.

Henry said that if a full-time position came up, she'd be interested. As we sat discussing hours, I remembered the comments that had come from customers concerning the drinks. Idly, I wondered if the early morning crowd would be enough to hire Henry for that. Time to take a risk, go big or go home! In the end, we agreed Henry would work from seven in the morning until two in the afternoon Monday to Friday and Saturday from seven until three.

So Henry ended up full-time as well, and I hoped the shop made enough money to cover the staff and give me and Reid a living. Henry looked ecstatic at the job offer and accepted at once. When she left, I had a quick look at today's coffee sales and saw they'd doubled from yesterday, Henry definitely was a good investment.

There was a knock on the door, and I glanced up and recognised Jett standing outside. Jett wore a pair of faded tight blue jeans, worn at interesting places and a plum thermal and his cut over the top. He was smiling as I made my way and opened the door.

"Good day?" Jett rumbled in his deep voice, and I nodded as he stepped into the shop and crowded my space.

"Seemed busier than yesterday, I'll have to compare the days later. I met Emily and Slick, they seem nice people. Emily is nuts, but let me do a quick run-through," I said as I walked away. Quickly I began checking everything was shut down. Once I was satisfied it was, I walked back to where Jett was leaning against the counter.

"Slick was grumping that Emily beat him to some books. Man's pissed but singing your praises," Jett threw at me. In return I shrugged, I hadn't done much, just served Slick, he'd been kind to me.

"He seemed nice, he was interested in the shop and books we stocked. I need to do a bank drop if that's okay?" Jett gave me a nod, and I grabbed the deposit and my bag and set the alarms and locked up.

"Let me take that," Jett said as he walked me down the street. He took the deposit off me and tucked it into his cut. Once hidden, Jett gently but firmly dragged me into the crook of his arm and kept his arm around my shoulders. I shivered slightly in the chill air, but the heat from his body kept the cold at bay. Once I'd done the bank drop, I looked at him.

"Wanna go eat?" Jett asked me, and my stomach rumbled in agreement, I blushed.

"I'm starved," I told him, Jett frowned.

"You not eat today?"

"I grabbed a sausage roll and a bacon cob."

"Bacon cob?" Jett asked, sounding confused.

"It's what the English call bread rolls," I told him, laughing.

"Okay," Jett mused, "what do you fancy?" I bit my tongue to stop myself blurting out him.

"Anything, I could eat a horse."

"You're not on a fancy-schmancy diet or shit like that?" Jett asked. I glared.

"Do I look like I need to lose weight?" I bit out, Jett grinned and squeezed my waist.

"Fuck no, you're perfect, but women get stupid shit in their heads. Steak and ribs?" Jett thought I was perfect. I looked at his mouth as he spoke and I felt a shiver run through me, this beautiful man thought I was perfect. Jett impatiently gave me a little shake, and I blinked.

"You think I'm perfect?" I blurted and blushed deeply,

was it possible to sound anymore gauche?

"Yeah Sin, I think you're fuckin' perfect. Now I need to eat woman, steak and ribs sound good?" I nodded, and Jett kept that arm wrapped around me as he led me down the street away from the huge Rage forecourt. Jett walked towards the other end of our block, keeping an arm around me, where there was a fancy restaurant.

We walked in, and I thought the girl at the front would drool. She looked stunned as she eyed Jett from top to toe. Jett looked hot, incredibly hot, and I saw lust hit as he smiled and asked for a table for two. The waitress gave me a disgruntled look and led us to a table in the middle of the room. Jett shook his head and pointed to a more secluded table with low lighting.

A grim little smile aimed at me, the waitress marched us over to it. I sat down opposite Jett, and she handed us two menus. Keeping her attention on Jett, she asked us if we wanted drinks, I ordered a diet coke, and Jett ordered a Coors. With a winning smile at Jett, she told us the server would be over soon. Jett paid her no attention, which did wonders for my ego.

He put the menu on the table and reached for my hand. Jett's thumb made lazy circles as I studied him over the top of the menu. The damn man sent me a wink, and I buried my head back in the menu.

"Trust me?" Jett asked, using his other hand to pull the menu away.

"With?" I asked.

"Feeding you." I put the menu down and nodded. Another girl came over, and her gaze flew straight to Jett. Jett wasn't paying attention, but I was, and I hid a giggle as the busty blond fluffed her hair as she approached and thrust her boobs out. Without looking at her, Jett placed our order, and I listened open-mouthed. Were we expecting company?

It was apparent Jett could eat tons but holy hell, how did Jett keep that incredible body? Jett ordered a mixed platter starter, two lots of ribs and steak with fries, salad, onion rings, garlic bread and breaded mushrooms. He chased that up with the bread basket and topped it off with ordering mixed chicken wings. Jett gave me a disapproving look when I said I wanted my steak well done to his medium-rare. To finish, Jett ordered two more drinks and told her, we'd order dessert later.

"Are other people coming?" I finally asked when the waitress left and returned with a breadbasket. Jett shook his head with a grin and picked up a roll and cut it open and began buttering it. He offered it to me, and I took it and watched as his long fingers did the same to the next one.

"I'm hungry like you."

"I'm starved, so you must be way beyond that," I told him as I broke a piece of roll-off and popped it into my mouth. Jett watched me intently and bit into his own. Fascinated, I watched Jett's mouth chew and his throat ripple as he swallowed. I'd never thought watching a man eat could be sexy, but now I rethought that.

"Had a rough day," Jett broke into my thoughts, taking another bite. I made a pout at him, and his eyes warmed.

"Sorry to hear that."

"Ordered a part for a custom build, the system says it's here but couldn't find it. Lowrider, Ezra and I searched all day for the fuckin' thing. Tore the storeroom, garage and clubhouse apart lookin' for it, can't find the fucker anywhere. Gotta order another part, pissed at that. Expensive too which gonna eat into the profit on the build," Jett fumed. A furrow appeared on his brow, I nodded, I could understand that.

"Custom build?" I asked.

"I design and build bikes from scratch, Rage has a few brothers capable of design in the club. A customer tells me what he wants, I draw a few designs, and the client comes back and picks the one he wants. Then I make changes, if the client has any, once a design is agreed, the customer has to sign a contract and pay half upfront.

Then we start the build, a build can cover anythin' from replacing an exhaust to specialised paintwork. Texas and I do the paint jobs. Another prospect Hunter learning the trade, he's got talent, so with the three of us, we'll have it covered.

Drake's good, but he enjoys getting dirty, Drake likes to rip them apart and build them up. He doesn't mind bold, straightforward designs, but Prez loses patience with the small details, and a lot of my designs has small details. Drake can do it, chooses not to."

"Prez?"

"The club President, Prez, that's Drake."

"So how do you start the builds?" I asked, curious.

"Say a customer wants a Harley Street Rod customising, Rage will pick up the bike if the customer doesn't have one. Then rip off the shit client doesn't want and replace it with shit he wants. Sometimes we strip a bike down to a frame, sometimes it's just a paint job. Depends on the client, for an enthusiast cost doesn't always come into it. They know what they want, and they'll pay it no matter what."

"The bikes cost a lot of money?" I asked.

"If I'm buying the bike, and redesigning and repainting, it can cost anything from forty thousand up. If the customer has a bike, anything from twenty thousand up. Depends on the build and what customer wants doing. On average, Rage custom-designed bikes sell for fifty to sixty thousand each. But we've sold bikes for a shitload more than that."

"Oh my god," I breathed, Jett smiled.

"Rage MC, we're the premier bike design in South Dakota, not just Rapid City. When Drake went into this, he toyed with the idea of starting the garage in Sturgis. Chose not too because although Sturgis is the bike capital, it's also fuckin' cut-throat there. Some of the shops are lacklustre and sell crap.

With us being here it ensures we aren't battlin' them for business. Word of mouth spreads, and people will travel. Rage has a fifteen-month waiting list for orders at the moment which is why we're training Hunter up. Could use another four or five of us." Jett let go of my hand which he had still been holding all the time as our starters arrived. My eyes grew wide at the amount of food on the platter.

"Wow, that's a lot of food."

"Hungry," Jett grunted. He picked up a chicken stick and bit into it and chewed. I picked up a loaded potato skin and placed it on the small plates that had been delivered.

"So you, Drake, Texas and Hunter are the designers and custom painters? I thought everyone would be mechanics?" I asked as I cut into the potato.

"Nah, not all of Rage are into designs and shit, some brothers got no talent in custom design. There is other shit brothers can do if they aren't mechanics. We have the bar, and the store, the shops, Manny and Gunner don't work in the garages. They tend to run the parts and the Rage stores.

Besides Manny and Gunner, we always have at least one brother at the shop and one at the parts store. Take Mac, he prefers the bar, so it's left to him to manage alongside a Hellfire MC brother. The bar usually has two brothers present, other than Mac and Rooster, four altogether two Rage, two Hellfire and we take turns."

"Hellfire MC?"

"Rage's brother club, different club names but the founders of both clubs were brothers. Drake and Chance are cousins, we interact a load with them. Chance is as fuckin' nuts as Drake. Maybe more so as Chance raised Drake," Jett chuckled.

"Shop and store?" I asked, reaching for a couple of tempura prawns. Jett moved the platter away and picked up a prawn and held it to my mouth, I smiled and bit into it.

"The store holds parts customers wanna buy for their bikes and cars. If we don't have a part in stock, we'll order and hold it until the customer picks it up. The shop sells Rage merchandise. It always did okay, but now it's become popular because of Drake's old lady Phoenix.

Phoe's kidnap and beating made the papers. Plus we sat down on phones during a fundraising weekend which got us a lot of publicity. Rage was interviewed locally and nationally, which got our name out there more than it had been. Don't get me wrong, Rage was always well-known, but since the fundraising shit, we became known all over the country.

The shop sells tees, vests, hoodies, jackets with our motto or Rage in cool lettering. Items don't have our full patch, but it has Rage MC or a part of the patch. Shop sells mugs and shit too. Sell other lines, boots, helmets and shit, makes a decent whack for us."

"You say us? How does it work?" I asked as Jett held out another prawn to my mouth. I bit it and began chewing.

"We run a month behind. Texas takes the money earned by the bar and splits it between Hellfire and us. Then Texas takes our half, and the profits from the store, shop and garage and adds it together. Texas tracks what each has brought in before adding it all together. Brother takes out taxes and stuff, and the pot is split between us. Drake's decent like that, owns the garage and owns the store, could keep the money to himself.

Instead, the Prez puts it into the pot. Got a lot of respect for that, Rage MC owns the bar and Drake signed over the shop to the club, Drake did own that too. Full brothers get an equal cut and prospects take a lesser cut of the pot. Once we make full brother, we get the same."

"How many brothers in the MC?" I wondered.

"Fourteen brothers and four prospects," I winced.

"You must have second jobs?" I couldn't see how they'd get a decent living from that cut. Jett swallowed a mushroom and smiled.

"Nah Sin, not one brother takes home less than eight k a month, I take home a minimum five, and that's on a bad month." My mouth dropped open, eight thousand a month?

"How much?" I blurted in shock.

"That's a bad month, Sin. Custom builds, fifty k a piece, four a month? Eight twenty-five k pieces a month if we don't have fifty k ones. Bar makes a huge profit, people wanna be around Rage, the shop does a decent turnover, store too. None of us ever take home less than that."

"Holy shit," I muttered.

"Also have a pot we pay money into, Texas and Drake insist on it. Texas takes ten percent of the net profit and puts it into the pot before the cuts are sorted, then he dishes our cuts. A brother has an accident, his house burns down, needs legal help, that pot is there and don't need to pay it back. It's family Sin," Jett said, watching me, I swallowed a lump in my throat.

"That's sweet. The pot and family thing."

"Your dad and Reid must be the same?" he asked. The waitress came and cleared our plates away, and I sat back and sighed.

"We didn't have money like that to throw around, but Dad and Reid have the same sense of family. Reid was disowned for going to university. Can you believe that? What parents disown their kid for going to university and not going down a mine? I don't understand that, Dad literally adopted Reid, he loved him so much.

Dad didn't have family, he was cut off when he was younger, probably why he took to Reid so easily. Dad wasn't an easy man, like me, he had issues socially, we both preferred being curled up with a book than partying in a bar. What money we had, Dad made stretch, especially when I got accepted at college so early and then onto Oxford.

Both times I stayed with foster families. The families were vetted by the college and Oxford. I know most of the money from the shop paid for my education. Dad would hunt down rare books and manuscripts and sell them at a significant profit. It's where I got my love of literacy."

"Manny said you were a child prodigy, you're how old?"

"Manny has a big mouth," I muttered, and Jett grinned.

"I went to college just after I turned thirteen. Dad wouldn't let me go to Oxford, I was too young, I stayed at college for two years and moved to Oxford at fifteen. I stayed at Oxford for four years, came home when I was nineteen, and I've been working in the Museum in Pierre for four years. Just turned twenty-three Jett."

"I'm twenty-five," Jett replied. "Did college like you but at the normal age, rode around a bit. Did odd jobs working in garages but somethin' was missin'. Found that missing thing eighteen months ago. Hung around a while and then applied to join Rage. Found what makes me whole." The waitress brought our dinners, and we carried on asking each other questions. I found to my delight, Jett was dry and funny.

The food was wonderful, the steak was done just right, and the ribs were dripping in barbeque sauce. At first, I wondered how to eat them. Delicately I began cutting the meat off the bone until Jett laughing shoved a rib under my nose and forced me to bite it. They were delicious.

"Pick it up Sin, don't worry about gettin' sauce everywhere," Jett smirked, and I gave up and dug in. By the end of the meal, there was a pile of wet wipes in front of us. But the food was gone. I sat back with a huge sigh and rubbed my very full tummy.

"I don't think I've eaten like that since Dad's death. Thank you, Jett." Jett's eyes darkened at the mention of my dad's death and lit up as I thanked him.

"Want dessert?" Jett asked, and I shook my head. "They do an amazing chocolate orange bomb here," I groaned, I loved chocolate orange, anything chocolate orange!

"Oh, hell. Yes!" I snapped laughing, and Jett laughed.

"Never seen eyes get so big," he teased. I poked my tongue out at him daringly.

Without a word, Jett lent forward and dragged my head to his and kissed me soundly in front of everyone. I heard a cough and sat back from Jett and looked dazed at the waitress tapping a pen against her pad. She glared at me and smiled at Jett. Bitch, I thought as I gathered my bewildered thoughts together. Jett's kisses blew me away, the world could end, and I wouldn't know in his arms. I looked at Jett and saw him watching amused.

"Huh?" I said as I realised the waitress had strutted her stuff away.

"Ordered for both of us," Jett smirked and sat back, folding his arms behind his head looking supremely satisfied with himself. Damn that man and what he did to me!

Chapter Four.

Jett remained a gentleman throughout our date, he was funny and courteous, completely ignoring the waitress, despite the constant attempts to gain his attention. When Jett paid the bill, I was shocked to see the waitress hand Jett a receipt with her phone number. On leaving the table, I snatched the receipt from Jett's hand and ignoring the amused twitch of Jett's lips, I stormed over to the surprised-looking bimbo.

"My man doesn't need your phone number. What type of tart are you that hands her phone number to a guy when he's on a date? Are you seriously that desperate?" I said loudly, drawing attention from other tables. The woman grew red and opened her mouth when another voice interrupted.

"Is there a problem? I'm the manager here," a man asked, appearing from nowhere. Jett arrived next to me, a hand on my waist.

"Is there a problem?" I asked the manager, looking incredulous.

"Well, yes, you look irate."

"I'm freaking irate. I'm on a date, and this idiot of a bimbo has been thrusting boobs in his face whenever she's approached the table and sending me dirty looks. We came for a pleasant meal. Not a chance for a tart to try and gain attention by being the biggest slapper in the restaurant. Then the stupid bitch gives my date her phone number in front of me, what the hell?" The manager looked shocked at my tone of voice and didn't want me causing a scene, tough!

"Oh, wow, um," the manager stuttered, and I cut him off with a wave of my hand.

"Is this how you promote your food and establishment? Whore out waitresses, so men return? We wanted a quiet, peaceful meal, not to watch the bimbo of the year thrust boobs and ass at us. The waitress's attention to my date was very attentive, she was as rude as shit to me. I'm disgusted," I snapped, pointing my finger at him and then her.

"You go, honey, she's been trying to eye fuck my man for the last hour. And he's wearing a ring!" another voice chimed in, and I heard Jett chuckle.

"My husband spilt water, and she offered to pat him down!" a second voice chimed in. The whore in question tossed her hair back in defiance, but there was a red tinge to her cheeks.

"Any idea who this man is? Rage MC? From what I understand, Rage holds a lot of influence around these parts, same as the HQ for the Phoenix Trusts. Phoenix, who is a friend of ours, just imagine how your business will look when Rage and the Trusts get done with you!" I said waggling an angry finger in the man's face. The manager turned puce.

Okay, maybe I was being over the top, I didn't know what Rage and Phoenix would do. But the threat worked well as the man hurried the bimbo out of the way and promised us, he'd manage this. With a glare, I turned my nose up at the staff and gathering my icy pride around me. Smugly, I slipped my hand inside Jett's and led him out the door. Still glaring, I hissed a second 'tart' at the woman still manning the podium, she blanched.

Outside Jett tugged me into a doorway and grabbed me in a bear hug and buried his head in my neck. His whole frame shook, and I thought for a few seconds that Jett was angry, then I realised he was laughing. Jett finally lifted his head and looked at me trailing a finger down the side of my face, I leant into Jett's hand, and he cupped my face.

"Shy and retiring? Not fuckin' likely. Artemis or Marsha, even Phoe, I could see making a scene like that, didn't think you had that in you kitten."

"I'm not a pushover," I said pouting, "confrontation is something I shy away from. But I'm not afraid of it."

"No, kitten you ain't," Jett said his eyes warm on my face, he tilted my head and kissed me. As usual, Jett controlled the kiss, and I was a hot, wet mess by the time he finished. Jett left me clinging to him dazed as always and slanted a slight smile in my direction.

"Love seein' that look on your face, makes me feel good," Jett said huskily. The evidence of how our kiss affected Jett pressed into me, and I cupped his cock through his jeans. Jett let out a groan as I squeezed gently and he grabbed my hand.

"Jett," I sighed.

"Told you kitten, gonna do this and you right," Jett replied, I narrowed my eyes.

Shy I may be, but I knew I wanted Jett and where exactly I wanted him. I hissed at him, and Jett's eyes widened, and he laughed again. Jett dragged me out of the doorway and slung an arm around my shoulders, he drew me against his body and into his warmth. Still stunned by the kiss, so I didn't realise Jett was leading us towards Rage until we were nearly on the forecourt.

"Jett?" I asked, suddenly dragging my feet, he stopped and looked down at me.

"What's up kitten?" Jett asked.

"I'm not ready for that," I told him pointing at the clubhouse, Jett's face darkened.

"Why not?" Jett's voice had an edge to it.

"Because I'm not, they're overwhelming," I whispered, picking up his barely hidden anger, I didn't know what I'd said wrong.

"I'm a biker, nearly a full brother, I'm Rage. You tellin' me that you're okay with me one on one, but you don't want to meet my brothers?" Jett growled, I pulled away from his shoulder and looked up at him.

"What are you talking about?" I asked, confused. Jett put his hands on his hips and glared at me.

"I'm Rage, I'll have my patch one day soon kitten, and won't be ashamed of wearing it." I bit my bottom lip and took a step back at the anger in his voice. Jett wasn't hiding it now.

"I didn't say you had to be ashamed of your brothers or MC," I stuttered, panic swirling inside me. And I wondered how Jett read that I was prejudiced against his brothers in the fact they overwhelmed me.

"Don't want to meet them because they're overwhelming? Because Rage is loud and brash and real men? Because they belong to an MC, they ain't good enough for you?"

"Yes, they overwhelm me, they're..." Jett cut me off with an angry noise, and I paled.

"Forget it, don't need to be dating a judgemental cunt. Thought you were different." Jett grabbed my elbow roughly and dragged me in the opposite direction and led me to where my car was parked.

"I'm not being judgemental," I gasped at Jett as he let go of me abruptly by my car.

"Wanna meet my brothers or not?"

"Not…" Jett cut me off again.

"Glad I found out now. See ya around." In shock, my mouth dropped open as he strode away in a long-legged gait.

I stood there for a few minutes shocked, I'd no idea what had just happened. Jett disappeared onto the forecourt, and then anger sparked. How dare Jett judge me? I hadn't deserved that, I'd been trying to explain that I feared saying or doing the wrong thing. Before I knew it, I scurried after Jett across the forecourt and barged through the doors of the clubhouse.

Men turned and looked at me, some impassive and others with sneers on their faces. My own face was expressive and flushed with anger. The target of my ire stood in front of me, with a foot on a stool leaning into Drake. I stormed up to Jett, and he glared at me, Jett opened his mouth, and I poked him hard in the chest with my finger and shouted first.

"How dare you, you arrogant numpty! If you shut your mouth instead of being a judgemental asshole, you'd have understood what I was trying to explain. I wasn't judging your brothers or your damn MC. Who the hell am I to judge anyone? I'm a freak!

I was trying to tell you, I was afraid, afraid of saying or doing the wrong things. That I like the brothers, I've met, and they're good people. But my social skills and anxieties make my conversation stilted, and I come across a stuck-up bitch. And I didn't want to cause a wrong impression and shame you!

That I didn't want them to believe that I was judging them because I can't fucking converse easily. I freeze up in large crowds, your brothers are such significant personalities they're overwhelming. And I'm well aware of what happens to my mouth when I'm overwhelmed, *I fuck up*.

If you'd shut your mouth and listened, you'd have heard I want to meet them, but not all at once, maybe in smaller groups to start with. Instead, you shouted at me for being judgemental, and you were rude, you called me the C word! I was terrified and ashamed of embarrassing you, but you didn't care about that.

I don't know the women in your past who may have been like that, but I'm not judgemental. Being freaking shy, is a curse but I'll tell you this, I'm damn glad you showed your true colours tonight. Because I don't want to be around someone who uses my shyness and lack of social grace against me and as a reason to shout at me!" With that, I turned on my heel and stormed back out. Manny's grin caught my eye as I did, and I shot him a glare.

Drake turned to Jett and raised his eyebrows, amusement in his eyes. Jett gazed at his boots and flicked his gaze up at the brother Jett admired most in the world.

"Fucked that up, son," Drake murmured.

"Sin was fuckin' magnificent," Jett mused.

"She's mad as shit," Ace said, leaning over and pushing a beer at Jett.

"Fucked up, we'd such a good time at dinner I forgot about Sin's shyness." Jett rubbed a hand over the back of his neck.

"Yeah, you fucked up," Drake agreed again. Jett shot him a look.

"Yeah," Jett drawled.

"Better get after Sin and fix it," Ace suggested.

"I'll let Sin cool down first," Jett said, and multiple shakes of heads met him. "What?"

"You let her be for a day or so, she'll stew on it, women do, and Sin will make it bigger than what it was," Drake said ruefully. He looked at Phoe who grinned, Drake was pussy whipped and didn't care who knew it.

"Sin will calm down," Jett insisted.

"Makin' fuck up number two," Ace told Jett, and Manny laughed.

"What's a numpty?" Texas asked whipping out a phone to look it up. He showed the screen to Hunter, who managed a smile, rolling his eyes, Texas showed it to Drake who snorted.

"Girl was fuckin' fantastic, didn't think Sin had that under her hood. Better give chase brother," Manny said.

"I'll let her calm down," Jett insisted.

"Told Sin this will be fun," Manny said to Lowrider, who grinned. They looked up as Ezra's phone beeped and the man rose to his feet in a fluid motion and began moving towards the door.

"Ezra?" Drake called out.

"Got somethin' to do, be back later," Ezra called over his shoulder. Lowrider turned with a frown to Drake.

"Ezra got pussy on the go?" Lowrider asked, and Drake shrugged.

"Not said anything."

"Ezra never says shit to anyone," a small redhead said popping up under Ace's arm. Ace looked down at his old lady.

"What do you know killer?" Ace asked, and his wife grinned up at him.

"Not much, want me to find out?" Ace groaned, and Jett caught his eyes.

"Club ain't prepared for two brothers to go down together," Texas whined to Drake whose face settled into anger and concern. Drake's gaze followed Ezra's exit.

Drake's relationship with Phoe hadn't been smooth sailing, and there was no way anyone could mistake Ace's and Artemis's courtship as anything, but a full out war. Marsha and Fish were the only couple who'd an easy time dating. Nothing came between them, and they'd been smooth sailing apart from one blip, they desperately wanted kids, and it hadn't happened.

"Club will manage anythin' that comes our way. Don't let Sin stew if you claimin' her, will make it rocky." Drake slapped Jett on the shoulder and tucked Phoe under his arm and picked up his beer.

"Woman got to learn that I wear the pants," Jett replied and missed seeing Artemis roll her eyes. The brothers thought they wore the pants and the women let them!

When I got home, I saw Reid's car wasn't in the drive, and the house loomed dark and empty. A frown crossed my face, as Reid wasn't supposed to leave until the morning and I got out the car. A tremor of fear run through me, Reid was right I hated coming home alone to a dark house, it always scared me. As I opened the front door, I reached out and hit the switch and light flooded the hallway.

I reset the house alarm and locked the door behind me. Ramses came scurrying towards me yowling, and I bent down and picked the annoyed cat up. Sadly, I carried Ramses into the kitchen and flipped on lights. At least Ramses loved me! Once there, I put Ramses down and pulled out his food. Ramses yowled as he threaded himself around my ankles and then stuck his kitty head in the bowl.

A note sat on the counter, and I read that Reid was staying at a hotel near the airport as he'd an early flight out. I frowned, but there was nothing I could do, lonely, I walked into my living room and turned on a lamp. Once the room dimly lit up, I turned off the other lights bar the upstairs landing light. I curled up in my armchair and gazed at the wall.

Tonight, I'd had such a lovely time until Jett blew it. Jett had been so nice until his harsh words, I was still reeling he called me a judgemental cunt. I'd never been called that word before, and it had shocked me to my toes. Jett's face had taken on an ugly expression as he took my words out of context and I hadn't liked it.

I didn't date, not even in college, I'd had the odd dinner date but never a relationship, so I didn't know how to handle one in real life. In my opinion, which was what mattered, Jett had well and truly overreacted. Jett hadn't listened nor had he attempted to listen.

I'd liked Jett from what I'd experienced with him, and now my emotions were all over the place. Sexually, Jett attracted me, but there was no way I'd to allow sexual attraction to let me be treated so poorly. Reid would be furious if he knew what happened tonight, he'd shown me I deserved respect. And if Jett couldn't (and after tonight, he very clearly couldn't), give me respect, then I had to leave him by the roadside.

Reid had picked me up after several disastrous dates in Oxford. Men thought because I was shy, I'd be easy. Dates hadn't ended the way they wanted, and it hurt when harsh words had been exchanged. Reid waited in the side-lines to pick me back up and rebuild confidence in myself. Self-esteem had always been a problem for me, but I'd gained confidence with each experience.

Somehow my essays and gradings in University built up my ego, I'd found my courses easy, academia was pure. My lack of confidence came from being the youngest person in Oxford, and that was where Reid stepped in. Obviously, I hadn't been able to go to parties with everyone else in my courses, because I was too young. Reid made sure I did things like bowling, played pool, went for picnics and movies.

Reid had his own group of friends, but he always checked in with me for breakfast or lunch each day. He'd found a natural balance of spending half a week with friends and then the rest with me. That was a quality I'd loved him for, we'd kissed once, just to see if anything could come of it. Both of us had such an intense feeling of wrongness, we'd agreed never to repeat the kiss!

Thinking about what Reid had done for and shown me, I decided there and then that Jett and I were finished. Yeah, I'd wanted to explore the sexual attraction between Jett and myself, and I'd sensed something in the fledgling relationship that had been promising. Instead, Jett showed himself to be a total asshole tonight, and I wasn't up for having an asshole in my life. Dad and Reid set excellent examples of what to aim for in a partner, and Jett lacked those qualities.

Lonely, I sighed and looked down at my feet. Was I so inept socially that I was doomed to be alone for the rest of my life? Did I not deserve a partner who understood how to handle me carefully and lovingly? I thought I was worth that and as my father had taught me, what I thought mattered. Determined, I rose to my feet and went to bed, determined to avoid Jett.

I succeeded excellently the next day which happened to be Sunday. With the Reading Nook shut, I drove to Pierre as there was a market on Sundays. I wandered around the market stalls looking for anything that would catch my interest. I found three books worth buying and bought soaps and bath bombs from my favourite stall. For lunch, I walked to the old deli I'd used, when I worked in Pierre.

From the book market, I paid a visit to three bookstores that I'd used while there and sometimes I'd found bargains. To my disappointment, nothing caught my eye today. In an attempt to keep busy and my mind off Jett, I did some early shopping for Christmas presents for Reid and bought a couple of things. When I next looked at my watch, it was five o'clock, and I was surprised the day had flown. As I walked back to my car, I bumped into a man, Drew, I'd worked with and accepted his invitation for dinner.

Drew wanted to discuss a project I'd been working on, and he'd now inherited the task. Politely asking for my advice, I agreed to talk Drew through the plans and ideas I'd had. Drew begged me to return to the museum and take the project back. He made me laugh, and while I appreciated that I was missed, I told him no. It was only a business dinner, but it had felt nice to laugh after yesterday's disaster, it gave me the ego boost I needed.

Darkness had fallen when I got back to my car at eight and drove carefully home. The weather changed, and rain lashed at the car in sheets. While I was a confident driver, I was still wary as the storm made seeing difficult. I pulled into my drive finally and gave a sigh of relief, scrambling out of the car, I entered the house and went to bed alone again.

With Reid away, it was my job to open the shop in the morning and barely awake, I greeted Zoe, Henry and Penny. It was disgusting how they looked far more awake than I did. Penny had been in the shop an hour baking for the morning rush, we'd given her a key to the store. When we entered, the smell of delicious pastries met us, and my stomach growled.

A few minutes later, the door pinged as the first customers, from Phoenix's HQ came in for coffees. But they soon bought the excellent smelling pastries. Penny had several batches on sale, some in the ovens and she was rolling and making more as she went.

Bacon and sausages were sizzling, so Penny could offer a breakfast menu of pastries, bacon, sausage or egg cobs and offered golden syrup oatmeal. She wouldn't fuss with anything else and kept the breakfast menu simple. I was worried how she'd cope, but Penny calmly had everything under control, now she wasn't operating the register or making coffees.

Despite my hesitancy at first, Henry was definitely a godsend. Customers only waited as long as it took to make the coffees and I was on hand to help keep the queue moving. Zoe was operating the book register, and I heard her ringing up several sales. Phoenix's staff were content to pick up a book and sit and read before starting their shifts. In a hard decision, I kept the Vault locked until I could be down there watching the valuable books.

New customers had seen the people inside, and they came in out of curiosity or because they'd popped in over Friday and Saturday. I was praying they'd keep up their repeat business. By eight-thirty, we'd been open an hour and were buzzing.

Andy strolled in and grunted, and Henry offered him a latte, Andy snatched it from her hand and walked upstairs. I was working out Andy wasn't a morning person. We hadn't had anyone who'd gone upstairs this morning, so I assumed students didn't enjoy early mornings much like Andy didn't.

Come half-past nine the rush for coffee and pastries slowed down to a crawl and we took a sigh of relief. Penny came out of the kitchen to check how many were left, and we laughed when she saw the empty trays! She said she'd have to adjust her baking each morning as she'd underestimated the sales. To everyone's surprise, it was the English pastries that flew off the shelf quickly.

The sausage rolls, Cornish pasties and porkpies literally disappeared as soon as they were put on the shelves and Penny appeared smug. She told me she was making sandwiches, cobs, and tomato and basil soup. In addition, Penny was making a cream of chicken soup, pulled barbeque chicken and the chilli and rice which would appear to be set to be a daily dish. She'd also bake extra pastries, Penny with a nod to the health-conscious was preparing a healthy salad with either chicken or tuna.

Penny kept Andy from the buns and cakes baked for the lunchtime rush, which appeared to be a full-time job! The shop remained busy in between the breakfast rush and lunchtime rush, so book sales were doing okay. Zoe and I had time to fill several internet orders, and she popped out to get them mailed.

Andy was upstairs helping several students who'd heard about the shop. And they were signing up to our packages, which cheered me as word of mouth often did wonders for a business. I'd had two elderly ladies come in who asked if they could hold a weekly book club here on Monday mornings. Thankfully, my morning was keeping me busy, and I couldn't think about Jett or the horrible things he'd said.

The old ladies had been using the local library, but they'd been asked to leave as the library needed the room for better-paying customers. On speaking with them, I informed them they could use the Dickens window seating arrangement if it was big enough. They clapped their hands in happiness and told me it was perfect. Their delight made me smile, and it was with pleasure, I told them they were more than welcome. I waived any charge and agreed with them that as long as they bought a coffee or two or had a sandwich, they were welcome.

The old ladies, grateful at not being charged, promised to let everyone know about the Reading Nook. Bless their hearts, they took a couple of our flyers to hand out to other groups they attended. It may not bring in big bucks, but if they bought our food and drink and ordered their books from Reading Nook, it was still a sale. In truth, I'd have felt guilty charging such elderly ladies a rate.

I'd been on edge, expecting someone from Rage to turn up and yell at me about Saturday night. But no one from Rage came, and I relaxed gradually as the morning passed. I dealt with a further phone call just before lunch from what sounded like an elderly man. He inquired whether we'd an area he and his Cold Case Club could use on Tuesday nights.

I described the Dickens area and also our StudentZone upstairs. The gentleman asked if it was possible to make an appointment to have a gander and asked when the Reading Nook closed. When I told him we shut at six, he informed me they usually met at seven until ten. We discussed how the Reading Nook could accommodate him as Reid had made sure we'd licences that allowed us to stay open late. The gentleman made an appointment, and I got ready for the lunchtime rush.

Henry offered, bless her, to take her hour between half-past ten and half-past eleven, before the lunchtime rush hit us. Zoe was going between twelve and one, Andy would go at half twelve till half one and Penny when she basically wanted to go. I'd argued with her to make sure Penny had a set time, and she asked me if I could cook as well as her. Penny won.

At about half twelve, I saw the back of a black-haired man standing in the counter queue wearing a Rage cut. I stiffened up wondering if it was Jett and then he turned around and I saw it was a brother I hadn't yet met. A sharp gaze wandered around the shop and came to light on me. He took in my frozen stance and his mouth quirked in amusement, I shot him a glare and ignored him, when I next looked up, the brother was gone.

The lunchtime rush was busier than I expected, word of mouth had got around to local offices and businesses. We were rushed off our feet until two o'clock. Despite my internal warnings to run and hide, I handled myself and the customers well. Penny grabbed me at two and discussed making custom made wrapped sandwiches and taking lunch orders. That was something I hadn't considered, but it made sense as a few customers had to wait for food, as Penny made sandwiches to order.

In the end, we agreed on a chicken and mango, pulled pork, pork and apple with stuffing, beef and blue cheese and obviously the usual, pastrami, cheese, ham and tuna. Penny would use three different types of bread, white, wholemeal and rye. I agreed to give it a go and see how sales did.

Penny said we could either use a book or take slips in the morning until nine am, for lunch orders. And she'd prepare them and the customers could pay in advance. The customer just had to pop in and collect their order. Although I'd planned for the café area of the shop, if I was honest, I wasn't too clued in with what foods to serve. I was trusting Penny to lead me up the right path.

We'd been so busy that I hadn't had time to question myself once that day. I'd just collapsed in a chair when the shop cell phone rang, and I dealt with a very pushy buyer interested in the Lady Downing and Marshall papers. Penny brought me over a chicken salad sandwich, the last sausage roll and a hot chocolate with whipped cream. I politely informed the buyer that no, I wouldn't remove the letters from the auction and sell them to him.

"I'll up the offer," the pushy buyer told me, and I sighed internally.

"Sorry Mr Rouse, but those letters are part of the auction, and I will not be removing them for a private sale. Besides the offer you're making is below the reserve price. And I'm certain those letters will sell for more than the reserve price," I told the man firmly. Mr Rouse made an annoyed sound down the phone.

"I'm a private collector, I want those papers," Mr Rouse's voice got louder.

"Then please bid on the auction, it will go live this Friday."

"Want to buy them now." The feeling this guy had never been told no was overwhelming.

"I understand that, but I'm not willing to take the letters off the auction site. I hope you'll bid on them on Friday, but I will not remove them."

"My family had connections to the Marshall's. The idea of those letters in someone else's hands makes me shudder. This is a matter of family pride," Mr Rouse snarled. I held the phone away from my ear as his voice rose in decibels.

"I understand. But I don't know how many times I can tell you, I'm not removing those papers," I said firmly.

"How about I offer ten percent over the reserve price?" A short laugh escaped me.

"The answer is no. Mr Rouse, we're going around in circles, so your best bet is to bid on Friday."

"I'll ruin you," Mr Rouse shrieked down the phone. I sat up straight, my eyes staring out of the window.

"Mr Rouse, you may try, but my reputation is one of the best appraisers in the business and trying to ruin it will work against you. In fact, I may now pull the letters…" Mr Rouse interrupted me.

"Thank you, I'll send the money over at once."

"I hadn't finished Mr Rouse, I may pull the letters and publish them myself. I do not respond well to blackmail, nor do I enjoy threats. If you want those letters so much, then I suggest you bid on Friday. Have a good day Mr Rouse," I told the irate Mr Rouse calmly and hung up the phone. With a sigh, I sank back in my chair and rubbed my temples, picking up my coffee, I sipped it, my mind whirling.

"You eat today?" A voice rumbled from behind and my body tensed.

"Why would that matter to you?" Jett moved around the armchair and sat down in the armchair opposite.

"Need to eat, kitten," Jett replied, leaning back and stretching those long legs of his out in front of him. As usual, Jett looked good, a black tee and faded black jeans. He had on heavy motorcycle boots, a silver chain from his belt to his pocket and his cut.

"What I do is not your concern," I replied coldly, I stifled the part of me that yelled, 'Yippee sex god in front of me, jump him!' Entirely inappropriate, that train of thought! Jett raised his eyebrows.

"Disagree there."

"No disagreement, since you called me a cunt, I'm no longer your concern." I heard a gasp, looked over my shoulder and saw Zoe scurrying away. Irately, I looked back at Jett and saw a flash of guilt, and then anger crossed his face.

"Fucked up," Jett replied, I nodded.

"Yeah, you did, you were aware I was inept, shy, that I struggle to explain myself, that I'm afraid of social situations. You ignored that and thought I was judgemental, in your self-righteous anger, you cut me off every time I tried to explain. And then finally you called me a cunt." I rose to my feet and looked down at Jett.

"Kitten," Jett drawled, I narrowed my eyes.

"Goodbye Jett, I choose not to be around you and the stick up your ass and the chip on your shoulder." With great dignity, I turned on my heel and walked away, I heard Jett get to his feet and come after me. Jett gently this time, took my elbow and turned me around.

"C'mon," Jett said with a small smile, which damn it, made him hotter. My temper sparked which it tended to do around Jett lately!

"Is that how you do it? Insult and hurt someone and think a smile will make everything better? God, what a mistake I nearly made with you." I fought the two parts of me, one that wanted to curl in a ball and die and the other wanted to jump Jett's bones. Jett hurt me with his cruel words. Jett called me a cunt, how was I meant to get over that?

"Fucked up, if you can't forgive me, then you're not what I thought you were." Jett rubbed a hand at the back of his neck, and my eyes narrowed, and I bit hard.

"I see, you can insult and belittle me and I'm meant to get over it and forgive you?" I poked a finger in Jett's chest, and his eyes flashed. "You hurt me with those words, you treated me no better than a piece of shit on your shoe. Now because I won't fall at your feet that makes me a bad person? Someone you don't want to know? You twatwaffle! How about I go insult one of your brothers, seriously insult them. And then tell you that you have to forgive me or you're not the person I thought you were.

Oh my god, your ego is immense. How do you fit your head through a door? I'm not the person you thought I was if I don't forgive you? Well, guess what, you're not the person I thought you were! And I don't like you, I may stupidly, be sexually attracted to you but I've got more respect than to go to bed with someone who calls me a cunt!" I shrieked. Jett gazed at me for a few seconds and stormed out, I turned around and saw Zoe, Henry and several customers standing there open-mouthed.

"You get this floor show every day?" a customer asked Zoe, who shook her head vigorously.

"Don't think so."

"Well you just got yourself a regular customer honey, and you go girl! Don't let any man treat you like you're a piece of shit!" The customer grinned and wandered away. I stormed downstairs and locked myself in the Vault, I was furious, beyond furious and I'd never felt so alive. The blood was pumping through my veins, and I could pull my hair out in temper.

I was silently shocked at myself, I'd never had a temper until Saturday night. Yes, I stood up for myself if I was pushed, but screaming and shouting? What was Jett doing to me?

Jett stormed towards the door of the Reading Nook and caught sight of Manny standing near it grinning. Jett glared at the brother who laughed and then fell into step with him. Long strides marched furiously across the street to the forecourt, and Jett slammed into one of the bays. Drake looked up startled as Jett kicked the wall.

"Sin ripped him a new one," Manny said, still grinning. Jett spun and scowled.

"Fucked up twice now son." Drake wasn't asking a question.

"Told you not to let her stew, Sin's stewed all right," Manny said with laughter in his voice.

"She's done, I'm done with her," Jett growled. Manny tilted his head and looked at Drake.

"Well if you're done, you got no problem if I make a move brother." The last word barely left Manny's mouth when Jett spun and grabbed Manny's thermal and slammed him against the wall. Jett got into Manny's face.

"You don't touch Sin," Jett growled. Manny shoved Jett back and straightened his tee laughing.

"Yeah, you ain't done," Manny laughed. Jett slammed a punch into the wall and stormed out. Minutes later, his bike flew out of the forecourt.

"That's a brother who needs to get laid," Manny grinned at Drake, who shook his head.

"Playin' with fire brother," Drake grinned.

"Sin called him a twatwaffle!" Manny roared with laughter, and Drake joined in.

"Numpty, twatwaffle. Girl's got an inventive mouth," Drake said grinning.

"Gonna stoke a fire," Manny smiled.

"Yeah, stoke the fire, our dumb prospect gets his head out of his ass, worth it. Sin is Jett's one. Be nice for a normal 'one.'"

"Girl won't know what'll hit her when the prospect wises up," Drake mused.

"Going to warn her to buckle up?" Manny asked curiously.

"Why the fuck would I do that? Jett's gonna twist himself in knots over her, be fun as you said. Sin will run him ragged, and then Jett'll pin her down, thinking girl's worth the effort."

"You romantic shit head, you're matchmaking," Manny said, surprised. Drake grinned at him.

"What's our most basic principle?" Drake asked abruptly. Manny glanced at Drake.

"Family," Manny said at once.

"Can't have family, if you ain't got pussy, nice, classy, sweet, clever pussy like that. She'll make good family," Drake grinned, and Manny looked surprised still.

"I gotta warn brothers to buckle up? Fuckin' president of an MC, matchmaking." Drake threw his head back and roared.

"You met your brothers? Fuckin' warn 'em, they won't listen. None of ya do, too fuckin' stubborn with your heads up your asses." Drake wandered back to the build he'd been working on. Manny stood and stared at Drake for a few seconds and returned to the parts store.

I came out of my sulk when my appointment arrived on time. Mr Kenna, who was as I guessed elderly, seemed to be aged around seventy. The charming man had white styled hair, brown eyes and was thin but well dressed. He was politely spoken and told me that the club needed somewhere to meet once a week. The cafe the Cold Case Club used had shut, and the members were cramming into random living rooms, and there was never enough seating.

On being asked Mr Kenna informed me, the club had roughly twenty members. When I asked what the Cold Case Club did, Mr Kenna spoke with enthusiasm about how they picked up crimes that hadn't been resolved and attempted to resolve them. The club had given the police clues to cases over the years which resulted in several arrests. It wasn't hard to see how proud Mr Kenna was of his clubs' actions.

The club comprised several retired police officers, a judge, two retired doctors and several other well to do members. Mr Kenna enquired about food and drinks, and

I showed him what we offered. We agreed if the club wanted food, he'd need to phone in an order each Tuesday morning. As the club wanted the Reading Nook to open after closing time, he asked about rental payments. Naming a price I thought was a fair figure, and Mr Kenna turned to me in shock.

"Young lady is that per week?" Mr Kenna asked me, I nodded, wondering if I'd over-charged.

"Dear girl, we paid twice that at the café and they were open. How about this figure?" Mr Kenna named a figure, and I shook my head, thinking it was too much. Finally, after a lot of back and forth, we agreed on a number in the middle. Still, Mr Kenna insisted the food be charged at what other customers paid. He told me I was saving the club money and the cafe also charged for food outside the room rental.

Once we reached an amicable agreement, I showed him the Dickens window seating arrangement and how it could be shifted to seat twenty or more. Then I took Mr Kenna upstairs to the StudentZone. He wandered around and asked about the laptops and several other questions. Curiously Mr Kenna, asked if we'd wipe boards and I nodded, and he said the StudentZone would suit the club better.

Quickly discussing with Andy, I named a small fee for using the laptops which I could tell appealed to Mr Kenna. The Cold-Case Club could have their meetings and research at the same time. Mr Kenna nodded his snow-white head when I finished. Slyly Mr Kenna asked if I'd draw up a contract for three months to extend it afterwards. I agreed and said I'd have it ready by the end of the week.

Whether he realised it or not Mr Kenna had given me another idea for the shop to make money. There was bound to be more clubs out there needing somewhere cheap, warm and pleasant to hold their meetings. Mr Kenna casually spoke of several other clubs, with a twinkle in his eye, and said he'd pass the word. I nodded eagerly and received a handsome smile.

You could have knocked me down with a feather when Mr Kenna asked about my father's paranormal club and where that was now being held. I stammered out I didn't know that Dad had a paranormal club, and Mr Kenna shook his head in mock despair.

He gave me a contact number for the man who ran it and said that Dad let the club use the shop for a similar fee. It would be worth seeing where that was now based. Offering advice, Mr Kenna, told me to set an hourly rate, as it would only be fair they were all treated the same. I agreed with him and said I would contact them.

I was shocked that Dad had belonged to a paranormal club. Yes, Dad and I didn't meet up on Thursday because that was my day to stay late at the museum, that's when he attended his club. I wondered how many more secrets Dad had from me and my mood bombed a little.

When I received an email from Reid, I perked up, he'd secured the books and trunks and arranged to have them shipped back. Reid said the papers looked interesting in the trunks and to hang tight until he got home. I shot him another email, telling Reid about the reading club and about the Cold Case Club. Reid, so mature, sent a picture of clapping hands back.

Chapter Five.

Reid kept me updated during his trip to England, he'd been gone a week now, and I was missing him like mad. He had attended a couple of sales and found several bargains, and also done some valuations for someone who'd contacted him. Then two days ago Reid had travelled to Scotland, attempting to authenticate papers allegedly belonging to Robert the Bruce. The documents had popped up in a private sale, and Reid paid rock bottom as they hadn't been validated. Reid would authenticate them when he got home, he believed they were authentic, or he wouldn't have bid.

I gave a sigh, Reid was a law unto himself and was running through the funds we'd put to one side for purchases. The Lady Downing sale happened tomorrow, it opened online at nine in the morning and closed at seven in the evening. There'd been loads of publicity over it and a lot of queries.

Mr Rouse had been extremely pushy over the last few days, and I finally had Celine answer the phone and tell him I wasn't available. He'd upped the offer a few times, but not enough in my opinion, the papers would sell for far more than Mr Rouse was offering. I'd had Andy check the site was in working order. Andy had been busy posting the authentication documents online next to each item.

In a long discussion with Reid, I'd mentioned my concerns over Mr Rouse, but he'd said that there wasn't much I could do. Mr Rouse wasn't the first person who we'd come across in our line of business who thought he was entitled. On taking Reid's advice, I shrugged the concerns off, despite the chill in my gut that said something was wrong.

Business was booming, and I'd not had time to sit down and read through the reports. I'd intended to do them daily, but they'd been pushed to one side dealing with other things. The auction was taking up a lot of time which irritated me. We really needed to find a manager, but the last few interviews had been duds. Today after I shut the doors, I curled up in the Dickens window and began scrolling through the reports.

The drink counter was clawing its deficit back one cup at a time, and it was doing remarkably well. Far better than Reid and I ever assumed it would. As I read the reports, I was surprised how the sales increased daily.

The food counters were flying, chilli and sandwiches being the leading sellers at lunchtime, but the English pastries were leading the way for breakfast. Including the bacon, sausage and eggs cobs. I looked at the sales, and any worries were assuaged when I read how well food sales actually did.

The book sales were also doing better than predicted, and so were the internet packages. Online orders looked healthy, so I was happy three hours later when I'd finished going through them with a fine-tooth comb. The time was nearly ten o'clock at night, and I got wearily to my feet intending to go home and have a bath and hit the sack. Tonight, I was shattered beyond belief.

Tiredly bending to pick up my briefcase and laptop, I completed the walkthrough and then set the alarm. I shut the door firmly and waited for the beep to say the alarm had set. Without warning, I was shoved face-first into the brick wall, and my head slammed against it, rattling teeth. Blood dripped from my nose and shocked I put a hand out when a hand grabbed me and banged my head for a second time into the wall.

Blackness swirled in my vision, and more blood began to drip down my forehead. Stunned, I finally gathered my shattered thoughts and screamed. In an instant, I was spun around, and a fist hit me full in the mouth, and I collapsed on all fours. A hard kick landed in my ribs and wheezing, I gasped and rolled to one side.

Curling in a ball to minimise the damage I heard my briefcase opened and then emptied. A low growl was aimed at me, and I cringed. A second kick landed on my head, and I screamed loudly, and then someone knelt and grabbed me around the throat.

"Where are they?" a voice snarled, I didn't know what he was talking about. Where was what? Hands scrabbled at my clothing and tore my blouse open and lifted my skirt. Fearing the worse, I screamed again, and those hands closed around my throat again. I began scratching at his hands, and my feet hammered the ground. A weight settled over me and bile rose in my throat. No, this couldn't be happening!

A hand pulled my skirt up, ripping it, and fingers groped between my legs. Violently twisting my hips upwards, I tried and failed to get the weight off me, a cruel hand grasped my breast, and I flinched in pain.

"Where are the Marshall papers?" the voice snarled. The Marshall letters? This was about them? A hand forced itself between my legs and my body tensed. My mind was whirling in fear and pain, and I began struggling as the fingers slipped around my panties and tore them from me. No! I would not be raped on my doorstep!

"Where are the fucking papers?" the voice snarled again. I shook my head as I tried to free my hands which were pinned to my sides. The assailant's weight was smothering me, and his fingers crept ever closer to violating me. I screamed one last time, and a fist smashed into my mouth.

"Let her go!" a voice shouted, and the pressure lifted from my throat. Gulping, I screamed the word help and then the attacker was gone. I heard shuffling footsteps, and then polished wing tops appeared. The blows to my head had made it hard for me to focus, those wingtips faded in and out.

"Police, we need the police, she's been raped. The Reading Nook near the Rage garage. Please hurry the girl's bleeding, she needs an ambulance," a calm voice said hurriedly into a phone. A figure bent over me, I cried out weakly and shuffled away.

"Sinclair, Miss Sinclair, it's Earl Kenna." I blinked out of swelling eyes and recognised the snow-white hair. Hoarsely, I tried to tell Mr Kenna what the attacker had said, but Mr Kenna covered me with his coat and kept making soft calming noises. The entire time Mr Kenna sat near, not caring that his immaculate pressed pants would get dirty. Bless him, Mr Kenna held my hand and made soothing noises, while he kept talking on the phone to emergency services. I couldn't stop shaking, and my vision remained blurred, I was so grateful for that calming, soothing voice.

Minutes later blue and red lights appeared and a police car came screaming to a halt in the middle of the road. Two officers jumped out guns drawn and aimed at Mr Kenna. Calmly he told them, he was the man on the phone and had witnessed the attack. The police officers holstered their guns and came running over to us. One of them spoke into a radio and then a second car came screeching around the corner, sirens and lights blazing.

An ambulance followed behind, and a third car arrived and began setting up a cordon. The EMTs' knelt taking stock of my injuries. Gently, they rolled me on my side, and I cried out in pain and then laid me back down on a backboard. Gladly, I gave up fighting to stay conscious, aware of the red and blue lights surrounding me, I gave up the ghost. Darkness swallowed me whole.

"Police and ambulance outside in the street. A girl's been attacked," Lex grunted as he strode into the clubhouse. Drake looked up and glanced around, he counted Phoe, Silvie, Marsha and Artemis. Not one of their women.

"Whereabouts?" Drake asked, getting to his feet. Lex looked uncomfortable, and Drake got a sinking feeling.

"The Reading Nook, police have the shop cordoned off," Lex scratched his stomach and looked at Drake. Drake's body stiffened, and then he left the clubhouse with the majority of his brothers on his heels. Jett was working at the bar, so may not be aware the incident involved Sin.

Rage pushed their way through the crowd that was gathering and saw EMTs' working over a figure lying crumpled on the ground. The EMTs' were working hard but not looking frantic. That meant the victim was stable.

"Drake," Phoe whispered and pointed. A white-haired man stood talking to the police. Apache got close enough so he could hear and Drake watched Apache blanch. There was a slight commotion as the EMTs' lifted the backboard and Drake saw a woman's fragile, slender hand fall off it. As they got closer to the ambulance Drake's gaze caught ripped clothes and a figure covered in blood.

"Brother, it's Sin," Apache said, drawing close, "girl's been attacked and raped. Old dude witnessed and interrupted the attack. Called it in." Drake spun on his heel and rubbed a hand over his eyes. Sin and Jett were meant to be an easy one, a normal one, blood and pain had yet again found one of their women.

"Get Rock, Blaze and Ezra over to the bar. Get Jett out of there and lock him down, I'll tell him, no one else."

"Bit fuckin' late," Ace muttered, and Jett appeared at the side of the cordon. His worried gaze raked across them, and the tension left his shoulders as Jett spied the four old ladies present and accounted for. Jett ambled over to them and tilted his head in the ambulance's direction.

"What happened?" Jett asked. Ace stepped behind him, and Apache and Drake moved closer. Jett frowned. Lowrider and Ezra appeared at his sides, and Jett tensed. Tension flooded his body again as he turned slowly and looked at the place the attack had taken place. Jett's eyes took in the shop and the fact the police stood around near the doorway but not entering it.

Anger sparking, his eyes took in the blood showing on the dark ground in the torchlight of the police officers attending the scene. Jett's gaze hit the cordon, stopping people entering the scene. He turned and saw the white-haired man talking to the police and his hands mimicking what he'd seen. He watched as the old man's hands closed around his own throat and showed the officer how he'd seen someone being strangled.

Jett finally looked at the ambulance, and he moved. Ace locked arms around him and held him back, and Jett began roaring. Officers turned in Jett's direction, and the old man looked shocked. Ezra and Lowrider added their own weight, and they stopped Jett moving forward.

"Is Sin fuckin' in there?" Jett shouted, tossing his head in the direction of the ambulance that was stationary, but its engine was running.

"Yeah," Drake said bluntly. There was no way to sugar-coat this.

"Sin alive?" Jett hissed at Drake and Drake nodded, "let me the fuck go!" Jett dragged Ace, Ezra and Lowrider forward a step.

"Not until you got a lock on your emotions," Drake said firmly. Jett's head snapped towards him, and rage shot out of his eyes. Drake met Jett glare for glare.

"Let me the fuck go," Jett spat every word at Drake.

"Not until you get a fuckin' lock on it," Drake spat back, "Sin doesn't need this." Drake pointed at Jett's heaving chest.

"Sin needs me."

"Girl don't need your anger, hear me?" Drake got in Jett's face, and Jett growled.

"Get out of my way brother." The argument became moot when the ambulance pulled off sirens going. A police officer approached the men warily.

"You know her?" he asked.

"Sin's mine," Jett snarled, "where she goin'?"

"RC Regional," the officer asked, observing Jett cautiously.

"Let me go," Jett hollered at those holding him. Drake looking in his face, nodded as he realised Jett finally had a loose hold on himself. The minute Jett was free, he was across the street and on the back of his bike. Rock and Ezra were behind him.

"Drake," a voice said. Drake turned to Detective Antonio Ramirez and his partner Eric Benjamin, known as Ben.

"Ramirez, Ben," Drake acknowledged.

"You know the victim?"

"It's Sinclair Montgomery?" Drake asked and got the confirmation. "She's Jett's."

"Ms Montgomery's in a bad way, nasty assault. May need more than Rock and Ezra with Jett," Ben said. Drake looked over his shoulder as Lex, Ace, Texas and Gunner peeled out of the clubhouse. Drake turned back to the cops.

"The witness saw her being attacked and hurried over to help. Ms Montgomery was fighting the assailant, her clothes ripped. Witness says she was raped, but we're not sure on that yet, the hospital will run tests," Ben gave it to Drake straight. Phoe gasped, and Silvie moved closer and wrapped her arms around Phoe.

"Let's go," Phoe said, looking wide-eyed at Drake. Drake looked to Ramirez.

"Anything else?"

"Know anyone called Marshall? That's the name Ms Montgomery gave us before passing out," Ramirez asked. Drake and everyone around him shook their heads.

"Keep me updated," Drake said, and Ben cocked an eyebrow at Drake's order. Benjamin wasn't close to the MC like Ramirez was, and didn't take orders from Drake. Ramirez just gave them a look and turned his back on them. Drake grabbed Phoe's hand and dragged her toward his Dyna Glide.

"Slate, Blaze the bar," Drake ordered the prospects who shifted their asses. Drake kicked his bike stand and peeled out in the hospital's direction.

Shit wasn't good when Drake arrived. Jett was towering over everyone in the waiting room, and the vibes coming off the prospect were dark and dangerous. Rock and Hunter stood either side of him. Ace stood in front of Jett containing him and his volatile temper. Texas and Lex stood at the nurse's station trying to get information.

Everyone else in the waiting room was giving the huddle surrounding Jett a wide berth. Drake walked over and checked on his prospect, seeing the man still had a grip, Drake walked over to Texas.

"Won't tell us shit except Sinclair's in theatre. Doc Gibbons on his way, the prospect called him," Texas gave Hunter a chin lift. Drake thanked Christ that one of his brothers had wits about him. Drake picked up the vibes coming off the brothers surrounding Jett. They were pissed and wore a burning need for blood, they fed Jett's temper as well as Drake's own.

Despite Drake's outer calm, he was murderous. Sin was an innocent woman, whoever this Marshall was, he was a walking dead man. Sin was a Rage old lady, whether or not his stupid prospect had finalised his claim. Drake had known that although Jett had fucked about this week, he'd no intention of giving up on the girl. Jett was smitten, the stupid fucker just hadn't admitted it to himself. Drake watched as his wife ignored the dangerous vibes and shoved her way through the brothers surrounding Jett. Phoe pushed under Jett's arm and wrapped herself around him.

Jett jumped, dragged out of dark thoughts as Phoe wrapped arms around his waist and he slowly wrapped an arm around Phoe and held her tight. A curvy body pressed into his other side, and Jett looked down as Silvie wriggled her way in. Silvie burrowed into his body, and her arms crossed over Phoe's as Silvie wrapped around him. Marsha tackled Jett from the front, and Jett dropped his chin to the top of her head.

"Those women," Fish muttered to Drake. "Prospect won't move if they're wrapped around him."

"Miracles," Drake agreed. Jett raised his head and gave Drake a helpless stare. Arms slipped around Drake's own waist, and he looked down at the diminutive red-head wrapped around his front. Drake put his arms around Artemis and held her tight. Artemis held him back just as close.

"You lose it, Drake, they'll lose it, you need to be strong. Let them calm Jett, and I have you," Artemis breathed. Drake took a deep breath and dropped a kiss on her head and then held onto her tightly. Artemis was right, if he lost it, they'd all lose it, Drake's brothers looked to him to lead.

"Manny's on lockdown in the clubhouse," Lowrider said approaching. Drake looked up startled.

"Manny?"

"Brother likes her. Liked Sin for Jett," Lowrider tilted his head in Jett's direction. "Manny's raging overheard the old man saying Sin been raped. Got Slick and Mac sat on him," Lowrider replied. Ah fuck, now Drake had two brothers to worry about, not that he wasn't worried about the rest of them. Lowrider's eyes promised retribution.

Jett held the women tight in his arms, and some of his anger leeched out of him. He couldn't lose it without hurting one of the old ladies, and that was the last thing he'd ever do. Jett looked over to Drake and saw the man with Artemis pinned to his front. Fuckin' women knew Jett would never harm them, so he was pinned the same as Drake.

Phoe tucked her head into his shoulder, and one of her hands rubbed his back. Silvie was rubbing his stomach and Marsha just held him. There was a grunt next to Jett, and he stared into the burning gaze of Ace. Marsha followed Jett's gaze, and he heard her gulp and Marsha gave Jett a final squeeze and then plastered herself against Ace.

Ace had taken five bullets for Phoe, he'd lost his own woman when some of his brothers betrayed him. Out of Rage, Ace was the one who'd protect the old ladies even against his brothers. Ace's arms slowly lifted around Marsha as she whispered shit to him. Ace closed his eyes, but when he opened them, Jett could see the man was barely holding on.

"Phoe," Jett whispered. Phoe looked up, "Ace." She looked over and sighted the struggling VP and Phoe reached out and touched Marsha on the shoulder, and they swapped places. Everyone saw Ace visibly ease up as soon as Phoe's arms wrapped around him. Phoe was a better choice to calm Ace than Artemis because Artemis was a killer. She'd go ballistic over this and Ace would encourage his old lady.

Jett wasn't aware how much time had passed, but Doc Gibbons finally appeared. Doc wandered over to them, looking old and tired, he rubbed his eyes and stood in front of Drake. They spoke briefly, and Jett pulled free of the women and marched over to them.

"How is she?" Jett bit out.

"Beaten badly but no rape thankfully. Rape kit was done and came back clear, Sinclair's been informed of that fact. The witness saw the man on top of Sinclair, and her skirt pulled up and assumed the worse." Jett's shoulders dropped and eased instantly. Jett's unspoken fear that Sin had been raped was alleviated. He'd been burning with the thought she'd lost her virginity through rape. Jett's white-hot anger bled out and left a simmering boil instead.

"Injuries?" Drake asked.

"Sprained wrist, bruised ribs, swollen face, black eyes and a bruised but not broken nose. Sinclair's got a gash on her head that's been stitched. Her spleen ruptured, it's been removed," Doc said matter of factly.

"Sin out of surgery?" Jett asked. Doc nodded, "Want to see her."

"You're not family," Doc replied.

"Get me in there, or I'll rip this hospital apart with my bare hands Doc. Get me fuckin' in there. Sin gets a private room as well," Jett insisted anger creeping back into his voice.

"They won't let you in, son," Doc shook his head. As Jett moved towards Doc, Phoe intervened and got between them.

"Doc, make the hospital manager aware I'm here," Phoe pointed at herself. "And that I could be persuaded to make a nice donation if my guys are allowed in Sin's room." Phoe smiled sweetly at Doc, who rolled his eyes and waddled away.

"Ten minutes Jett," Phoe said, placing a hand on his arm. "Give Doc ten minutes, and they'll let you in her room."

"I'm staying," Jett grunted. Phoe patted his arm.

"I'll make sure the donation says that." Drake rolled his own eyes at his wife and dragged Phoe into his arms. Phoe would always find a way. Money meant nothing unless it got her what she wanted. Phoe was right, ten minutes later Drake, Ace and Jett were being escorted to a private room where Sinclair lay.

Jett froze in the doorway when he laid eyes on her. Sin looked so tiny and fragile in the bed, and from the door, the extent of Sin's injuries was noticeable. Doc hadn't mentioned the terrible damage to her throat, it was black and blue and livid finger marks could be seen against her pale skin. Sin's left eye was swollen shut, and there was a bandage across her forehead. Her poor nose was double its usual size, and her lips split open.

Jett staggered back, and Drake's arm shot out to support him. Visibly pulling himself together, Jett walked over to the bed and saw her hands were bandaged up. Sin had fought her attacker, shit his woman had fought. Her chin had a nasty scrape on it, and so did her nose which added to the swelling there, her bottom lip was puffy Sin's left wrist was in a bandage, and from the way she was lying, her ribs were taped up.

Jett sat down in the chair next to the bed and reached out and picked up her bandaged hand. He gently stroked

Sin's blood-soaked hair away from her face and touched her undamaged cheek gently.

"Find him, find this Marshall and hold him," Jett forced out to Drake. He sensed Drake's and Ace's anger at his back.

"We will I swear," Ace grunted, and then he left the room.

"It's the Marshall letters, he wants them. Tell Reid, he knows," Sin whispered hoarsely. Her damaged vocal cords pitched Sin's voice low and harsh. Sin turned her head towards them with a wince. Her one eye studied Drake and Jett, and then she looked up at Drake.

"Make Jett leave, he called me a cunt." A single tear tracked down her cheek, Jett made a noise and touched it with a finger.

"Can't leave you, Sin, I can't," Jett whispered. She closed her eye and turned her head away.

"What are the Marshall letters?" A voice asked, and Drake twisted and recognised Detective Benjamin standing there.

"No idea but her partner will," Drake said, "anyone got Reid's number?"

"Yeah," Jett said and pulled his phone out of his pocket and tossed it at Drake. "Reid's in England, keep ringing until he answers."

Drake left the room and dialled Reid who fortunately answered on the first set of rings. The man was horrified and began scrabbling to book a flight home. As Reid surfed for a quick flight, he told Drake everything he knew which wasn't much. A guy called Mr Rouse had been pushing for a private sale claiming he was related to Marshall.

Sin had refused the sale several times, but he'd kept phoning. Reid told Drake to get hold of Andy as every potential buyer for the online auction had to register, and Andy could dig out the details. Drake passed the information over to Ben and told Reid he'd stay in touch. Ben phoned Ramirez who'd remained at the scene and got the information police were looking at the paperwork in Sin's briefcase.

"Ms Montgomery say anything else?" Ben asked as he walked back into the room. Jett shook his head and kept watching. Ben sat his ass down in a chair in the corner, and Drake sat on the other side of the bed.

"This shit with your women getting hurt needs to stop Drake," Ben sighed. Drake looked at Ben.

"This ain't linked to the club, this is about her work and the shop. Nothing to do with Rage but you can bet your bottom dollar it will be. Find the bastard before we do or you'll never find him." Ben bristled and leaned forward.

"You telling a cop that you plannin' a murder?" Drake held Ben's eyes.

"Tellin' a cop, better find Rouse before we do or you'll never find him. Not said shit about murder," Drake said back just as quick.

"This man's body turns up Drake we'll be lookin' at you," Ben warned.

"Won't be a damn body," Jett muttered, and Ben peered at him and then glanced away. Fucking Rage, Ben didn't know why and how or why Ramirez dealt with them.

I came to wired up and bone sore, my face felt like my skin was stretched taut, and I couldn't open my right eye. From my blurred vision, out of the window, I saw the sun was just rising. I looked at the wall, and a large clock announced it was half-past seven, I assumed it was Friday, but I couldn't be sure.

I peeked and saw a pair of legs stretched out by the side of my bed. Despite the tightness, I frowned as best as I could with the bandage on my head. I looked up and saw Jett asleep in the chair next to my bed. Jett's arms were folded across his chest, and he had a pillow under his head. He looked tired.

I turned my head, and Manny sat on the other side, Manny was awake and watching me, he looked tired too. His thermal was rumpled, and his jeans looked dirty and torn, but he was staring at me, and a small smile lifted the corner of his mouth.

"What day is it?" I croaked hoping I didn't wake Jett. My throat felt like it was on fire and even swallowing hurt.

"Friday honey," I pushed myself up wincing, and Manny got to his feet and helped support me.

"I need to leave, I've got to open the shop," I told him. Manny sent me a look that I couldn't mistake.

"Apache has the shop covered, he's opening it, you're going nowhere," he said firmly.

"I have the auction to do." Manny lent forward and put a finger over my lips, I winced as he touched them and Manny lightened the pressure.

"You need to shut up and rest your throat. Asshole nearly fuckin' crushed your trachea. You need a pad to write shit on, the cops will be here soon, and they'll expect you to talk. The shop is covered, and the auction will be, one of your girls is calling your computer guy. He'll deal with shit. Sit back and rest." Manny didn't flinch as I glared at him out of my good eye and his face took on a soft edge as he stroked a finger down my cheek.

"Ah honey, your beautiful face, I'm so sorry. Rage will get him, I swear we will," Manny promised.

"What do you remember?" a sleepy voice asked. I turned my head, and Jett sat up, rubbing his eyes and then staring at me, concern and guilt were written all over Jett's face. I pursed my lips which stung a heck of a lot and folded my arms as best as I could across my chest. I turned my head away from Jett back to Manny. Manny smirked and sent me a wink which led to a low growl from the guy I was ignoring.

"Want to tell me what you remember, honey?" Manny asked, and I nodded. I tried shifting and winced. Manny put out his arm, and I clung to it and moved around in bed and turned my back on Jett. When I looked back at Manny, he was grinning and sent a shit-eating grin at Jett over my shoulder. The growl sounded again, louder and far more pissed off.

"You know who did this?" Manny asked, stretching a leg out and hooking his chair with his foot and pulling it closer. Manny sank down into it, I nodded my head.

"You said last night, your attack was over some letters?" I nodded and mimed writing, and Manny gave me a pad next to the bed. I began scribbling stuff down as much as I could remember and then handed it to Manny. Manny read it and then passed the pad over my bed to Jett.

"I'll get Hawthorne on this," Jett said, and I heard him leave the room. Manny lowered his head and looked me in the eyes.

"Jett's eating a shit load of guilt over this Sin, prospect promised your brother you wouldn't be alone, and asshole left you alone. Jett fucked up twice, and this is the third fuck up, man's not sleeping too well." I cocked an eyebrow at him, Jett had been sleeping when I woke up.

"Sleeping," I whispered to Manny, and even that word hurt.

"Prospect fell asleep an hour ago, man's runnin' on fumes and caffeine. Jett's a good man, my brother, but fucker's stubborn and an idiot sometimes." I snorted at Manny and damn it that hurt my nose, I nodded instead.

"How much longer you gonna make him pay?" I narrowed my eyes, telling Manny that Jett would pay through the nose before he got back in my good graces. I honestly didn't want a relationship with Jett, not after what he'd said to me. Jett wasn't what I thought he'd be, but I sensed there was good in him, so maybe we could be friends. I wrote this down and told Manny who grinned again.

"Told him, it was going to be fun," Manny said insanely, he touched my cheek again gently. "Honey, you like him a fuck load. Don't deny it, you wanna make Jett pay, do it, but he's got you locked in his sights. Can fight all you want but you'll go down." I sent Manny, a 'we'll see' look, and he chuckled. A knock at the door interrupted us, and two strange men entered, who I didn't know. I clung to Manny's hand, shifting towards him as fear caught me unawares.

"Ramirez, Ben," Manny said, sitting back.

"Manny. Good morning Miss Montgomery, I'm Detective Ramirez, and this is my partner Detective Eric Benjamin. We'd like to ask you some questions if you don't mind." I looked at Manny and made wide eyes, he sat forward in his chair and picked up my bandaged hand.

"I'll be here," Manny promised. I leaned closer to Manny and gave the two police officers a nod. Jett came back in as they were questioning me and Ramirez sent several confused looks at the two bikers. Ramirez couldn't be any more obvious that he'd heard I'd been seen with Jett, and yet it was Manny I was turning to for comfort. Ben looked amused as Jett's face settled more and more into black annoyance.

The detectives asked questions like, if I hadn't ever met Mr Rouse how I could be confident it was him? I told them I recognised his voice. They informed me the shop camera at the front had got a shot of the suspect, and they were running the image through their databases. They showed me a picture of a man in his early forties with dark hair and a thin face. He wore a vee necked sweater and a shirt underneath.

The man who attacked me looked ordinary, I'd expected to see a monster. I recognised him from my attack and gave an identification. Ramirez told me Mr Rouse appeared to be on the run, but they had a bolo out on him, and local PD's had been sent his picture. The attack had been recorded, and I was thankful that Reid had put cameras outside the shop entrance.

The two detectives left after an hour of asking more questions and me slowly writing answers. My hands were bandaged, which made writing difficult. But after worrying at my right hand with my teeth, Manny had torn the bandages so I could grip the pen better. Jett remained standing at the end of my bed his arms folded

"Get Drake the info brother," Jett muttered to Manny. Manny looked at me with a question in his eyes.

"I'm fine," I whispered. Manny rose to his tall height and bent over and dropped a kiss on my forehead, which led to a loud growl from Jett. Manny winked and left the room.

"He's being too familiar," Jett growled. I looked at him out of my non-swollen eye.

"I like Manny," I whispered, putting emphasis on the word like. Ensuring Jett knew I didn't like him very much, Jett's eyes narrowed in reply.

"Can like him all you want, but Manny keeps his fuckin' lips away from you." My eye narrowed at his possessiveness.

"We got nothing between us, you can't tell me who I want to kiss me," I whispered, and his back went rigid. Jett's shoulders went back, and anger hit me.

"You're mine, I'm claimin' you. Whatever game you playing Sin, you don't pit brother against brother," Jett snapped. Yeah right, I'm not a possession to be claimed! On the other hand, ouch, I wouldn't pit brother against brother, that would be wrong, but I wouldn't lie down and take Jett's attitude. Throat killing me, I angrily wrote my thoughts and underlined possession and flipped the pad to face him. Jett's eyes narrowed, and then he sent me a grin.

"You're mine, sweetness. Get over your mood and get on board, or I'll make sure you get on board." I wrote again and flipped Jett the pad. His eyes narrowed as he read what I had put, and then he threw back his head and laughed.

Jett was stunning, pure memorising stunning beauty when he laughed like that. My mouth went dry, and I swallowed hard and hurt my throat again. I didn't see what was so funny about writing 'fuck you', but Jett found it amusing. Rolling my eye at Jett, I closed it and ignored him until I slept. I woke up a few hours later and found Drake and Manny at my bedside. I peeked for the annoying man who'd been bugging me and discovered him gone.

"Sent prospect home for sleep babe," Drake drawled looking tired. Drake ran a hand through messy hair and leaned forward, taking my hand in his. The big President of Rage held it gently.

"Reid will arrive in a couple'a hours, got hold'a him last night, Sin," Manny said. I gave him a nod. I needed Reid, I made typing motions with my fingers, and Manny drew an over the bed table near and I saw my briefcase and laptop sitting on it. Thank God they hadn't been stolen. I looked up at the clock and saw it was nearly midday.

"The shop?" I croaked to matching frowns.

"It's open although the police didn't let people in until around ten. Henry was taking orders and passing them out of one of the side windows. Customers were disconcerted, but they kept queueing," Drake told me.

"Okay."

"Shops fine, your staff are kinda pissed, they'll be here when their shift ends. Andy is staying and locking up tonight, and a member of Rage will walk female staff to their vehicle or take them home. They're covered, girl," Manny said, and I touched his hand.

"Fuck Jett for seein' you first," Manny murmured with a smile, and I made wide eyes. I snorted and then winced as a sharp pain shot down my nose and made my eye water.

"These Marshall letters, they that important?" Drake asked, I shook my head frowning.

"Elizabethan porn," I whispered. Drake's eyebrows disappeared into his hairline.

"As in sixteenth-century Elizabethan porn?" Drake asked, looking confused, I nodded.

"Holy shit, didn't think they'd have porn," Manny said, I snickered which hurt like mad.

"Not quite, they were raunchy love letters sent by a courtesan Lady Downing to her many lovers. The letters are explicit and definitely hot stuff," I whispered.

"They worth someone gettin' the shit beaten out of them?" Drake growled, and a flash of fear hit me as I felt my head slam into the wall again. I raised a hand and touched my forehead, and Manny's giant hand covered mine.

"We're here, girl," Manny soothed me, I shook my head at Drake.

"They were written by Lord Marshall, the main advisor to Queen Elizabeth. Marshall was a staid man who was faithful and loyal to his wife. These letters throw a different light on the man. It is true though, that Lady Downing was able to bring many a powerful and private man to her boudoir," I croaked. Then my voice cracked.

"Fusty old love letters led to this?" Manny asked disbelief in his face and voice.

"These show Lord William Marshall in a very different light from what history has cast upon him. The staid uptight Lord who'd the ear of the most powerful female in the world had a sexy dark secret. I can't imagine the family would want them to come to light," I pushed my voice to its limit.

"Doesn't lead to a beating. Fuck I'd think the family would rejoice in knowing their ancestor had a kinky past. Takes away the stuffiness about him," Drake drawled. I shrugged. It wouldn't bother me, but these letters showed the man had a passionate affair with Lady Downing. I don't know, it wasn't about me.

"Did the proper descendants register for the auction?" Manny asked. I nodded, I pointed at the laptop and Manny dragged it over and I opened it up and logged on. I tapped in the address for the auction site and brought up the owner's page. Curiously, I clicked on the auction page for the Marshall letters and my mouth dropped open. The auction had already hit six figures.

Amazingly, the letters were already twice the reserve price. I scrolled down to the private information only I could see on the bidders and saw that Marshall's alleged direct descendant was leading the auction. I turned the laptop and pointed it at Manny, who leaned closer, and I got a whiff of his scent. Manny smelt of lemons and spice, and it was a clean, healthy smell. I liked it.

Manny's eyes narrowed as he read down the bidders, and he made a noise. I peered up at his face and shrank at the anger there. He turned the laptop to Drake and Drake gave a sharp nod, pulling his phone out Drake sent a message. As they communicated silently over my head, I clicked on the other pages and saw that so far all of them had met their reserve prices. Even better, most were doing well above what Reid and I had predicted.

Manny remained looking over my shoulder his eyes slightly wide at the figures being touted on the pages I was clicking on. I began humming happily for a few seconds before stopping when it hurt my throat. Yeah, Reid may have spent close to our budget in England, the dratted man. But with these figures, well into the mid-six-figure range, we'd easily make back what had been spent on the papers. Including what Reid had spent in England, we'd still be in the black with a wonderful large buffer.

"Can't believe people would pay so much for musty old love letters," Manny said, sounding faintly perplexed.

"Lady Downing was famous, as was her liaisons. She's notorious in historical circles so people will bid. The fact that we've letters from several important figures in history makes them more valuable. There had been rumours of powerful lovers but never proof until these salacious letters. History is worth money," I whispered. Manny sat on the edge of my bed and flicked through the site himself. Drake gave him a look, and then Drake turned his attention back to his phone.

"Several museums are bidding too. I bettin' many of these are private collectors though," Manny said. He pointed at a few names, I nodded.

"Some of them will use a proxy, they'll hire a company to bid, give that company a limit and then let them do the bidding. Some are people who sit at the laptop bidding for themselves. Others are like you said, museums who'll have an admin staff watching the bidding."

"Did you do this?" Manny asked, settling back against my pillows, I nodded. "And you know the values and shit?" I nodded again and respect flared in his eyes.

"I loved finding old papers and so on, didn't enjoy losing them in bidding wars though."

"Museum gave you a budget and wouldn't budge on it?"

"Yeah."

"And you guess how much this shit is worth?" Drake asked, I nodded again beginning to feel like a nodding dog in the back of a car.

"I don't guess, I know, I often get a second valuation to back up my original one. A lot of professionals do that to make sure we aren't over-valuing items. Reid is the best out there, he's young for this business, but he knows his shit."

"And you, young lady have an impeccable reputation, you're in the top ten for valuations and authenticating items. Well known across the world," a voice spoke from the door and to my surprise, Mr Kenna stood in the doorway. The elderly gentleman held a bunch of peach roses with baby's breath threaded through them. I gave him a painful smile as he hustled forward.

"Mr Kenna," I whispered. He looked at Manny, who reluctantly shifted his ass and sat back in his chair. And Mr Kenna took his place at my bedside and leant over and studied my face. He pursed his lips, and his eyes narrowed on my injuries, and then he picked up my hand and dropped a kiss on my bandages. Mr Kenna turned to Drake.

"I know who you are," he said, Drake gave him a chin lift.

"Twenty-four hours," Drake said curiously. Mr Kenna relaxed, and he returned Drake's chin lift. I wondered what the twenty-four hours was about.

"That will do young man," Mr Kenna replied. "Sinclair, you look remarkably better than last night my dear child, but not as beautiful as you usually are." I tried to give him a smile. Out of the corner of my eye, I saw Drake sit up and then Manny did. Mr Kenna took note as well.

"Quick twenty-four hours, I can stay with the child," the old man said. Drake shot Mr Kenna a look.

"Two prospects will be here soon, Slate and Hunter, you'll stay," Drake didn't ask the question, as much as he told Mr Kenna. Mr Kenna nodded.

"Sinclair won't be alone. Please give him my regards too." I looked up at Mr Kenna, and it clicked.

"No!" I hissed, reaching out and grasping Manny's wrist, "don't get into trouble for me." Manny looked down, anger in his face, and then it softened, he bent down and dropped a kiss on my head.

"No trouble girl," Manny reassured and left before I could stop him. Scrabbling, I reached out for Drake and just caught his hand.

"Drake please, no trouble," I whispered a tear trailing down my face. Drake reached out and touched my cheek catching the tear on his finger, he looked down at it and then up at me.

"No one raises a hand to a Rage woman, no one babe, he'll live, but he'll never lay a hand on a woman again. No backlash, I promise," harshly Drake spoke and then followed Manny. I looked helplessly to Mr Kenna.

"If I was twenty years younger dear child, I'd be out that door after him," he told me, and I settled back lost in thoughts. Rage had found Mr Rouse, I knew it even without them telling me. I just hoped they'd take him to the police, then I remembered the rage in Jett's eyes and the anger on Manny and Drake's face. I prayed Mr Rouse would make it to the police station.

Chapter Six.

Jett scowled at the man who stood shaking in front of Rage MC. The brothers were in Rage's mess room, a building far from the clubhouse and hidden in the forest where Rage did wet work. Jett stood surrounded by his brothers, while the man kept looking for a way out. Jett noted Rouse's bruised and broken knuckles, Rouse was a foot taller than Sin and weighed twice as much as her. This man had beaten Jett's woman over stupid letters, put Sin in hospital, Jett didn't feel charitable.

Jett took two steps forward, and the man's frightened gaze came to Jett's face. Rouse swallowed audibly and coughed to clear his throat. Jett watched, his face a mask of fury.

"I wasn't aware the woman was linked to your gang," Rouse finally said fear in his tone.

"No? So if Sinclair wasn't, it would have been okay to beat a defenceless, innocent woman?" Drake asked from behind Jett. Rock and Lex had found the man, tracked Rouse by his photo, and they'd found the cowardly asshole at home. Hawthorne had met them there, arriving minutes later. The man sported a bruise on his chin where Lex had clocked him and knocked Rouse out. Hawthorne, Lex, and Rock had piled Rouse into a van parked outside his home and brought Rouse here.

"All she had to do was give me the letters!" Rouse shrieked.

"The letters weren't fuckin' yours to take, they were Sin's, and hers to do what she wanted with," Manny growled.

"I offered to pay, that bitch wouldn't pull them. Greedy bitch kept saying they'd sell for more than I was offering," the man whimpered. He kept stepping backwards and banged into Ezra who pushed Rouse forward back into Jett's range.

"Sin's in business to make money. Sinclair told you several times how to buy them, and you wouldn't listen, and that gave you the right to beat a woman half to death? Nearly rape her? Sin's a virgin, you nearly raped a virgin!" Jett roared and his inner beast released. Jett let rip with a hammer blow of a right hook and sent the man flying.

"Bitch shouldn't have been so greedy. I'm descended from William Marshall's family, those are my family papers. Bitch had no right to them!" Rouse shrieked again, and Jett threw another punch and knocked him backwards into Lowrider, who again, pushed Rouse forward.

"That gave you the right to attack her?" Jett roared. "To rape her, if that old man hadn't come along, would you have stopped?" The truth shone in Rouse's eyes, and Jett lost control. Long minutes later, Drake pulled Jett off him. Rouse lay on the floor conscious but bleeding heavily, Jett had broken his ribs and nose. Rouse spat two teeth out from a bloody mouth.

"Guess what my woman gonna do now? Publish those papers and spread your shame over the news. Everyone will know your families dirty secret," Jett sneered, and Rouse shrieked in denial.

"Pick him up," Manny said, stepping forward, "Sin's my friend." And Manny let rip. Drake was next, Lowrider let slam with a punch that lifted Rouse off his feet, and they heard something snap inside the man.

"Put that asshole in the van," a delicate voice spoke, the brothers looked surprised at seeing Artemis.

"Artemis," Ace said on a sigh.

"I'm the only one who can take Rouse in, Rouse resisted me bringing him in, that explains his injuries. I've the bounty hunter licence." Artemis pulled out a wicked knife and crouched down where Rouse lay.

"Honey," Apache said, warning his wife.

"Fuckin' lucky it's the brothers, Rage want you sent down. They have contacts inside, rapists get a shit ride in prison," Artemis hissed at the bleeding mess on the ground. Rouse opened his eyes, groaning, if Rouse wanted sympathy, Artemis was the wrong person.

"If it was me, you'd be sliced and diced and chopped into small pieces. Your piece of shit body would never be found, Sin's my sister, she's Rage, one of us. If it was my choice, I'd be carving you until you screamed and even then, I wouldn't stop, I'd dish more than a beating.

You won't speak of this because if you do, you won't know where or when I'll come for you, but I will. And then when I do, you'll fucking scream, alone in the darkness, terrified and unable to see where I'll stick my knife next. Tell the cops everything you did to my girl and don't force a trial, no plea deal and fuckin' admit to attempted rape. Breathe one word concerning Rage… I'll find you. Put that bastard in the van," Artemis told Apache and reached up and gave Ace a kiss.

"Rouse'll reach the PD?" Apache asked his daughter-in-law.

"Bastard will reach it, might be bleeding a tiny bit more but he'll reach it," Artemis said. Walking forward she kicked Rouse in the ribs and then his head, knocking Rouse out. Artemis wriggled her ass out of the doorway.

"Your fuckin' wife scares the shit out of me sometimes," Lowrider told Ace as they picked up the man.

"Woman fuckin' scares me too man, great ain't it?" Ace grinned, and they carried Rouse out.

"Going to get my girl," Jett said, and Manny put a hand out.

"Make it right this time brother." Jett's eyes searched Manny's face.

"Fuck, you want Sin," Jett growled.

"What's not to want? Sin's sweet, fuckin' beautiful, sexy as hell, funny, everything a brother looks for. Make it right this time, or I'm taking a shot," Manny said firmly.

"Brothers don't steal a brother's woman," Jett carried on growling.

"You haven't been inside Sin yet *prospect*, which leaves the girl free. Make it fuckin' right," Manny got in Jett's face, "if you ain't guessed, Sin's special. An old lady in waiting, most of us would take a shot." Jett looked at the brothers. Lex and Ezra met Jett's stare with a nod, shit Jett's brothers were interested in his woman.

"Claimin' her," Jett warned.

"Then fuckin' claim Sin before I take my shot. Still a prospect, yeah, you'll make a full brother. But at the moment unless you're inside Sin, a brother can lay claim," Manny sneered. "And Sin likes me better than she does you at this moment." Jett spun on his heel and hit his bike, the bike roared off in the hospital's direction.

"You're walking the fuckin' line there," Drake warned Manny.

"You and I fuckin' know the prospect's pissing this up. This will motivate the prospect, if not, I'm in the sidelines, waiting, I've declared interest now it's in Jett's hands. No fuckin' line if Jett ain't been inside her," Manny replied.

"Prospect's claimin' her," Lowrider said.

"Then prospect better stop fuckin' messing shit up, or I'm makin' a move," Manny insisted. He turned as Ezra's phone began beeping, Ezra pulled it from his pocket and looked down with a frown.

"Gotta go," the man said, walking towards the door. Drake's hand shot out.

"Need anythin' brother?"

"Nah, all good. Be back later."

"Pussy brother?" Ezra narrowed his eyes.

"Said I gotta go, brother," Ezra shrugged Drake off, giving off back away vibes and left them alone.

"Want me to go with?" Lowrider asked, tilting his head. Drake shook his.

"Ezra will tell us when he's ready, brother's always been one of the private ones."

"Fuckin' pussy, screwin' your heads up," Texas boomed. Drake shot the man a stare.

"Can't wait for you to get fucked up brother," Drake snapped back. Texas threw back his head and roared with laughter.

"No pussy will ever chain me."

"Who's taking bets on that one?" Lex asked as they left, Rock gave him a slap on the shoulder.

Surprised, I looked up as Jett walked into the hospital room just before five o'clock. I studied him, and my gaze fell on Jett's bruised and broken knuckles. Sharply I drew a deep breath and checked the rest of Jett's body for injuries. Not finding any, my eyes finally moved to Jett's face.

"Rouse won't ever hurt you again," Jett whispered, sitting on the bed. Jett reached out and traced my cheek with his knuckles. At Jett's gentle touch, the sobs I'd been holding back broke free and sounded dreadful with my damaged throat. Jett shifted his ass and drew me into his arms.

"It's okay Sin, the police have Rouse, and he won't get near you again. Swear it, sweetness," Jett said, holding me as tight as he dared. I shuffled forward, nearly climbing on Jett's lap and buried my head in his neck. I'd been so scared last night, it would take a long time for the overwhelming terror to fade.

When Mr Rouse had been on top of me, I'd feared the worse. And when Mr Rouse began strangling me, all I could see was Reid alone and Jett blaming himself. Life didn't flash before my eyes, as people say, Reid and Jett had, and how they'd be alone. I wrapped my hands in Jett's tee and clung, as I did so, a sense of safety came over me. Jett kept a tight hold on me in one arm, and his other hand stroked my back.

"Let it out Sin, fuck let it out," Jett soothed, and I began calming.

Even though Jett had called me a nasty name and said cruel things, Jett wouldn't physically hurt me, he'd watch over me. Jett's knuckles spoke to that fact, if he'd been done with me, then Jett wouldn't have come last night, wouldn't have stayed all night. Jett's knuckles wouldn't be split and bruised, no, Jett had me. That's all I needed, I calmed, and I lifted my head to gaze at Jett.

"Sorry for being a bitch," I spoke in a harsh, tortured whisper.

"Sorry for being an asshole, sweetness, you were right, I was a total twatwaffle." I smiled, and Jett grinned ruefully.

"Yeah, you were," I agreed, and Jett's grin turned into a chuckle.

"Doc's are springing you later tonight. Take you home and feed you, Reid will be home when we get there, Drake called Reid, tellin' him you're being discharged."

"I haven't got anything to wear," I whispered. Jett picked a bag up I'd missed him putting on the floor.

"Got you shit. Phoe guessed your sizes."

"That's kind of her," I muttered, "have I time to watch the end of the auctions?"

"Yeah, docs won't be here for an hour. Let's get you ready, want a shower? There's blood in your hair." I gave Jett a nod, and he helped me into the bathroom where he ran a shower. Jett cocked an eyebrow when I ordered him out but left on the condition I leave the door open. I'd agreed with a sigh.

Somehow, I sensed I was just seeing the beginning of Jett's protective streak. The bandages got soaked through as I washed my hair, and I thought the nurses might be angry, but it was cleansing. I was washing Mr Rouse away. I scrubbed my hair vigorously jostling my ribs and hurting my head, but it was worth the effort as I saw blood washing away.

I turned the shower off and wrapped a thin, scratchy towel around me that luckily fell to my knees. Briskly, I towelled myself dry and then called out to Jett who looked mad when he saw the state of the bandages. Jett slipped the hospital gown back on and went to get a nurse to get dry dressings. The nurse clacked her tongue at me but deftly replaced them and then helped me get dressed.

When she pulled the curtains back, Jett was waiting outside the door talking to a doctor and holding a wheelchair. The doctor gave me forms to sign, and Jett filled in my insurance details, which I told him. Jett deftly manoeuvred me into the chair and then whisked me away. Once outside, I drew in a deep cleansing breath, and spied a new truck, when the door opened, Slick climbed out. Together Jett and Slick gently lifted me in and settled me in the new truck.

Jett's ass hit his bike and followed Slick and me home. I looked down and saw Slick's knuckles were faintly bruised, I bit my lip gently and looked up at the man. Slick gave me a quizzical smile.

"Is there a brother without spilt or bruised knuckles?" I asked. Slick grinned widely at me, and I guessed that was a no. The lights welcomed me home, which warmed my insides and Reid dashed out of the house like the hounds of hell were after him. He opened my door, and waves of fury rolled off Reid and hit me.

"Next time you wait for me," Reid snarled at Slick as he gently helped me out of the truck. I was confused, had Reid expected to pick me up from hospital?

"There won't be a fuckin' next time," Jett snarled at Reid. Reid turned and gave him a stare that made Jett step forward. "No one will touch Sin again, over my dead body."

"You fucked up mate, I left you in charge of precious treasure, and you fucked up, look at Sinclair! Then you take away my chance to lay Rouse out," Reid snapped, Jett didn't back away. Okay, Reid was pissed that everyone got a shot in at punching Rouse apart from him. I glanced at Reid, and he checked me head to toe, and then turned back and continued glaring at Jett.

"Yeah, I fucked up, this is on me, and I'm gonna make it right. Sin won't ever be afraid again, she didn't need to see you with blood on your hands," Jett shot back at Reid.

"You ain't welcome mate," Reid said, angrily.

"Hey," I interrupted.

"Ain't leavin' her so get your head around it," Jett said back getting into Reid's face. I looked at the men towering over me and sighed. Sharply, I gave them both an elbow in the stomach and frowned at them.

"I want to get indoors. Stop pissing on my leg both of you, it's not Jett's fault, I should have sold those letters," I rasped.

"Not your fuckin' fault," Jett said as Reid snapped at me.

"You didn't ask for this, those letters were our property. The fucker attacked you, the asshole better be suffering a shit load of pain. And banged up in the nick," Reid said, looking at Jett and receiving a sharp nod.

"Then can I please go get comfortable, and I'm hungry," I whispered plaintively. Before I could blink three sets of hands, shot out to help me. I sighed again. Wonderful. Three overprotective males. Between them, they got me into the living room, and I settled down in amongst my fluffy, comfy throw pillows.

Reid remained standing, legs splayed apart, arms folded and beyond pissed. Jett matched his stance, Slick gave me a wink and left, slapping Jett on the back. I sighed and kept swapping my gaze between the two irate men in front of me. Neither was prepared to give an inch.

"Okay you two, please knock it off," I said wearily. Instantly both men relaxed, and an apologetic expression crossed Reid's face.

"I'm sorry honey, I let you down, I trusted your safety to other people and look at what happened." I sighed loudly as Jett immediately snapped his gaze in Reid's direction.

"I'll be watching her from now on in," Jett snarled.

"You'll be doing shit," Reid snapped back poking at Jett with a finger.

"Gonna stop me?" Jett sneered back. Reid met his sneer with one of his own.

"Oh yeah bud, I'm going to stop you, and you're not getting near Sin ever again," Reid squared up to him.

"I'm not a bone," I whispered. Both men looked at me, "look at you, testosterone, preening and bulging muscles. You, Reid, are my brother, the one man who'll never judge and always be there. Yet you stand here snarling like a rabid dog at the man who effected vengeance for me against Rouse." Jett relaxed minutely and sent Reid a triumphant grin. Reid curled his lip.

"You, you let me down twice, you don't get to say what I do and when I do it. You had no bigger right than Reid to exact vengeance, Reid had first claim to that act. Jett, you insulted and hurt me and then think you have the right to go punch someone. You're wrong," I said to Jett, and his face looked crestfallen. Then I saw that look, one I was learning to recognise but wasn't sure what it meant, crossed Jett's face.

"Claimin' you Sin, so whatever you think of me get over it. Not going anywhere," Jett said, stubbornly his arms crossing back over his chest as he looked at me.

"I'm not an item to be claimed." Jett grinned. Damn him, my traitorous heart fluttered.

"You're mine," Jett refuted my words.

"I belong to me."

"We'll see," Jett kept grinning at me.

"I'm hungry." I turned to Reid and ignored the annoying, grinning man.

"I'll pop out honey, get Chinese," Reid said and looked at Jett.

"Not leaving," Jett refused to budge.

"Please Jett, I'm tired, and I don't want to watch you and Reid glare at each other all night. It will just make a nasty atmosphere, and I want to relax," I asked him sweetly. Jett's eyes narrowed, and he tilted his head towards me.

"Give you tonight Sin, but we gonna talk babe," Jett replied. He spun on his heel and left.

After an hour of Reid fussing over me, I was ready to kill him. Reid's guilt shone through even though he had nothing to feel guilty over. He refused to leave me alone after Jett left, and ordered food to be delivered. Reid fluffed cushions and lifted my feet onto a footstool, put my kindle and the tv control near where I could reach. He'd moved a small coffee table next to the sofa and put everything on it.

Reid ran himself ragged not wanting to sit and talk. The food was delivered, and he served it up, and we ate in an uncomfortable silence. He kept glancing at me and wincing every so often, and I put my fork down and frowned.

"Stop it, Reid," I whispered.

"Stop what?"

"The guilt trip, I don't think you sent Mr Rouse after me. Neither one of us could have realised what Mr Rouse's obsession would lead to and if we had, we'd have taken precautions. It wasn't your fault you went to England, it's not your fault Jett was a prick, and we had an argument so please for my sake stop the guilt." Reid sighed and placed his chopsticks down with a clatter.

"What happened with Jett? He was meant to watch your back."

"Jett made a snap decision and was a total prick, I told Jett to stay away, and he did. I don't need judgemental people in my sphere, and Jett can take a hike. Jett misjudged me, and I didn't like it, now Jett thinks he's in with a chance, but I'm not so sure."

"Jett doesn't think so," Reid parried back.

"I honestly don't care what Jett thinks. He did me wrong, and we're both aware I can hold a grudge, I'm holding one. Now get over yourself, I don't need your guilt I need you. Jett has to prove himself, not you." Reid shuddered, laughed, and I grinned back.

"You never did mix your words, Sin," Reid said still chuckling. But he picked up his fork and began eating again. My shoulders relaxed as tension fled from them, pressure I wasn't even aware I was feeling. I changed the subject.

"Shall we check at the figures from the auction? When I checked at the hospital, the figures were putting us solidly into the black. The sales should even cover your excess in England," I teased Reid, and he gave me a rueful glance.

"You going to love the items I got my mitts on, I got some great first and second editions and three signed copies of famous books. I'd a quick gander through those trunks, you won't believe what I discovered."

"No?"

"One trunk had papers from Elizabeth of Hardwick. Letters and so on, I've no idea what exactly but they were curious."

"Reid! I think I've had more than enough of Elizabethan England for a lifetime." Reid just chuckled and informed me the trunks arrived next week. He'd had them flown out, the books were also coming in a crate. Reid relaxed back and began telling me about the treasures he'd found.

I didn't realise how the attack had affected me until Monday came and Reid offered to take me to the shop. Reid insisted that he didn't want me to work but just curl up in an armchair so he could watch over me. A wave of panic welled up inside, and I shook my head vigorously. His eyes narrowed, and Reid tried to bully me into going. Quietly, I told him I needed a few more days, and Reid guessed I was avoiding the shop.

Reid pulled his phone out reluctantly and sent someone a message. And then after making sure I'd everything I needed, Reid left to go to the shop for a few hours. I wondered if Reid had texted Jett, I'd avoided Jett all weekend. Reid had taken a phone call from Drake late Saturday asking if it was okay that the old ladies come to visit and I'd shaken my head furiously. He asked Drake to give me a few days.

Reid had a few arguments with Jett, but after I broke down in tears and Jett heard he backed off. I was relieved, I'd been safe in his arms, and while I didn't blame him for the attack, I wasn't ready to face Jett again so soon after his statement. Infuriating man Jett was.

Jett tried phoning me, and I'd ducked calls pretending to be asleep when Reid answered my phone. Jett wouldn't let me mess around forever, but for now, both men in my life were leaving me be.

Tuesday came and went, and so did Wednesday, by Thursday Reid was frustrated and annoyed. I hadn't left the house once, and I could see Reid was worried. My bruises were beginning to heal, but I felt so self-conscious, I was the girl who'd nearly been raped. My throat remained a vicious mess, and I'd taken to wearing scarves. Something Jett didn't comment on when he finally wrangled his way over Tuesday and Wednesday night. Generously bringing food to share but with Reid present, Jett couldn't do or say much.

Reid asked if I was going to go into the shop today and I'd made a non-committal reply. It was now Friday, a week since the attack. I looked down at my hands which were now unbandaged and healing and missed seeing Reid's concerned glance. Yesterday morning led a huge fight between Reid and me. I shouted I was safer at home and he'd shouted back that if I didn't face the shop soon, then I never would.

Reid stormed out, frustrated and angry, and I locked myself in my bedroom. I'd shamelessly used Reid to avoid contact with anyone else. The shop staff had called and sent flowers and baskets, Rage old ladies had done the same. I hadn't had to face anyone and Reid hadn't pushed for that, even though Reid pushed me to leave the house!

I was still curled in a ball when bike pipes outside roared and then the front door open and shut. Booted footsteps clumped up the stairs and then a knock at my bedroom door, I guessed it was Jett.

"Go away," I shouted at Jett swallowing tears. Instead of going away, the annoying man opened the bedroom door, and my mouth dropped open. It wasn't Jett, it was Manny, and he looked rough. Manny's face was gaunt, and he looked like he'd lost weight, not that you could really tell, Manny remained as big as ever. He stood in my doorway and scratched his chin.

"Nope, not doing that woman," Manny said finally and walked into my bedroom. I watched him warily, I hadn't seen Manny since the hospital.

"What do you want?" I asked rudely, I didn't care anymore. People wouldn't leave me alone, damn it, I wanted to be alone.

"Need to come with me, get out of that bed, woman." Hell no, I shook my head vigorously. That was not happening! Manny placed his hands on hips, and for the first time, I realised how attractive he was, Manny was lean but well built, tall and muscled. His hair flopped over his forehead, and I was tempted to smooth it away from his brow.

"I'm healing here," I mumbled as Manny watched me. Manny shook his head.

"No, you're licking your wounds woman and that ain't safe or healthy. No one wants to upset you princess, so it's down to me to drag your ass out of that bed." I stiffened at his words and narrowed my eyes.

"I'm still healing," I repeated.

"No, you're licking your wounds. Damn it, woman, I thought you'd have more guts than this."

"Than what? To want to be safe? I didn't mix well with strangers in the first place, the shop is doing fine without me, I'm not needed there." I folded my arms across my chest and stared at Manny.

"Fuckin' pussy," Manny swore, my eyes became slits, "thought you had courage, that you were a strong woman.

Sin, you're a coward, Jett's better off without you." Manny ended on a sneer. My head sunk down at the harsh words, and tears crept into my eyes. I swallowed hard, I wouldn't let Manny see me cry, no one will ever see me cry again.

"Sorry to disappoint you," I whispered, I sensed rather than saw movement and the bed dipped, and Manny sat on my bed.

"Where's my girl gone?" Manny asked gently, "talk to me." Manny inadvertently pressed a button, and my mouth opened, and I couldn't stop the words.

"I'm terrified, I can't breathe, I keep seeing the fist hitting my face and then hands on my legs and up my skirt. Rouse touched me there Manny, touched me and if he hadn't been interrupted, Rouse would have been inside me with his fingers a second later. I'm dirty, I keep scrubbing myself down there, but I still feel fingers pressing against me trying to get inside. So shaming," I wailed and arms folded around me. Manny held me tight as I shook and gulped loudly, swallowing back tears.

"Sin," Manny whispered hoarsely. Manny's voice broke me, I pulled my top to one side, and Manny's eyes zeroed in on the finger marks on my breasts.

"Why didn't you report the marks at the hospital?" Manny asked gently, one arm wrapped tightly around my back and the other buried in my hair, holding my head into his shoulder.

"How could I? The doctors did the rape kit, and Rouse hadn't gone all the way. I didn't want everyone to know how dirty I was. Rouse marked me." A growl vibrated against the top of my head. A kiss dropped gently on my head, and then Manny gently forced my head up, so I gazed into his eyes.

"We beat the shit outta that man Sin, now I see we should' a done more. You ain't fuckin' dirty, you could never be dirty, you're so fuckin' beautiful it hurts to look at you, honey. Beauty and innocence shine from you, fucker tried to beat you down and failed. Shouldn't have said what I did.

Ain't got nothin' to be ashamed of, nothin', you hear me? Jesus honey, fucker forced himself on you, didn't the fuckin' docs see the marks on your legs and breasts? There had to be some."

"That's why they did the rape kit. The doctors thought the marks meant Rouse had raped me, he didn't. Rouse just got very close to it," I whispered.

"Rouse may not have got a part of himself inside you Sin, but it was rape. He was a second away from violating you. Rouse violated your emotional state, violated your security and violated your body. A man doesn't have to shove his dick inside a female to violate her. He can violate her many ways. Fuckin' people think rape means a man forcing himself inside a woman, lots of ways to rape a woman." Manny grasped me tight in his arms again.

"I can't sleep Manny, I'm terrified of being alone, but I'm terrified of being with people. I can't tell Reid what has happened, he'll flip, he won't know how to cope. Jett and Reid stare at me as if I should be over Rouse's attack.

I can't, I close my eyes and Rouse is there, in my head forcing hands up my skirt, fingers pinching and pushing to get inside. I'm showering six, seven, eight times a day and still can't get rid of Rouse and get clean." I broke off with a swallowed horrible sob and Manny dipped his head to mine.

"Ah honey, no wonder you wanna be left alone. Ain't

good shutting yourself up, can't conquer this until you face it. You need to visit the shop, but I won't let anyone push you for the next few days," Manny said as I stiffened. "Trust me?" Manny asked, I nodded against his shoulder.

"Okay," I whispered, deciding to trust this rough and ready man. Manny had a gentle side he hid under his gruffness.

"Want anythin'? Chocolates? Food? Snacks? Books?" Manny asked.

"There's a set of books I ordered from the shop. They should have arrived by now," I whispered. I pulled back from Manny, wiping my eyes and looked at him. Manny gave me a crooked smile and rose to his feet.

"Get you some shit and then stand guard, okay honey?" Manny bent down and touched my face gently. "You can sleep while I'm here 'coz I'll beat the shit out of any nightmare that wants to bother you." I gave a rueful chuckle, and with a wink, Manny left me alone.

"Are you fucking kidding me? Sin's terrified. What you going to do about it?" Reid yelled at Jett just as Manny entered the shop. Manny hitched a hip on the counter and watched the two men who were glaring at each other, anger flaring between them. Drake took a step forward to get between them, and Reid paced forward and got in Jett's face.

"What you think I been doing?" Jett yelled back.

"Playing with your dick from what I've seen. Christ, work it out, this is her haven, Sin's daddy left her this, she's made it work, gave Sin something of Dad back. Then a wanker attacks her and makes Sin's safe place not safe," Reid carried on yelling. Not caring in the slightest, the shop was full of customers watching.

"Fuckin' know that," Jett bellowed not backing down. Zoe made a tiny noise and backed away from the yelling men. Manny glanced at Zoe and sent her a reassuring smile, Zoe didn't smile back.

"So what you gonna do about it?" Reid snapped. Jett dragged hands through his hair.

"What you want me to fuckin' do? I'm at your place as much as I can be, Sin don't want anyone with her. She's pushin' everyone away, I offered her cameras and shit, Sin turned me down."

"You offered," Reid sneered. Manny had to agree with Reid's opinion of that.

"Yeah, I did."

"How thick are you? You don't offer Sin shit, you tell her. Someone has taken Sin's haven from her, tried to steal her peace of mind, and you offer to do shit? You don't fucking offer, you fucking do it, yeah Sin will throw a tantrum but so what? She'll ease up the minute she knows she's being watched all day every day. Put it together, Sin's struggling for control, and she can control that. Sin can control not leaving the house, so she is. Stop letting your guilt let Sin lead you around by your dick," Reid yelled again. Jett stiffened and got straight in Reid's face.

"She's not leading me around by my dick," Jett snarled.

"No? Then fucking get on the phone to your mate. Sort shit out and give Sin, her safety back, fucking hell, do I have to spell it out?" Reid stormed away.

"Wow, I'm definitely drinking here every day," a woman whispered. Jett looked at her, and she winked. Jett dragged his phone from his pocket and punched in

Hawthorne's number.

"'Bout fucking time Jett," Hawthorne said, answering, "thought the brit would've beat shit into your stubborn head."

"What the fuck?" Jett snarled.

"Dude's right, stop letting Sinclair lead you around by your dick."

"You got cover here."

"Well, yeah, Jett. A Rage woman got attacked of course we covered her, Sinclair's been covered the night after it happened. Minimal coverage. I'll have someone there in an hour we got shit set up to go here. You owe me one hundred bucks, I lost my bet."

"What bet?"

"Office bet, bet it would take you another day to put your foot down with her." Jett snorted.

"Who won?"

"Davies, he even bet on the brit punching it into your head. Fucker won the pot, nice one k for him," Hawthorne laughed.

"Jesus," Jett said, finally letting go of his anger.

"From now on in, the moment Rage shows interest in a woman, we're wiring her up," Hawthorne sniped, "tell Drake I'll take a marker." The connection cut. Manny stepped forward, looking at Jett and then at Reid.

"No one is gonna force Sin back to this shop until she says so," Manny stated. Jett spun on him, and Reid came storming back.

"What did you say?" Reid snarled going toe to toe with Manny.

"Back the fuck off Reid now! You heard me, man. Sin comes back when she's ready, not when you two think she is." Manny stood his ground facing the two snarling men and the frowning Drake.

"Mollycoddling Sin will do shit," Reid spat. Manny leant forward and grabbed the man's pristine white shirt.

"You haven't fuckin' asked Sin why she won't leave the house, neither of you have. Neither of you fuckin' asked why she can't sleep, and when Sin does, she wakes up screaming. Neither of you has bothered to fuckin' ask why Sin's showering six times a fuckin' day." Manny shoved Reid back and let go of his shirt.

"Rape kit was negative," Drake said softly as Jett stared at him with stunned eyes. Manny met Drake's eyes.

"More than one way to rape a female. Rouse was shoving fingers inside her when the old man stopped him. Asshole had fingers at her entrance, you get me? One more second and he'd have fucked Sin with his fingers, destroying her virginity. One fuckin' more second, she said. Sin felt Rouse starting to push inside, more than one way to rape a woman, I don't need to be telling you that. Spent two minutes with her today before I knew Sin needed to spew.

You two fuckwits have been with her nearly all the time, and neither one of you picked up that Sin's hurting bad. I've seen the bruises on her breasts, she's got Rouse's fuckin' fingerprints on them. Sin's ashamed, you just accepted that Rouse didn't shove his dick in her. And that meant no rape," Manny spat at the two pale men. Reid made a gagging noise and left the room quickly, Jett stared at Manny in horror. Sin had nearly been finger raped. Jett hadn't thought to questions the scrapes and cuts on her inside thighs, he'd just accepted the doc's appraisal. Oh shit, when would he stop fucking up with her? Manny met Drakes gaze.

"That fuck out on bail?" Drake nodded. "I want

Artemis," Manny said, surprising Drake.

"Not a brother?"

"Artemis. She needs to strike a blow for Sin, a woman needs to take Rouse down, I'll back her up."

"I'm coming." Manny spun around looking at Jett's face. Inside Manny acknowledged the pain his brother suffered at what he'd just heard, but Manny was furious. Jett needed to pull his head out of his fuckin' ass and take a proper look at the girl they both desired.

"You're not wanted, Sin told me," Manny hissed. Jett paled more and then took on a mulish expression.

"Sin's mine, I claimed her."

"Don't give a fuck, you get me, prospect? Told you to get your head straight or I'd be banging' in a claim. I like pussy, like Sin more, girl's got class, you want that type of class in your bed, any man does. That woman has options, I'm letting Sin know she got options. You don't fuckin' listen," Manny snarled at Jett.

"I said she's fuckin' mine," Jett replied. Manny leaned into Jett's face.

"Then for the last time, stop laying down the law and start listening to Sin and reading signs. Got your head so far up your ass prospect, you think you're all that. Look at Drake and Ace, learn a lesson. You don't, I'll get in before you do and you lose her, I'll treat Sin like the precious thing she is." Manny spun on his heel and left.

"Claimed her first," Jett yelled at Manny's back.

"You and Manny acting like Sinclair's a fuckin bone to chew over. Manny's right, the woman is class pussy. You get sweet and clean in your bed, prospect and you'll live a good life. Keep doing what you're doing, and you'll lose Sin and be fuckin' sour and dirty pussy for rest of your life. Start looking out for your woman and get your head outta your ass," Drake told Jett and followed Manny from the shop.

Three days later, I glared at Jett as he pulled into a parking space outside the shop. He'd turned up at nine o'clock at the house and let himself in. Which meant that Reid had given Jett a key. We'd quarrelled before Jett gently yanked me out of bed and into the shower. Something was bugging him, and I could tell Jett was based on a precipice, I was wondering how far I could push.

Turned out not to be that far, Jett threatened to shower me himself and grumbling I got in before Jett could make good on his threat. Jett was pacing outside my bathroom door when I emerged with a towel wrapped around me. He told me in firm tones to get dressed and meet him downstairs in ten minutes, or he'd dress me himself.

Beyond furious, which was good considering that for the last few days, I'd alternated between fear, horror, shame, and pure terror. Three nights ago Reid had come home looking shell shocked and had treated me with kid gloves. Reid stopped his insistence that I leave the house and accompany him to work. Jett had hovered all weekend, alternating between solicitous and cajoling.

Between the two of them, they'd pampered and spoilt me during the weekend. I'd shot Manny several texts asking what he had told them, and the damn man kept ducking me. A gut feeling said Manny had said something, but when I dialled Manny's phone, his phone rang out. I'd pin Manny down if it was the last thing I did.

Once dressed, Jett had bundled me out of the house and into a truck. He'd strapped me in despite my constant questions and then drove off, which led us to here and now. Sat outside the shop on Monday morning. I sent Jett a look that should hopefully make his balls shrivel up and die, and Jett returned a shit-eating grin. Jett turned in his seat towards me and slung an arm around my shoulders, dragging me closer.

Jett gazed into my eyes, and I swallowed. He raised his hand and gently brushed a finger down my face, and Jett's grin faded into a serious expression.

"Sin I know, babe, the bruises, the fingers. Manny told me," Jett whispered, and I stiffened in his embrace.

"Manny had no right," I muttered and dropped my head. A gentle but insistent finger tilted my chin back up, and I was staring at Jett again.

"Manny had every right. Sweetheart, how could you think you're dirty? You are the most beautiful thing I've seen. Quiet and shy but with a fire that burns deep inside baby, I've seen it in your eyes. That fucker won't ever darken your life again. Rouse paid a hard price for attacking you. Now we know what Rouse tried to do, that fucker won't walk again." I shuddered under his words.

"Don't want anyone to get into trouble over me," I muttered ignoring the first stuff he'd said.

"Claimed you Sin. Get you don't know what that means in full but let me tell you somethin' it does mean when a man like me claims a woman. It means no fucker lays a hand on you and walks away a free man, means he bleeds and suffers and I have your back. Means the MC has your back, means that you don't live in fear Sin and that you feel safe." Jett leant forward to make sure I got his point.

"This claiming? Does it mean that I'm your possession? I don't like that idea," I told Jett searching his face for something, but I didn't know what. Jett's eyes crinkled, and he smiled.

"No it means that you're mine, I get to look after you, get to make sure you're happy. Break my back, making sure that you have anything and everything you need." Okay! I thought about that not realising that Jett was watching my face carefully.

"What do you get out of it?"

"You, I get beauty in my life," he said, and damn it, wow, Jett thought I was beautiful.

"All I seemed to have done is cause you trouble. You're speaking of hurting someone, making them bleed." I watched as Jett's expression closed off. "You're not going to just hurt him, are you?" I whispered realisation suddenly hit me.

"You don't need to worry, ain't the club taking care of it. Artemis is, striking a blow for a sister," Jett said his tone making no bones about us not discussing it any further.

"So we're dating?" I asked, confused and deciding to change directions. Jett smirked and my breath caught in my throat.

"If you wanna call it dating sweetness, we'll call it dating. Exclusive dating, no other man can lay a finger on you, I'll kill them." I blinked at the emotion behind his words and then pulled away slightly.

"No other women for you?" I asked, I needed Jett to confirm that I wouldn't be the fool who sat at home, while Jett was out chasing skirts.

"There will be no other women Sin I promise. I want this, what's between us, burning for you and what we can be," Jett said his eyes staring into mine.

"You won't judge me again? Call me the C-word again?" I whispered. A look of guilt crossed Jett's face, and he cupped my face in his hands.

"Try to give you time to explain Sin, in future. Can't promise I won't erupt from time to time but will try to let you explain. Got a temper, ain't no mistaking that, I'll blow, but when I do, you get in my face, and you shout like you did when you stormed the clubhouse. That was so fuckin' hot."

"It was?" Jett nodded.

"Dick hardening hot baby, wanted to lay you bare and fuck you over a table. If the clubhouse had been empty, I'd have been balls deep inside you bent over the bar." I blushed furiously. Jett stroked his thumb pads against my cheeks smirking.

"I'm not my brothers Sin, told ya that before. Didn't go through what they did to get the club clean, but I got my own demons, my own darkness. It's too soon for me to tell you but I will one day, when I know you're bound to me body and soul. When I know, you're claimin' me back and will always have my back."

"Give me the chance to prove that," I whispered, Jett, shook his head.

"Not you that's gotta prove shit baby, fucked up three times with you, not aiming for a fourth. You gonna hold back I know that, it's for me to break those walls down and make you mine." I sighed at Jett's words and leant forward to kiss him, Jett allowed me to brush my lips over his, and I cupped his face.

"I told you, I'm socially awkward, I'm shy and come across stuck up and stuff. I've never dated, just the odd dinner date here and there that never went beyond the first date. So much easier to be locked in the Vault with my papers and artefacts.

I'll try, I'll try to be more open and more social, but I can't meet everyone at once. It terrifies me. There's your brothers, the old ladies, that's what they are called, yes? There are the women who hang around your club. I haven't met their like, but I've read enough books on the women who hang around there, and I have seen Sons of Anarchy." I took a breath and Jett kissed me and stole it from me.

"Just don't judge us Sin, I know I was wrong last time, and I jumped the gun. I'll stand between you and the whores, that's my place to."

"I don't have to mix with them, do I?" I asked afraid Jett would say yes, I knew what women, skanks, wanted when they hung around an MC.

"Nah. The old ladies yeah, but not the club whores, whores ain't in your circle. The old ladies are good women, strong and proud to be a brother's heart and soul. Old ladies have their own clique, Phoe, Artemis and Marsha don't mix with club whores. They only hang with each other," Jett said with a light in his eyes. I realised that Jett wanted that, wanted what his brothers had.

"Okay," I nodded and then allowed Jett to lead me into the shop.

Chapter Seven.

When Jett opened the door, I faced Reid, Zoe and Penny. The three appeared a contrast between hopeful and worried. Zoe was wringing her hands together, and Penny was chewing her lip. Reid was hoovering and fiddling with his watch, a nervous thing he did.

"Hey," I said inanely. What else could I say?

"Oh, my gosh boss, great to see you back." A hurricane flew towards me and an arm wrapped around me, and Henry was grinning in my face. She held a coffee cup in hand and presented it with a flourish.

"Thanks, Henry," I said, and Jett's hand touched my back. I leant back against and sank into his comforting presence.

"I made your favourite, sausage rolls with pickle and cheese," Penny said as her welcome back. Shyly, giving Penny a small smile I watched as Zoe pushed Henry to one side.

"Didn't make you anything but did get you chocolates," Zoe said with a grin and pointed at Reid. "Boss man opened them and ate a few." Reid looked affronted at being outed, Jett snorted.

"The Vault needs you Sin, means you don't have to stay upstairs," Reid said. "Those trunks arrived at the shop Friday, and I locked them in the Vault. Thought maybe you'd start cataloguing today. Everything you need is downstairs, and someone will constantly be with you." Reid sent a sharp stare towards Jett.

"Got me this morning and Silvie this afternoon," Jett muttered. His hand gave me a slight push towards the stairs leading to the Vault. I soaked in the heat from Jett's palm before cupping my coffee and walking downstairs. Several new cameras dotted on the shop floor came to my attention, and I made a mental note to ask Reid.

"Thought you'd want to go through the sales reports, you'll be ecstatic and make a start on those trunks and books this morning?" Reid said following us down the stairs. Breathing deeply, I drew in the basement's smell and smiled. The basement smelled like home, parchment, paper and preservatives.

"Sure," I replied realising Jett and Reid waited for an answer.

"The Vault has CCTV and remember the door locks from the inside," Reid said. Un-necessarily reminding me facts I knew, I gave Reid a glare, I wasn't a child.

"Reid, I'm aware, did help design the Vault," I chastised, and Reid grinned.

"Really need to get shit done baby girl, honestly, I think we've hit the mother lode with some of that stuff. Price it up and add ten percent, I promised Montague that we'd give him ten percent. If we add ten percent, it won't cost us anything." I rolled my eyes at Reid and his business sense. I shooed Reid away and entered the Vault with Jett on my heels.

Jett looked around curiously, and I realised that Reid

must have missed out showing him the Vault. The room was large and uncluttered, the back wall was filled with shelves. The right-hand wall was full of glass cabinets, holding the stuff needed to preserve documents and restoratives. The shelves held items such as gloves, Ziploc bags, two handheld vacuums, microfibre cloths and plastic sleeves, all used for protecting and cleaning documents. The remainder of the shelves was filled with the other paraphernalia used on our treasures. There was a double sink to wash hands and equipment.

The left-hand wall was covered in a metal wall of drawers and plastic containers. This is where we stored items that we were working on. Reid had taken up a tenth of the wall with items he'd worked on, as the drawers had labels slotted into the label inserts with his writing.

The door wall had several tall safes which stored valuable prints, documents and letters. The centre of the Vault was dominated by two large worktables, each held four book stands of various size and a pristine work surface. There were several high-backed stools and two comfy armchairs. Over those was what was basically hospital tables that mounted over a bed, on our case they were draggable cover the chairs, enabling people to work from the comfy chairs.

"Guess I shouldn't poke around," Jett said and sank his long body into an armchair. He tucked one leg under himself and cocked his head. Jett waved a book in my direction.

"Don't you got work, sweetness?" Jett asked and grinned. Mock scowling at him, I made my way over and brushed my lips across his mouth. Jett's hand shot out and held the back of my head, where Jett deepened the kiss to such an extent that my toes curled and my fingers clutched his tee. I blinked at Jett bemused when he ended the kiss and smiled into my eyes.

"Get to work Sin," Jett muttered and looked down at his book. Well!

The trunks and crates stored on the left side of the entrance which we'd left empty for that purpose and I dragged the top box from the pile. I pried the lid open and washed my hands before asking Jett to lift the crate onto a rolling lower table. Jett pushed the table over to the middle work table and went back to reading. Deftly, snapping on a pair of gloves I began gathering the items I'd need to start examining what was in the crate.

Finally set up I peered inside the lid and began lifting out documents and parchments one by one. Examining them individually, I began placing each one carefully inside a plastic sleeve, labelling and entering it onto the Vaults laptop. I started creating piles on the two adjourning tables. I had to fight the temptation to read several of the papers. Every so often, Jett's eyes flicked to me as I concentrated on making piles of business letters, personal letters, pamphlets, and so on.

This took all morning as I carefully separated the items in the crate and protected them until I could study them further. Once I'd done, so I put them into drawers and labelled the fronts up. Reid dragged me upstairs for lunch, and after, I headed down again. Jett and I spent a scorching ten minutes saying goodbye and only stopped when Silvie came downstairs chirping happily. Silvie helped drag down a second crate that was decidedly heavier than the first. Silvie happily perched on a chair after pulling on gloves, to hand me the items I requested.

I enjoyed spending time with Silvie, she asked so many questions, and for once, I found I didn't mind, as they weren't stupid questions. She helped by handing me sleeves and labels and Silvie tracked them carefully on the laptop and then placed the items into corresponding piles. Reid poked his head in and told me he was going across to Rage, and I waved Reid away. Reid laughed and disappeared.

At the bottom of the crate was the reason it was so blasted heavy. A wooden, locked chest that was very old, lay there wrapped in a sheet. Carefully with Silvie's help, I lifted it out and then unwrapped the cloth. A solid wooden box ornately decorated with a solid brass lock and hinges. Carefully I vacuumed up the fine dust covering it, and my eyes widened as I stared in shock at the top.

My heart sped up, and my palms began to sweat. I blinked, but the plaque adjourned to the top of the chest, didn't disappear. Dampening down my excitement, I ripped off my gloves and washed my hands before pulling on a fresh pair. I walked back to the box, shaking and stared again at the plaque.

"Oh, my freaking hell," I exclaimed stunned, Silvie looked up.

"What is it?" Silvie asked.

"The Hellfire Club," I whispered, Silvie, blinked at the box.

"Huh?" Silvie said, yeah that's exactly how I was feeling.

"Read that out loud," I demanded not sure if my eyes were playing tricks on me.

"Says 'The Order of the Knights of St Francis, 1752'. Underneath it says, 'Property of the Orders Secretary.' Does that mean something?" Silvie asked, tilting her head.

"Oh, my freaking hell," I repeated and looked into the crate for a key. Something dull caught my eye, and I reached in and pulled out a small key. "Please fit, please fit," I begged as I inserted the key into the chest and carefully twisted the key. A little effort made the lock finally turn, and cautiously I opened the chest and rested the lid on a book stand.

Silvie came to stand next to me as I peered inside the chest and lifted the first book on top. Carefully I opened it and nearly dropped it, my hands were shaking as I put the book down and locked the chest. I undid my necklace and slid the key on, I spun on Silvie whose eyes were wide at my actions.

"I'm going to trust you, I need to get Reid, do not let anyone in, not staff or customer. Please, Silvie, I'm trusting you. I'm going to lock you in, please don't touch that box or let anyone near it," I begged her. Silvie nodded bright-eyed at being part of something important, and I left the Vault and locked the door. Once outside I broke into a run and flew out of the shop startling Zoe and a few customers.

Fast, I sprinted across the road to where the Rage forecourt was. A couple of men around a bike jolted at the sound of my heels pounding the pavement. One came towards me, brow creased in concern, it was Rock I thought.

"Where's Reid?" I blurted out, catching my breath and skidding to a halt.

"Clubhouse," Rock said, tilting his head and studying my flushed cheeks, "lady, you okay?"

"Oh my god no! The Hellfire Club!" I stuttered at Rock and ran towards the clubhouse. I flew through the double doors and skidded to a halt. I took a few seconds to adjust to the dim lighting, and I searched the room for Reid. Drake, his VP. Ace and Jett were getting to their feet at my dramatic entrance, and I spied Reid at the bar.

"Sinclair?" Reid snapped out hurriedly getting to his feet.

"The Knights of St Francis! The Hellfire Club!" I shrieked at Reid. Reid looked at me as if I'd gone mad as he put his beer on the bar. Jett reached my side and tilted my face studying me carefully. A huge grin erupted from me and surprise crossed his face.

"Sin?" Reid asked. I bunny hopped on the spot and then jumped in a circle, and I wrapped my arms around my waist and laughed.

"The Order of the Knights of St Francis! Hellfire Club. Francis Dashwood. It was in the crate!" I couldn't get my words out to make sense. "You need to come, Reid, you need to come now!" I nearly screamed in my excitement at Reid.

"What the fuck has Hellfire got to do with you?" Drake asked. I stared at Drake, confused and then spun back to Reid.

"You need to come. Oh bloody hell, I can't believe this, the Knights of St Francis." I turned on my heel and jogged to the door, turning back and Jett moved towards me. Reid remained still, studying me.

"Pete's sake, hurry up Reid. It's the Order of the Knights of St Francis," I snapped at Reid. He finally began moving with a puzzled look on his face. I bounded out of the clubhouse and bounced off Rock who'd been entering.

"Sin!" Jett called, but I was too excited to heed him.

"Hurry Reid, hurry! The Hellfire Club, oh my god, the Hellfire Club!" Reid moved towards me, so I sprinted back across the forecourt and back into the shop and tore downstairs. Surprised stares from my staff followed me, but I ignored them. My hands were still shaking with excitement when I let myself back into the Vault and found Silvie hovering in front of the chest. I kicked the door shut behind me and dragged the key off my necklace and bounced on my heels as I waited for Reid.

Reid entered the Vault with Jett, Drake, Ace, Apache and Rock at his back. He was frowning at me as he closed the door behind him.

"What the hell Sin?" Reid asked, I leapt towards Reid and dragged him over to my table.

"Read it!" I exclaimed. Reid bent his head and checked the chest out and looked at the top of it, I saw when Reid finally got it. The stunned look of recognition that crossed his face mirrored mine.

"Shit!" Reid exclaimed. Reid tried the lock and nearly broke my fingers when I dangled the key in front of him. He unlocked in gently while I remained buzzing with excitement and pulled on a pair of gloves. Reid lifted the book I had done and opened it carefully.

His hands begin to shake as Reid put the book down and he looked across at me. I bent at the waist, laughing at Reid's stunned expression, I straightened up and giggled and bounced on my heels again.

"The Hellfire Club!" I shrieked throwing my arms up in the air and flew towards Reid as his arms came out and Reid lifted me up and spun me around.

"That's a list of members. That book!" Reid exclaimed loudly.

"Not only that but it records what year they joined, who inducted them, their donations and oh my god, everything. If that is in one book, what else does the chest contain? Did you see the name on the inside page?"

"No?"

"Montague! Lord Montague was the Hellfire Secretary. Can you imagine the sheer freaking value of that book? Just that one book? Can you imagine finally knowing for sure who the members of Hellfire were? We're going to change history!" I shrieked excitement rampaging. Reid put me down, and I spun as someone coughed. I'd been too excited to do more than take a vague note of those who'd followed Reid. And now I saw grim and curious glances and in Jett's case indulgent.

"Guessing there's no danger," Drake drawled, crossing big arms across his even bigger chest.

"Danger?" I asked, stopping bouncing.

"You came shrieking onto the forecourt and then into the clubhouse. Thought there was danger," Ace said with a stern tone. My excitement dropped, and I gazed to the grim-faced men staring back at me.

"Oh. I'm sorry," I said in a small voice, dropping my gaze, I hadn't thought of that. A hand closed around my shoulder, and I refused to look up.

"Hey, it's okay Sin, you're excited, we can see that. Wanna tell us what so exciting?" Jett said. I shook my head, the excitement faded now, and I toed the floor with my shoe. I heard a sigh, and a body stood in front of me, and a finger tipped my chin up.

"Tell us what this Order of the Knights of St Francis is then, girl. All that excitement and hollering, thinking you owe us an explanation," Drake said and offered me a panty-melting smile. I stared at Drake's mouth, how on earth did Phoenix get anything done with that smile around? Drake grinned wider at my dazed expression, and Jett huffed at Drake and turned me to face him.

That was worse as Jett had a gentle expression on his face and a half-smile tilting the corners of his mouth. Jett's eyes blazed down at me, and I shivered under his hand as they promised me something I'd never dared to reach for before.

"Sinclair. The Order of the Knights of St Francis? What links do they have to Hellfire MC?" I turned and faced Apache puzzled.

"Hellfire MC?" I asked, "no, the Hellfire Club."

"Hellfire MC is linked to us, a brother MC. You were shrieking about them," Apache drawled.

"No, I was shrieking about the Hellfire Club, the eighteenth-century Hellfire Club." I began bouncing on my feet again, as I looked at the wooden chest. Reid still hadn't moved and was gazing down at the chest in rapture.

"I don't understand," Silvie said, leaning forward.

"In the eighteenth-century Sir Francis Dashwood created a club for his friends. They were rakes, hellraisers, immoral and lawless. Dashwood called the club the Order of the Knights of St Francis. They held rituals and orgies and did the things polite society back then frowned upon. The order became known later on as the Hellfire Club," I explained and saw comprehension dawn on everyone.

"Shit," Reid exclaimed interrupting. He reached down into the chest, and I heard the rustling of papers.

"Don't damage them!" I yelled, flying towards him. Reid lifted his head and held out his hand, I skidded to a halt and stared. Nestled in his palm was two miniatures, one easily recognisable as Sir Francis and the second I vaguely recognised.

"Is that what I think it is?" I asked, rocking back into a

hard body. Someone's arms steadied my waist, and I reached up and patted Drake's chest absentmindedly. Reid carefully turned the miniatures and written on the back were the names of the portraits. Sir Francis Dashwood and Thomas Potter.

"I think there's more, carefully wrapped and stored at the bottom," Reid said, gazing at me.

"Portraits of the members! Oh, my word!" I yelled and threw my fists in the air, I couldn't for the life of me ever remember being so excited.

"There's personal diaries and more records and lots of letters. Can see what looks to be a donation list and fuck knows what else. This is huge, a treasure trove, I can see the edge of what I suspect is another miniature frame." I spun on my heel and threw my arms around the nearest person. Apache, the recipient, looked bemused. Jett looked irritated. Apache patted me on the shoulder, and I flew across to Jett and leapt, luckily, he caught me, and I wrapped my legs around Jett's waist. I bounced up and down, and Jett gave a pained groan.

"Can you imagine the treasures in here? Even one book about the Hellfire Club is worth serious money, but that lot as a collection? Jett, seven figures easily!" I exclaimed wrapping my arms around Jett's neck. Jett hooked a stool with his foot and sat his ass on the edge.

"Kitten, love how excited you are. But keep bouncing on my cock like that, and you're gonna get a different kinda excitement," Jett groaned. I wriggled in his lap and froze as laughter came from behind and buried my head in his neck.

"Everything's good Fish, Sin found somethin' historically valuable and got over-excited. Yeah, yeah, girl's good. Tell the brothers to stand down," Ace said, and I jammed even further into Jett's neck.

"Yeah, it's somethin' serious, and somethin' exciting, not sure what but the girl is hot to trot, and Reid looks like someone beaned him over the head. Whatever it is from what I'm following, it's huge," Ace said in reply to something asked.

"Huge is an understatement," I whispered into Jett's neck. Drake chuckled behind me.

"Will do brother, cancel the call to Hellfire. Tell Chance, Drake will contact him later," Ace ended the call and glanced over at me.

"So, woman. Want help with your fuckin' huge find and shit?" Ace asked, I nodded shyly. Jett scorched me with a kiss, and I got off his lap and walked with dignity to the table. Reid kindly let me take the lead, and Reid began explaining to the men how they could help.

To my surprise, they all seemed to be interested in how we took care of the documents. Without a murmur, Rage gloved up and helped hand over stuff Reid and I needed. There were several squeals from me and even from Reid as the afternoon passed us by. Reid and I put each item into protective sleeves, Apache and Ace labelled them up with what we directed them too.

Silvie entered them into the system, and Drake and Rock put them on the piles we had directed to be compiled. Jett gathered us items we required when we came across a damaged document or fragile piece of paper. We finally cleared out the books and loose paperwork and gazed down into the bottom of the chest.

"Wow," Silvie said as we gazed at the carefully wrapped a few dozen miniatures stacked neatly at the bottom of the chest.

"We hit the mother lode," Reid whispered in reverence.

I reached out a hand to Jett and squeezed it when he took hold.

"We've hit the freaking mother lode!" I repeated, and Drake winked at me. That was hot.

"You'll never complain when I go buying in England again!" Reid laughed.

Jett and the others left after a couple hours while Reid and I stayed late documenting everything. We'd mentioned security to man the store at night until we knew precisely what was in our hands. I knew the chest was something big, but how big, we weren't sure.

From what we'd seen so far, we'd a list of members, including code names for some, dates of joining and death or leaving. The diaries for the Hellfire Club members had to be read and catalogued. We'd letters from one member to another and several other documents which needed investigating.

There were the miniatures and at the bottom was a set of gold signet rings. There was one for each member of the Hellfire Club. Each ring had a stone set into it, a symbol and a set of initials carved into the back. We'd have to link up the rings, miniatures and member list. There had a set of heavy gold chains which I assumed meant, without proof yet, that there had been a hierarchy in the club.

The different stones in each ring, some held sapphires, others had rubies and so on, which lead me to the same conclusion of a hierarchy. Today we'd achieved separating the books, diaries and documents into piles. Tomorrow we'd begin going through them to see what we had. The other trunks and crates needed checking and also cataloguing, so we didn't know where to start.

Despite me hopping around Rage like a lunatic no one

knew we had the Hellfire Club chest apart from the Rage members who had been present. We'd explained to Drake what this meant and what the discovery was worth. Drake assured us that none of his brothers would talk and possibly endanger Reid or me.

Drake had given us a number for a company called Hawthorne's Investigations and told us to speak to a guy called Dylan Hawthorne who provided security. He'd also given us a direct cell phone number to Artemis, Ace's old lady who could help if Hawthorne's couldn't. Reid called Hawthorne's and was told that Hawthorne had arranged night security with two of his guys. Seems they watched the Vault after all.

Niko and Max would take the next few nights in the shop while they monitored our CCTV as well. Jett whispered that Hawthorne's was covering our cameras so this wasn't a big deal. I insisted on paying even though Dylan Hawthorne had said he'd take a marker, whatever that was. Drake had agreed, but I'd argued against Drake, and he must have seen me steal myself to do so, because Drake let me have my way.

While Reid, Drake and Hawthorne had a three-way conversation, I clicked on Hawthorne's website. I discovered that Hawthorne's Investigations was the premier private eye and security company in South Dakota. Which led to me knowing that when Reid told me how much security would cost, that Dylan Hawthorne had severely discounted his costings.

I added that favour to the mental tally that was building up. Hawthorne as he preferred to be called, just asked that his men have food and drink. And if we didn't mind if they helped themselves to books. I told Hawthorne, we'd leave a tray of pastries in the fridge and leave the coffee maker on for his men. Hawthorne replied that it was a deal.

After the Rage brothers had left and we'd finished sorting through the chest we began locking away the items in one of the large safes. The rest of the contents of the crates we put into drawers and locked up the Vault. It was nearly nine at night, and I yawned suddenly overwhelmed with tiredness. Reid slung an arm around my shoulder as he led me to his car, and before we reached the end of the street, I was asleep.

I woke up the next day toasty warm and with an unfamiliar weight across my waist and boobs. Frowning, I opened my eyes and stared at the vision of beauty in front of my face. I was tucked into Jett's shoulder on my side, facing him with one of Jett's arms across my boobs and the other arm wrapped securely and firmly around my waist.

Urgh, did I miss something last night? The last thing I recalled was settling down into Reid's car and zilch, not getting out or walking into the house. Silently, biting my lip, I lifted the bedcovers and saw to my relief I was in pyjamas, which led to the question of who changed me!

Reid grunted in his sleep and relaxed the tight grip he had on my waist, and I began to move out of Jett's reach. Once my legs hit the side of the bed, I got to my feet and crept into the adjoining bathroom. Shutting the door quietly, I brushed my teeth and washed my face. Still trying to puzzle it out, I opened the door and saw a pair of sleepy eyes looking at me.

Oh my, sleepy head Jett nearly stopped my heart. I had to remind myself to breathe as Jett sat up, and the sheet fell down his bare chest. Jett rubbed his eyes cutely and sent me a beatific grin.

"Hey baby," Jett rumbled, and he popped a mint into that sexy mouth. One of the mints I kept on top of my bedside table for some inane reason. I hovered by the bathroom door rubbing one foot up my leg in nervousness. My eyes couldn't move from that beautifully carved chest and muscles.

"Hey," I finally replied when Jett sent me a quizzical look at my lack of response.

"How you feelin'? You were out like a light."

"Who undressed me?" I blurted and saw lazy warmness in Jett's eyes.

"Would it matter?" Jett asked, I nodded tongue in cheek. "You did Sin, you roused yourself enough to strip and put pyjamas on," Jett laughed. No doubt Jett laughed at the outraged look on my face, he knew that I thought it had been him! I gave a low growl and tackled Jett on the bed tickling him, I didn't get very far. Jett adeptly flipped me onto my back and laid his lean muscled length over my body and kissed me mindless.

My hands slipped up Jett's back as he growled deep in his throat and deepened the kiss. Jett's skin was like silk over steel, muscles well defined that I could feel every clench and twitch as I ran my hands gently over his back. Hands grabbed mine, and Jett held them above my head.

"Kitten, I'll ask this once, are you sure you want this? Want me?" I nodded shyly, and a blush hit my cheeks, much to my mortification

"Yes, Jett, there's no doubt," I whispered back pushing my hips up against his large erection. Jett growled at me and lifted himself away from me.

"Sin, we need to take this slow, you're a virgin, and I'm big. Slow woman," Jett growled as I twisted my body under his. He sank his mouth back on to mine trailing light kisses across my lips and down my throat. That was sensitive, and I gasped, and Jett lifted his head with a wicked glint.

"That make you wet, baby?" Jett asked, and I nodded. With a glint still in his eyes, he dropped back to the hollows in my throat and kissed lightly. Jett leaned his weight onto me again bracing himself with his arms as I squirmed from his kisses. No lie, I was wet, and I wanted Jett, and we hadn't even kicked off foreplay!

Jett trailed kisses down towards the hollows in my shoulders and tugged at my top, pulling it down to he could bare the flesh there to his mouth. I ran my hands up his back, needing to touch perfection and lightly down to his ass where it clenched under my light touch. Muttering under his breath, Jett reached down and pulled my hands up.

"They stay above your head like a good girl," Jett grated as I thrust against his erection. I nodded, and Jett in one move pulled my top up and over my head. I instantly tried to cover myself, and Jett pushed my arms away and up again.

"Hold onto your headboard," Jett murmured as he gazed at my breasts. My nipples puckered under his gaze, demanding attention. The heat in Jett's eyes affected me, and I lost my senses as he took first one nipple and then the other into his hot, wet mouth.

Jett took time lavishing attention on my breasts while I clung to the slats in my headboard and let him do as he wished. I couldn't stop Jett even if I wanted to, I was hot, wet and desperate for something. These feelings were new to me, and I couldn't understand them, I recognised desire, but there was something else. Surrender, complete surrender to the master who was awakening my body.

Jett smirked as he raised his head and saw my flushed face. Slowly he began tugging down my bottoms trailing kisses over my stomach, and hip bones and then his mouth was there, right where I needed him! I cried wordlessly as he found exactly the spot that needed attention. Jett's tongue penetrated and licked, and his lips sucked and nipped, and I was a crying mess of desperation.

"Need to prepare you," Jett muttered as I begged him to enter me. He slipped one finger into my slick wetness and then a second. It didn't hurt, but it was uncomfortable, I thrust against Jett's fingers as he moved them inside me.

"Please," I begged nearly weeping. Jett sat up and yanked his jeans off, and I heard a rip as he opened a condom and slipped it on. He resumed his position over me and kissing me deeply Jett began to feed himself into me. At first, it didn't hurt, but I thrust up against him in impatience, and I gasped as Jett forced through my barrier and buried himself to the hilt inside me.

"Dammit, Sin!" Jett snapped, holding himself tight as I let out a low cry of pain. Jett looked down at me with fire in his eyes. "I didn't want to hurt you, baby." I let out another mew as I moved my hips under him and Jett's body tensed. Jett let me move against him, finding a rhythm that I was comfortable with. Tightly holding himself, so I could get comfortable with his size, Jett's jaw clenched.

"Fuck me," I whispered and dragged Jett's head down to mine for a kiss. Jett still tried to control himself, and that was not what I wanted or needed. I sharply thrust up again, biting lightly down on his lip, Jett growled in return, and he thrust hard into me. Jett held my arms above my head as he set the pace, slow and torturous.

"Bad girls get punished," Jett panted in my ear. I struggled to make him go faster, to give me what my body demanded. There was something building inside, and I needed it to release. Panting, I tried to force Jett to give me what my body demanded. Jett gave me a bruising kiss and gave into my frantic demands. The pressure built inside and I cried out trying to free my hands to grab Jett and force him deeper. But he refused to let go and then it hit me.

I'd never orgasmed like it, it swept over me like a tidal wave, and I screamed his name as I rode the crest. Never had I felt this feeling and for a split second, I rued what I'd been missing. Jett jerked inside me as my walls clenched around him, greedy and demanding. He rode the wave with me and then Jett tensed and warmth flooded my insides. Jett collapsed rolling onto his side and taking me with him, we lay side by side with him still inside.

"Fuck me, I'll never forget that look," Jett whispered. A long finger down what I was sure was a dazed and incredibly smug face.

"I never knew it could be like that," I mumbled.

"Baby I never had it go fuckin' hot, you were so fuckin' sexy." Jett dipped his head and kissed the tip of my nose and pulled out. I gave a disgruntled mew and Jett winked at me as he rose from the bed and strutted his tight muscled ass across the bedroom to the bathroom. A few minutes later, Jett came out, and my eyes dropped to his cock. He was at half-mast.

"Again?" I asked Jett and his eyes grew hot, and half-mast became full mast.

"What's on for today?" Jett asked as I snuggled into

his arms. This I liked, he didn't rush out of my bed and yank his clothes on. Jett lay under my duvet, stark naked, and happily cuddling my own naked self.

"I've got to go through the documents one at a time and start sorting time frames and cross-referencing. Reid will help as well. We have to scan the documents into the laptop, so we've a computerised record and then go from there. At some point, we'll call in a second expert to confirm our findings and probably a third considering the importance of this find."

"Sounds a shit load to do," Jett mused.

"Yeah. The payoff though in terms of historical fact and relevance will be insurmountable. Add to that, both Reid and I can publish not only our findings, but we might draft up a book or something. We'll have to contact Reid's friend and let Montague know what we have. That would be only fair," I mused. Reid gave a chuckle.

"Well, it seems like Montague had no idea of what he had, so I think it's all yours babe."

"Oh, no, no," I shook my head, "that would be wrong. If Montague had known what he had, he'd never have sold it to us so cheap. While they remain ours, we owe Montague the courtesy of telling him and giving him a percentage."

"And if Montague wants this shit returned?"

"He can't, it's ours legally, but we still owe him to let him know what we've found. We're going to have trouble getting Reid's head out of the Vault for the next few months. Once we start, it will go slow at first, but it will soon speed up. So hard to believe the treasure we've got on our hands, the Elizabethan letters were out of this world. The Hellfire Club discovery is a once in a lifetime find."

"So it's gonna give you guys a massive boost in your community?" Jett asked.

"You've no idea. Our reputations are solid but this type of find, and if we publish? Well, the sky's the limit for us." I wriggled in Jett's arms, excited again. Jett's eyes flashed at me, and he pressed his hard cock against me.

"I'm feeling a different kind of limit," Jett said huskily and bent his head to mine.

The next month flashed by. Reid and I took on another member of staff to cover us both being in the Vault. Reid and I spent each day working from eight in the morning till nine at night, reading everything and documenting and cross-referencing. Montague had offered us his congratulations on the find and been genial about it. Luckily, Montague wasn't holding on to any bitterness around his rash sale. He kindly asked us to keep him updated and that if anything personal to his family came up, would we consider his family?

Reid and I both assured Montague that is anything risqué or heinous came up, we'd copy it, but send him the originals and keep it from the public eye. It was the least we could do considering how generous Montague was being. Of course, we owned everything, but some things, friendship, wasn't worth losing over a family scandal.

Jett had been so patient with me. He arrived at nine every night and took me home, and we often woke up together. Jett brought me lunch and dinner, and when he'd finished at the garages, he'd come and sit with us sometimes for a few hours. Our relationship was going from strength to strength, which is why when shit hit the fan, I was totally blindsided.

Chapter Eight.

I hurried across the forecourt excitement beating in my chest. After a solid month of working full time on the Hellfire Club documents, I was taking a day off to spend with Jett. Jett had asked a couple of nights ago for me to take a day off so we could go out somewhere and I'd agreed. He'd been so patient, supporting me with my investigations into the chest's contents, I owed us both this. Jett hadn't once complained, and most men would have by now.

Manny raised a hand in greeting as he came out of one of the bays wiping hands on his jeans. Slowly strolling over and Manny shot me a wink. No matter how dirty Manny looked, he was still hot as hell.

"So where you two off too?" Manny rumbled squinting in the sun.

"Not sure, Jett said it's a surprise. But he told me to wear jeans and boots," I replied with a frown glancing at myself.

"Well, lady, you look fuckin' fine to me," Manny rumbled. "Come on, I need to change my tee, spilt oil on me," he said. Manny looking down at his messy tee, I snickered, which made Manny grin, and we began walking towards the clubhouse. Manny glanced just past me, and he frowned.

"Manny?" I asked.

"That's a piece of shit, nothing we'd work on," Manny said, tilting his head towards a car. I couldn't disagree with Manny, the car was a piece of shit. Rusted and two different colours, I'd be surprised if it ran.

"Maybe someone's visiting?" I asked as Manny opened the clubhouse door and I stepped through into the dimmer light.

I peered around for Jett and waved to Texas who was glaring at a woman. Texas's mouth tightened when he saw me, and I wondered what was going on. Surprised, I saw several of the brothers, Lowrider, Ezra, Ace and Apache, all looking strangely pissed. Phoenix and Marsha stood with Lowrider's arms wrapped around Phoe and she looked mad as hell.

"Hey Texas, is Jett here?" I asked the frowning man. The stranger turned around to face me, I swallowed distaste and tried to make sure it didn't show in my expression. Ouch, this woman was not attractive, blond hair hung limply and looked in need of a good wash and cut. Her face once could have been pretty except it was sallow and pinched thin. Bloodshot eyes peered at me, and her mouth had a huge cold sore in the corner, she'd chewed her lips so hard they were chapped.

The woman wore a skimpy, thin, dirty tank and a mini skirt which barely covered her ass. To my surprise, she held a toddler in her arms. At least the child looked a bit healthier than her mother did, the mother resembled a drugged-out skank.

"Jett's waiting for you girlie," Texas growled with a warning glare at the skank.

"I'm waiting for Jett," the skank said, and I looked at her in mild surprise.

"I'm Jett's girlfriend, anything I can do?" I asked, and Manny's hand suddenly clenched on my shoulder.

"Fuck no whore, I'm Jett's baby mama and fiancée." The bottom fell out of my world as Jett came into view, his eyes a burning fury, as Jett looked to the skank to me. Bile rose in my throat as I looked at the woman and the baby. Jett was engaged? Engaged to that? No way, I didn't believe it, wait, that was his baby? Shock rooted me to the spot, and I was grateful for Manny's hand on my shoulder, I looked at Jett with stunned eyes.

"What the fuck are you doing here?" Jett snarled into the silence in the room, I took a step back, and Manny's other hand came to my waist.

"We had a date," I replied. Jett's burning eyes came to me.

"Not you, babe, that cunt." Jett spat with a flick of his head at the skank. I swallowed. Jett was enraged, angrier than I'd ever seen him and I took another step back into Manny's body which had tensed. Tension radiated off Manny's body in waves. Was this Jett's baby? I was confused, Jett hadn't even glanced at the little one.

"Charming, is that how you greet your baby mama?" the woman sneered, leaning forward.

"Ain't my baby Dina, whatever the fuck you want you ain't gettin'. Get the fuck out," Jett stormed towards her. To my surprise, Jett put a hand on her shoulder and gave her a hard shove. Dina stumbled back against a chair and kept her footing, the toddler whimpered in her arms.

"It's your fucking baby, and I want what I'm owed. Want back pay and child support, your fucking ring back on my finger," Dina hissed.

"Ain't mine, why don't you go drain Martin's pockets for money," Jett got in her face and sneered.

"Kid ain't Martin's, kid's yours," the woman insisted. I reeled as the toddler pouted, and Jett's eyes stared back at me. Oh god, she was Jett's child, even if Jett denied it. A sinking sensation began in my stomach, and I saw our life together taking a massive hit. No way on earth would Jett walk away from his child. Jett's cutting voice cut into my musing.

"Let me get this right. Not laid sight on ya for three happy years, why's that? Yeah, I remember, I come home from work early. Find you screwin' my *fuckin' brother* in our bed, *our bed,* Dina. I always wrapped up, knew I couldn't completely trust ya, but Martin was taking you un-gloved. Go hit my *brother* for blood money. Fuckin' whore," Jett seethed. I stared at Jett stunned, this was his dark, his issue. Manny muttered 'shit' in my ear, and I wholeheartedly agreed, I was watching a train wreck.

"Martin was paying support until three months ago," Dina whined, tossing her dirty hair back.

"What, Martin catch you sucking another man's dick?" Jett sneered.

"No, we never got together, Martin blamed me for you walking out. Martin and his bitch wife want kids, and it wasn't happening. They went for tests and guess what lover, he's infertile. Little Ursula can't be his, which means she's yours." Jett rocked back on his heels. Stunned shock crossed his face, I felt a similar emotion. Dear god Jett had a kid, with that nasty piece of skank, I'd been right. Phoe pulled free from Lowrider and picked up her phone, she sent a couple of texts and slammed the phone down.

"You got proof it's Jett's kid?" Phoe asked into the

silence. "From what I'm hearing you weren't too bothered shagging two brothers, maybe you had more than those two." Dina hissed at Phoe.

"What you are saying bitch?"

"I'm saying you appear to be free with your favours if one can call them favours. So you weren't just fucking Jett and his brother," Phoe said, striding forward. The difference between Phoe and the skank was oceans apart. Phoe wore a pale blue blouse and a black pencil skirt. Phoe's hair was glossy and shiny and hung loose past her shoulders. Phoenix was the embodiment of sheer elegant class. My hands rose, and I clutched at Manny's forearm, which was across my chest now holding me up. Phoe got beside Jett and stopped.

"Oh fuck, someone rein Phoe in!" Manny muttered loud enough for Texas to move in Phoe's direction.

"Be grateful Killer isn't here," Ezra muttered, and I knew he meant Artemis.

"Drake, now, brother!" Lowrider snapped down a phone.

"Who the fuck you calling a whore?" Dina shrieked.

"If the shoe fits…" Phoe bit out, leaning forward. I saw at once why the men were worried, Phoe had a look in her eyes, one that couldn't be mistaken. Rage's President's wife was in full fighting mode, and Phoe was coming out swinging. It had been something I learned quick about Phoe, she loved Rage and its brothers, and God help anyone who crossed them.

"Oh, fuck," Ezra said and moved forward. The door to the clubhouse slammed, and Drake strode past me just as Dina slapped a hand out intending to hit Phoe. Drake caught Dina by the wrist, and I saw him squeeze. Dina winced in pain as Drake squeezed harder, he put his other hand up and shoved Dina hard, forcing her backwards.

"No fuckin' cunt raises a hand to my wife," Drake snarled. Dina took one glance at his face, wrenched her wrist free and stepped back. The evil bitch placed the toddler firmly in between them. Drake snatched Phoe around the waist and snagged her tightly to him, Phoe still glared at Dina, the look on Phoe's face was one I never hoped to see aimed in my direction. Now I saw how she could be a sister in Hellfire MC and Drake's wife, Phoe had hidden depths.

"Whore claimin' it yours?" Drake snarled tilting his head at Dina. Jett nodded as his eyes studied the toddler who was now staring at Jett. I saw recognition register at the same time it did everyone else. Despite the dirty face and shorn hair, she was Jett's image.

"Want a DNA test," Jett finally said, his eyes remaining on the little girl.

"You can have one, 'because despite that bitch there I only fucked you and Martin, if Martin's infertile then you're her father, and I want my dues. Want back child support from when she was born, want my ring back and on my finger. I want child support for Ursula."

"You think I'd put a ring on your finger again? Fuckin' threw the one and only ring you'd ever get from me in the sewers where it belonged," Jett said with a bitter laugh. Shit just got worse, Dina had been engaged to Jett. I clung to Manny's arm his solid body providing support.

"You did once. I want it again, or you won't get to see the kid, you'll give me everything I want Jett and I want a fucking shit load. Having this brat ruined my life, and I want compensation. I will have compensation, and I know you're making good fucking money now, you owe me that."

"You want compensation for having a baby?" Phoe breathed incredulously as Drake's arms encircled his wife. Drake was definitely holding Phoe back.

"Jett ruined my life, asshole broke off our engagement and fucking ran. Martin wouldn't marry me, and I was left with a baby I didn't want, I'm owed!" Dina shrieked. "If Jett doesn't give me what I want and when I want it, I'll make sure Jett never sees the brat. I'll fuck Jett up and his life, make the asshole wonder every day, where the brat is and if she's okay." Jett took an angry step forward, and Drake's arm shot across his chest, stopping him.

Drake jerked his head towards Ace and moving fast Ace tore the baby from Dina's arms and placed her in Jett's. Ace yanked Dina's arm out, and Texas stepped forward and began snapping shots with his phone.

"Cunt wants money to shoot up with," Drake snarled. Dina shrieked and kicked out at Texas who released her. "Don't give her that kid back prospect," Drake snarled.

"You can't take her, Ursula's mine," Dina yelled and tried to sidestep Drake. The brothers began forming a barricade between Jett and Dina. The air of anger and disgust rolling off them nearly choked me.

"Drake, give her back the baby," a male voice spoke from behind us. A smartly dressed man in a suit stepped forward, my eyes cautiously followed him. Dina took her chance and grabbed the child from Phoe who Jett had handed the little one to. The little girl gave a cry, and Phoe let go not wanting to hurt her.

"The fuck I do, bitch is whacked out on drugs and claimin' my brother is the kid's father. Ain't giving her back," Drake snarled.

"By law…" the man began, and both Drake and Jett snarled cutting him off.

"Ain't giving the baby back to the bitch," Jett spat.

"I will organise a DNA test this afternoon, Doc Gibbons will do it. We'll pay to put a rush on the results. Once we got them, we can act," the man said soothingly.

"Ain't leaving my daughter with that cunt," Jett growled, anger and resentment in every line of his body.

"You've no choice, anything else is kidnapping. I know a couple of judges here, as soon as we have those tests results, I'll have a hearing ready."

"A hearing for what? You ain't taking my kid away," Dina hissed, the man spun on her.

"Listen up lady, I have everything you said on camera. *Everything*. Including the fact you don't want her and that she's only a meal ticket for you to get money out of Jett. We now have photos of those track marks. And we don't even need them because I can get this into family court in two weeks and they'll still be visible. Jett's DNA comes back a match, no judge will give you custody over him."

"It's because of Jett, I'm addicted. Ask him! Ask him! Jett bought me the shit and got me hooked. No judge will give Jett custody!" Dina yelled, turning bitter eyes on Jett who paled. My heart spluttered, and for a few seconds, I wondered if Dina was telling the truth and then I looked at Jett. No, Jett hadn't got her hooked, how could I doubt him?

"That what your story's gonna be, bitch?" Jett whispered. "Don't touch drugs, never have, don't even smoke weed. Come here with my kid, to smack me down to support your habit and think I'm gonna let you walk away with my kid? Got another thing coming, if Ursula's mine I'm taking her." I gulped at the level of hate in his voice. Manny's hand moved in soothing circles on my hip, I couldn't believe this. How the hell had our day gone so badly wrong?

"You ain't getting shit, I'll tell the judge I was a good girl, a college girl with a future. And you came along on your bike and with your bad boy rep, that you ruined me. Got me drunk and hooked on drugs so you could control me and have your way with me and pimp me out, who she gonna believe?" Dina sneered. My gaze searched the tiny girl who was silent, she appeared terrified and scared, and she was looking green from being swung around so much.

"Jett, stop," I said. Jett's eyes snapped to me. "Keep Dina here with the child. Take her to the hospital and get the test done. Get the lawyer to rush the DNA results and take Dina to a hotel and feed them. Put a brother on the hotel's door, so Dina can't run. Call Hawthorne and Detective Ramirez." Jett gave a sharp nod.

"Ain't going to no hotel room, I'm staying with Jett," Dina sneered. She dug in her bag for something and pulling out a cigarette. To my disbelieving eyes, Dina lit it while still holding her daughter.

"Second-hand smoke is bad for kids," I told Dina, reining in my temper.

"Fuck you cunt, you know I was once like you. Sweet and innocent, till asshole got his hands on me."

"Fuck you, bitch," I said, leaning forward in Manny's arms, my temper flaring. Dina's eyes grew wide as I took a step forward and Manny drew me back. "You came here to blackmail my boyfriend, my man! You try to blackmail Jett into giving you money and shit, and you light up and smoke while your daughters on your hip. How do you think I'll believe anything you say?" I sneered at her, I met Jett's gaze and saw relief in his eyes. Well, what did Jett think I would do? Run out on him?

This complicated our future, but Jett was my partner, I turned back to Dina.

"You aren't going anywhere near Jett, he lives with me, and no way on earth are you staying at my house. You just made the biggest mistake in your pathetic whacked out life. Once we get confirmation Ursula's Jett's, we're taking Ursula, and I *fucking* dare you to stop us." Despite Manny having his arms firmly around my waist, I still managed to get my hands on my hips and glare at the scum smoking.

"Baby?" Jett asked gently, his eyes searching my face. Whatever Jett saw there reassured him.

"You claim me?"

"I claimed ya, baby," Jett nodded.

"Then I claimed you and the shit that came with you, you're mine." Jett's eyes blazed for a different reason, and Jett strode forward. Manny let me go, and Jett cupped my face and looked down into my eyes.

"Never understand what I did to deserve you," Jett whispered and took my mouth. I kissed Jett back, putting everything I felt into it, and I hoped Jett felt it too.

"Stop that you cunt!" Dina shrieked, stamping a foot. Jett broke the kiss, I leaned around him.

"You fucked up," I said, pointing my finger at Dina. "Seriously fucked up when you came here to screw with Jett." Anger showed in every word I bit out.

"We'll see whose man Jett is when he gets those results, he'll put a ring back on my finger," Dina sneered. "Jett wants the brat and to get Ursula, Jett got to have me too." I stormed towards Dina, anger burning hotly and this time Apache snagged me around the waist as I got within a foot of her.

"Jett's mine, he'll always be mine. Those results come

back the way I think they will, we'll both be seeing you in court. And honey, you got no idea who I am or what I can bring to the table. You have no idea who Jett's friends are. Believe me, I'll bring in everyone and anyone to prove Jett will be a better parent than you ever would be," I said firmly, getting into her face. I shoved my finger at her on each point I made. Finally saw doubt flickered in Dina's eyes and then she was back to being bold and brassy.

"Jett's a biker in an MC. No one will give a biker a kid."

"How much you willing to bet on that?" I asked and saw that doubt return. "Make sure Dina doesn't leave until we're ready for the appointment," I said to the room.

"Doc Gibbons can see us in an hour and a half," the suited man said, texting on his phone.

"Thanks, Steven, can you get that proposal started now?" Phoe said, walking over to the man and putting her hand on his arm.

"It will be drafted by this afternoon, and I'll file it and make a few calls. Even if Jett's DNA doesn't match, that child doesn't deserve a mother like that," Steven replied. I didn't hear any more as I dragged Jett out back towards his room. My mind was racing, and I was unsure how to say what I wanted to say next, we entered Jett's room, and Jett sank down on to his bed.

"That was so hot baby."

"Thank you," I muttered thoughts racing through my mind.

"Fuck! A kid!" Jett exploded leaping to his feet and smashing his hand into the wall. "Can you imagine what fucked up shit Dina has done to her?" Jett punched the wall again.

"I love you." Jett stopped punching and his body locked

up before turning to face me. Tears were in my eyes, and I was biting my lip hard.

"What?" Jett bit out, I wasn't sure if he was angry I'd said it, I couldn't read Jett for once.

"I love you," I repeated in a much softer voice. Seconds later, I was in Jett's arms, tumbling towards the bed, and he was ripping my clothes off me. I freed my hands and grabbed Jett's belt, moaning when I couldn't get it undone. Jett's hands brushed mine away, his mouth on mine, our tongues duelling. Seconds later, Jett was slamming inside me, and I was clawing him desperate for Jett to go deep and make me his.

This was not making love, this was claiming. It was hard and brutal on both sides, I bit him hard, marking him, making him mine. Jett tightened his grip on my hips as he thrust inside me hard, I scratched his back and sank my nails into his ass. Jett pushed deeper, and I dug my nails in deeper to force Jett even deeper. I screamed his name as I came, and seconds later, Jett yelled mine as he came with a forceful thrust.

"I love you Sin, I fuckin' love you to death," Jett said collapsing next to me. I panted trying to regain my breath to tell Jett what was next.

"Love you," I said lamely, and Jett rolled me into his arms and held on tight.

"Didn't want to rush you, but I fell in love with you the first time you curled in my arms heartbroken. You trusted me to protect you," Jett whispered, kissing the top of my head.

"Are you going to tell me about Dina?" Jett flopped on his back and covered his eyes with his arm. Jett took a few minutes, dragging a sheet over us, but he did finally speak.

"Don't want her in our bed but ya need to know Sin. Dina wasn't always like this, met her five years ago, Dina was in college, studying business management and doing well. At first, Dina was amazing, and we were solid. Stable enough that after a year she'd moved in with me and had my ring on her finger. Dina was funny and sweet.

Wanted the dream, white picket fence and a family, I worked hard as a mechanic back then. Money was okay, and we'd have a decent life, then Dina found new friends. New friends who got her into shit, I kept trying to get Dina clean, straighten her out.

Dina got kicked from college, and I'd be walking the streets for hours looking for her. I'd find Dina on her knees sucking cock for drugs. So many fights and I broke when I came home and found Dina in bed with my brother. Didn't do or say anythin'. I packed my bags and walked, while the pair of them hopped around getting dressed and tryin' to explain." I sighed, heartbroken for Jett.

"Your own brother did that to you?" Poor Jett, how awful to have your brother turn on you.

"Martin was always a jealous prick, he was two years older but bland and boring. My parents were proud of us both, though, but Martin's jealousy got out of hand. Martin was in banking, and I went into mechanics. Was just getting a name for myself designing, and Martin's jealousy shot into over-drive.

Martin claimed Dina seduced him and my parents knowing of her addictions and what Dina was puttin' me through, took Martin's side. Caused a rift in my family and we ain't spoken since." I was furious on Jett's behalf and then realised that if Jett hadn't had left Dina and his family, then Jett wouldn't have Rage. I told Jett that and he grinned and pulled me tight.

"Yeah babe, I wouldn't have my brothers or you. So Martin and Dina did me a favour, they just don't know it." I made my decision there, and then, I acted on instinct instead of thinking things through in my usual way.

"We need to get dressed and get our birth certificates," I informed Jett. My mind whirled like crazy, and he pushed away to stare me in the face. "After the tests are done, we need to go to city hall and get married. If we're going for custody of that little girl, we need to prove we're in a strong, steady relationship."

"You wanna get married?" Jett rumbled shocked.

"It's quick, no doubt about that, but Ursula's your daughter, dreadful name, we need to change that! The test is just a formality. Even if Ursula is your brother's kid, she's still your niece, and if the twatwaffle's washed his hands of her, then we can step up, right?" I asked Jett sitting up and drawing the sheets up to my chest.

"Best thing I ever did in my life was follow you that day baby. Don't know what I did to deserve you, but fuck I'll break my back makin' you happy every day of my life."

"And I'll stand by you every day of your life. Always and forever," I told him gently my voicing trembling with unshed tears. Jett pushed himself up on his elbows and kissed me.

"Need a house, mine is too small. I might get a mortgage on it, but I'm not kicking Reid out," I said with a frown.

"Fuck no. Reid stays there, we'll find a house, I got a fair bit of money put away. We can put down a decent whack," Jett said musingly.

"I don't have much in savings," I said, shaking my head.

"Hey, we won't be able to buy in Drake and Ace's area, probably not even Texas's. But we'll find somewhere nice," Jett said.

"You'll look around our area. I'll pay cash and no mortgage, and you can work out payments with Drake," a voice said from the doorway. We both looked up and saw Phoe standing there with her hands on her hips, glaring at Jett.

"Phoe," Jett said as I shrieked and pulled the covers up to my neck. Drake smirked at me over her shoulder.

"My area!" Phoe waggled a finger and shot us both a frown, I didn't know Phoe that well, but Jett did and he shut up.

"Phoe we can't afford your area. I'm sure you're in a super-duper area, but we need to think smaller and more reasonable," I argued.

"Our area, we can work a payment plan out. Now get dressed and get that damn test done. Steven is working on a draft for the courts, to apply for sole custody. Hawthorne is digging into Dina's past. Cunt's really fuckin' clueless who she's messed with," Drake rumbled.

"I'll get my P.A onto looking for houses. How exciting!" Phoe exclaimed and disappeared, her heels clicking loudly down the corridor. Drake stared at us, one at a time.

"Where you hear from?" Jett rumbled eyeing Drake.

"Buyin' a house in our area."

"Can't afford that brother," Jett rumbled in return. Drake gave him the dead eye, and Jett stopped arguing.

"My woman will end up with the entire fuckin' MC within ten minutes of us. Phoe wants that, she gets that," Drake growled. Jett rolled his eyes as I squirmed next to him, very awake I was stark naked under the sheet.

"Yeah," Jett drew out the word.

"Phoe will fuckin' hit the roof when you two announce you're married. Be warned," Drake smirked and left, shutting the door.

"Drake knows?" I asked Jett wide-eyed.

"Drake knows everything," Jett replied with a grin, "if he don't, Texas or Hawthorne will. Let's get this test done and get married." Jett stood up, my eyes trailed up his body, and I grinned as Jett's dick twitched towards me.

"You're gonna kill me," Jett muttered and walked into his tiny bathroom.

Four hours later, we were married and sitting in Steven's office in Phoe's HQ. I hadn't known Steven worked for Phoe and was one of the best in his field. Luckily Steven had experience in family law because of Phoe and the Trusts, which was in our favour. He sat down and explained the draft he was presenting to court and that we'd have the test results tomorrow by noon at the latest.

Steven had taken several depositions from witnesses who had been in the clubhouse at the time of Dina's bombshell, and he'd transcribed the video and made copies. He said he'd take ours in the morning, but he'd filed a custody petition and made a call to a judge who was a friend. The judge could see us in two weeks after she'd moved some things around.

We'd installed Dina in a good hotel, with a limit placed on how much Dina could order there. Hawthorne's was watching the door in case Dina tried to do a bunk with Ursula Jean Letitia, the poor baby. Jett had made a modest payment to cover their costs. Grumpily, Jett muttered something about changing Ursula's name as soon as he got custody and I was in full agreement.

Steven said we'd have a good case, with the depositions and the video, we were in a strong position. He informed us he was calling character witnesses, but that went over my head. All I could see was my husband in front of me and how tense and weary Jett was. Steven blinked when we told him we'd got married that afternoon, but he agreed that made us even more reliable.

I kept waiting for the panic to set in, but panic abandoned me. I was dazed but relaxed, there was no way I'd imagined being married by this time today. On my ring finger was a slim but heavy, plain gold ring. My other hand kept twisting it around, and despite my worry that we'd rushed things, everything felt perfect. Not the wedding of my dreams by a long shot but contentment and a feeling of righteousness hit me hard.

Steven asked about living arrangements, and we told him, we'd be house hunting tomorrow. He told us to find one as soon as possible, and he'd do the closure on it. We needed to be in the house by the court date, which didn't give us much time. I sighed, this would be a tight squeeze. We'd do it, with Rage and Phoe helping us, but even so, such a squeeze.

When we left Steven's office, Emily was waiting outside for us. Phoe's P.A. was sporting blue hair with purple streaks and was wearing motorcycle boots with denim dungarees and a pink tee. Emily was bouncing on her toes and began babbling at us. In short, she'd lined up five houses for us to view tonight, within a fifteen-mile radius of Phoe's home. I blinked at how quickly she'd done this and Emily grinned.

"Nothing is impossible when Phoe wants something done," Jett whispered as we followed a bouncing Emily outside. Emily handed us the details of the houses and then gave us a list of times. It was already three o'clock, and we'd viewings per hour. Jett jumped on his bike, and I climbed on after him.

I loved riding with Jett. Wrapped around his hard body and feeling the powerful machine throb between my legs. The first time Jett had taken me for a ride I'd been terrified, but now I felt the freedom in it. I pulled on my helmet that Jett insisted I wear, and Jett's bike growled as he pulled away. Like, a good half of the MC, Jett favoured a Dyna Glide, it was a beast.

To our surprise, Phoe was waiting for us at the first house. Phoe walked it with us and turned her nose up at it before we did. She did much the same at the second house, finding fault with the size of the yard and the fact it was overlooked. Unhappy, Phoe followed us to the third.

The third house was it for us, there was a hedge fencing the front yard in and a wraparound porch. The house was two stories with a basement and a large backyard. To my amazement, it even had a swimming pool. The inside direly needed decorating, but it was clean and solid.

It had an open lounge and kitchen area and two small downstairs studies, there were also two further rooms, one a playroom for Ursula and the other space a tv room. The upstairs held a full en suite master room and four bedrooms, two of which had adjoining bathrooms. There was a decent-sized family bathroom decorated in olive green, despite the disrepair the house was perfect.

Jett put in an offer there and then, he undercut by fifteen thousand and pointed out why. The realtor baulked at first until Jett said not to worry, we'd go elsewhere and then she became all business. Phoe pointed out that we were only a five-minute drive from her house and were in a decent area with good schools. I blanched at the price, but Phoe told the realtor it was a cash buyer and we needed it completed within a week, or the deal was off.

The realtor contacted the seller while we walked around the overgrown garden and looked out over the grass area. Phoe remained inside having a further check around, Jett began making plans on how to use the space, and I fell in with his vision. We were holding hands, and I'd my head on his shoulder when the realtor came back and informed us our offer had been accepted. The realtor offered to sit down with Jett and go through the paperwork, and I caught her eyeing Jett, like, she'd like to go through him.

"We're married, and if you want this sale, you'll keep your damn eyes off my husband," I snapped. She blushed and scurried away. Jett gave off a rumble of laughter and pulled me while I was huffing into Jett's hard body.

"Don't ever change baby, love when you get possessive, Jett chuckled dropping a kiss on my pouting mouth. Well damn it, I'd been standing there while the idiot drooled over him. Jett picked up my hand and looked at the simple gold band on it. Smugly, Jett raised it to his mouth Jett kissed my hand and then dragged me into a bone-crushing hug.

"Love you," I told his chest, Jett chuckled again and dropped another kiss on my mouth.

"I know, l love you too," Jett replied. He looked down at

his hand, showcasing his own thick gold wedding band. "Gonna get you some bling to go with that, we're doing things backwards. But fuck it all, gonna do it our way," Jett muttered. He crushed me against a tree while Jett made love to my mouth with his own. An embarrassed cough broke us apart, and I sent another glare at the realtor while Jett chuckled.

Phoe came bouncing down the steps that led into the back yard and harassed the realtor. Once the woman realised who she had in her presence, she became fawning and simpering. Phoe dismissed the realtor with a look and told us, she'd meet us back at the clubhouse.

It was hitting nearly nine o'clock when we got back. Pizza boxes lay strewn across surfaces, and it seemed everyone was there. The MC had kicked skanks out, and so only old ladies or close friends were present. Those included Emily, two women called Susan and Diana and a Japanese guy called Akemi who introduced himself as Artemis's brother. Kids were running riot through the clubhouse, and the adults were paying them little attention, trusting they were safe.

My mouth gaped as Eddie and Tony, Phoe's twin daughter and son dashed past me with their own pizza box. Jett had warned me the little girl was a handful, in fact, he'd called Eddie, a hellion! Drake tried to rescue the pizza but was told firmly by Eddie, "no Daddy! Girls night." Drake's mouth twitched, and the little girl sat her ass down in a corner with Silvie and stared balefully at her father. Lowrider got them napkins and left them to it.

Reid was there alongside my shop girls. Andy, as usual, nowhere to be seen. Reid was pacing back and forth as we came in and Reid rushed up to me and dragged me from Jett. Reid cupped my face and look down at me.

"You okay?" Reid bit out.

"I'm fine, everything is perfect," I replied. My hand rose to Reid's chest as he crowded me.

"You standing by him?" Reid glared at Jett. I coughed and waved my hand in front of his face. Reid's eyes bugged out as he saw my wedding ring, Reid looked across to Jett and saw his ring. Jett was watching intently. Reid dropped a kiss on my head and then strode over to Jett. For a second I thought he would congratulate Jett and then Reid landed a staggering right hook on Jett's jaw.

"What the fuck is wrong with you?" Reid roared. "First you stand on my toes when you take vengeance for Sin. Then you go head to head with me in my house, now you fucking marry my sister without inviting me?" Jett felt his jaw and then wriggled it side to side as I rushed to Jett's side and ducked under his arm.

"Owed you that," Jett muttered, "don't get a second brother, not without getting one in return."

"Married? They got married?" I heard a squeal and Silvie popped up next to us, grabbing our hands. "Oh my god, they got married!" she yelled.

"What the fuck?" Apache asked as he made his way over to us. Apache grabbed us both in a bone-crushing hug and set us back on our feet.

"You got married without us?" Phoenix asked, and I saw hurt flash across her face.

"A spur of the moment thing," Jett said.

"Yeah, what Phoe said," Lowrider rumbled from close by.

"But we're brothers," Rock complained, reaching out to hug me. Texas grabbed me next and then Fish.

"I could have planned a party," Marsha whispered sadly as she hugged us.

"I'm so mad at you two right now! Neither of you said a word this afternoon!" Phoe exclaimed, making her words a lie as she hugged us both tightly.

"Decided it would be better for Ursula, I fuckin' hate that name, if we're married and bought a house. Judge will look for shit like that," Jett rumbled. Drake nodded as he held his tearful wife.

"You don't look surprised Drake," Ezra said, turning to Drake and eyeing him curiously.

"Prospect did what I'd have done," Drake said, giving praise. Jett straightened, and I knew how deep that touched him. "Couldn't be prouder of you son, or you girl. Perfect, the pair of ya's. Wish you many fuckin' happy years!" Drake roared. Roars came back at Drake, who hauled me into his arms and squeezed me tight.

"Knew it girl, knew you were one for my brother, couldn't be happier. The instant I laid eyes on you, I got hit in the gut, what type of woman you are. Proved me right," Drake's whispered words made me choke up, and I hugged him back tightly. "One of us girl," Drake whispered again and dropped a kiss on my head. He gave me a final squeeze and let me go.

"Hit a brother again, you bring an army," I heard Apache laugh at Reid who grinned back as everyone joined in congratulating us with loud voices.

"Heck of a right hook for a book nerd," Manny teased, and laughter erupted.

Two weeks later, I sat nervously next to Jett with Steven beside us in the courtroom. Dina had been served the day after we got married. She'd been ordered to bring Ursula to the court with her. Whatever Steven had said to the judge had made her insist on the toddler being present. Behind us sat all of Rage MC, Phoe and Emily, two gay guys called Stefan and Bernard who were Phoe's close friends, and Reid. To my surprise, Dylan Hawthorne attended, alongside a state Senator and a Congressman. There was also Detective Ramirez present.

Jett winked and whispered to keep calm, we had this in the bag. Steven had a thick file in front of him which he tapped his long fingers on. Steven kept gazing across at Dina and smirking at her lawyer and making him uncomfortable. Dina had found money to get herself one but looked shell shocked, and although she'd tried, she still resembled a drugged-out whore.

It had been no surprise when the DNA results came back a full match. 99.9 percentage that couldn't get much better. Jett had immediately slapped in the petition, and the judge had ordered the hearing as Steven said. We'd been sitting an hour listening to Dina tell her lies.

Dina claimed she'd been at college studying business when she'd met Jett. Innocently Dina claimed Jett led her into the dark side of life and when he'd finished with her, Jett pimped her out to his brother. I wanted to get up and slap the smug lying bitch, but Jett kept a firm grip on me as if he could read my thoughts. Dina's lawyer wound up his questions, and Steven stood up.

"Miss Smith, we've heard a lot of testimony from you which under oath you swear is true. Starting with Mr Cutter got you hooked on drugs and is still taking them?"

"Yes!" Dina sniffed and dried a tear from her eye.

"So it would be a surprise to learn that over the last few years, Mr Cutter has undergone several drug tests for his jobs. The earliest dating from when Mr Cutter was eighteen and none of them has ever shown a positive result. Including one dating from less than six months ago," Steven asked, tilting his head at her. Dina's face hardened.

"They must be wrong," Dina said.

"I submit the file called test into evidence," Steven said, handing it to the court clerk who passed it to the judge. "As you can see, there have been over eight drug tests from various places Mr Cutter has worked, and they have all tested negative. Miss Smith is lying," Steven said. Dina shot Steven a harsh look and allowed a few more tears to drip down her face.

"I'm not," Dina whimpered, Judge David turned to her.

"Well, young lady, I have the evidence in black and white in front of me," Judge David said to Dina.

"Have you ever been arrested, Dina?" Steven asked.

"Of course not!" Dina snapped.

"I'll ask again, have you ever been arrested?"

"I gave you an answer."

"So can you explain why you have been arrested and charged with prostitution seven times? That you have a record of petty theft, being arrested five times for stealing from shops. And the fact you have three outstanding warrants dating less than three months ago?" Steven asked, my heart leapt as I saw Dina glare. Steven passed the judge another file, and she flicked through it.

"Who is Diego Martinez?" Steven asked. Dina grew pale and bit her lip. "Miss Smith, who is Diego Martinez?" Steven asked again, Dina shook her head.

"Don't know."

"Is he your drug dealer?" Dina bit her lip again. "Do I need to repeat the question?"

"Yes," Dina snapped, her face flushing in anger.

"So, in fact, you accuse Mr Cutter of taking drugs and hooking you on them, when we have evidence to the contrary. The truth is you hooked yourself on drugs and look to blame Mr Cutter," Steven stated, and Dina glared.

"Jett's in an MC," Dina hissed.

"Ah yes, that brings me to our next subject, Rage MC over ten years has owned an impeccable reputation for being a clean club. They ride their bikes, run the shops and their bar and do much for the community. I have a list here of things that the Club has done for charity and its local community.

Highlighted are the events that Mr Cutter himself was involved in, including building a bike to auction for the Eternal Trust, operating telephone lines during a Trust drive for funding. Mr Cutter's also helped rebuild a community centre and collected donations for the local orphanage.

Detective Antonio Ramirez, a highly respected officer in RCPD, is here to provide testimony as to the legitimate work the club does." The judge flicked through the pages that had been handed to her, and the court remained silent.

"I don't think we need Detective Ramirez's testimony to the court. Unless Miss Smith's counsel wishes to question him?" Dina's lawyer shook his head recognising he was on the losing side.

"We also have present Mr Andrew Wainwright, the Congressman for South Dakota and Mr Antony Parker-Jones the Senator for South Dakota. Both are willing to be character witnesses for Mr Cutter and his wife. Both Mr Parker-Jones and Mr Wainwright have known Jett eighteen months and have had a close relationship with

Mr Cutter and the club."

"His fucking what?" Dina exploded from the stand. Dina turned to face me, and I barely controlled a flinch. Hate blazed from her eyes, Steven turned towards her with a raised eyebrow.

"Excuse me?" Judge David's gaze snapped in Dina's direction.

"His fucking what? Asshole's meant to marry me not some skinny stuck up ho! I'll gut you, you stupid bitch," Dina continued ranting, her lawyer dropped his head.

"That's enough of that language," the judge snapped, and Dina shut her mouth.

"I also have a file complied by Hawthorne's Investigations. They have investigated Miss Smiths background, and many things have come to light. Mr Hawthorne is present to explain his findings and testify."

"You fuckers," Dina seethed from the stand. "You absolute fuckers," Dina screamed. The judge rapped her gravel and told the guard to remove her. Dina didn't go quietly, she went kicking and screaming. The judge banged her gravel and demanded Dina be held because of the outstanding warrants. Finally, order ruled again, the judge faced Dina's lawyer.

"You may inform your client, I am suspending her custody. Ursula will not be leaving with her mother today, and I will remove Ursula Cutter permanently from her care. I have seen enough today to see Ms Smith is an unfit mother. I also will enter into the record that Ms Smith will not be granted visitation rights." Dina's lawyer nodded. "You may leave," the judge said, and he scurried out.

"Now that unpleasantness is over, I'd appreciate being told why Mr and Mrs Cutter should get custody of a child they never knew existed." I gulped and clenched Jett's hand. This was it.

Steven, for the next few hours called his character witnesses, went through the reports in greater detail. He explained our marriage as proof of our dedication to Ursula and explained we'd bought a larger house and would move in soon. Steven produced our marriage licence and the deed to the house.

To my surprise, Antony and Andrew both took the stand. They gave glowing reports about both of us, even though I had only met them once, a week ago. Hawthorne and Ramirez also took the stand giving similar reports. My attack was brought up and explained away, our finances were studied in minute detail. I was thankful Phoe had insisted on buying the house and settled for us paying it back later, after the court case.

Phoe herself took the stand after we'd been questioned where the money had come from to buy our house. She'd explained our plan, that we get Ursula settled and buy what is needed for her. Jett would make a lump sum repayment and then make payments each month until the amount was repaid. The judge questioned Phoe deeply before giving an approving nod.

A few hours later, with Jett taking the stand and then me, stumbling through my testimony, I was staggered to find myself holding Ursula in my arms as we left court. We'd won, Ursula was ours. I was informed that I'd have to adopt Ursula to make her legally mine, I agreed, and Steven submitted the papers, already drawn up, with a grin.

Steven also submitted a change of name deed, and our little girl lost that awful name and was now called Amelia Abigail Cutter. Jett had picked Abigail, and I'd chosen

Amelia. Judge David signed off on the name change application and informed us to return in three months for the adoption papers to be completed. We were over the moon, and Steven had been back slapped and kissed so many times he looked giddy.

I stood on the steps with Reid, who had an arm around my waist. Reid clutched me closer to him and squeezed me hard, I leant into Reid with Amelia in my arms.

"I have a niece," Reid said with a big grin at the little girl who looked solemnly at him.

"Yeah, I have a daughter," I whispered. Who'd have thought six months ago I'd be married to a biker and have a daughter? Jett came over a massive grin on his face.

"Hog roast at the clubhouse. Are we ready?" Jett asked, taking Amelia from me. "Hello sweetie, I'm your Daddy, can you say Daddy yet?" Jett asked, dropping a kiss on her forehead. Amelia looked at him and sucked her thumb. The child worker who had been looking after her while we were in court approached us.

"I have a few concerns about Ursula's development," she quietly said.

"Her name's Amelia now," Jett replied, "what concerns?" Jett tucked Amelia under his chin.

"Her speech is undeveloped, and she's underweight. Amelia also seems withdrawn, I'd like to monitor her if neither of you mind. It appears from what I witnessed in court the mother had little interaction of a positive kind with her, and it has stunted her development." I watched as Jett's arms tightened around his daughter.

"Amelia's been traumatised," Jett mumbled, the child worker nodded her face serious.

"Very traumatised and very neglected. I don't have a court order, I could apply for one, but I prefer to help without one if we can manage that? It would mean I can keep an eye on her development and also report to the court if you needed me to."

"It would be welcome, any advice you can give us would be appreciated," I said looking with concern at Amelia. Amelia gazed back at me with serious little eyes, and I had a sudden awareness that Amelia had had no fun in her short life. Amelia was just over two years old, and I wondered how often she'd laughed. The child support worker gave us her card and left. I looked at Jett at saw a terrible sadness in his eyes.

"Shit," Jett whispered.

"We'll make it, we'll make Amelia's life fun and loving, and she'll get everything she needs from both of us. Mornings Amelia can spend with you, at the garage and afternoons with me in the shop and that way our daughter gets the best of both of us. We'll make her life full of goodness and beauty," I told Jett. He crossed to me quickly and dragged me into his arms.

"Like that Sin, our daughter." I touched Amelia's little face.

"Yeah, Jett, our daughter."

Ace hollered from the road where he was waiting with his SUV to take us to the clubhouse. We meandered down the steps and climbed into the SUV. Both of us suddenly aware of the commitment and responsibility we'd taken on, but not intimidated by it.

Chapter Nine.

The following day after the hog roast which had gone on until the early hours of the morning, I rose to check on Amelia. She slept in a cot in our room, and I was concerned that Amelia hadn't once uttered a single sound during the night. As I approached the cot, I saw Amelia's eyes were open, and she stared fascinated at the mobile above her head. Little hands reached out as if Amelia could grasp it.

"Hey, little angel, are you hungry?" I asked, looking at the clock. The time was seven in the morning, and Jett remained sleeping in bed. Amelia looked at me and closed her eyes.

"Hey, I see you," I whispered gently. Amelia's eyes popped open again, I was worried as she'd hardly eaten a thing last night. I was determined that Amelia gain a healthy weight.

"Want banana pancakes?" I whispered and Amelia's solemn eyes, her father's mirror images, grew wide. Okay, so Amelia understood me, now I just needed to get her to respond. I bent down and made to pick her up, and my heart stuttered as Amelia flinched. For a second or two, I paused, unsure what to do and then continued picking Amelia up.

With a reassuring smile, I picked Amelia up and hugged her. Reaching down, I picked up the teddy bear that Jett bought for her yesterday and quietly made my way to the kitchen. We'd bought a few toddler items intending to get the rest when we moved into the new house. The house was being decorated, and we'd decided it wouldn't have been healthy to take Amelia there.

Together we'd purchased a cot and bedding for Amelia, a car seat, pushchair and a highchair at our house, or as it had now become, Reid's house. Phoe and Drake held onto the items until yesterday when they knew we were bringing Amelia home. Luckily Phoe provided diapers and stuff, something we hadn't thought of.

Not knowing how court would go we'd only bought Amelia pyjamas and a few outfits. Today I was planning to take Amelia and get her hair cut into a far better style, it was apparent Dina had just shorn it off. I didn't know if Jett wanted her hair to grow, but I knew I did, I looked forward to brushing and plaiting it.

After Amelia's haircut, I intended to go clothes shopping with her and then get toys. Jett and I'd taken the week off work. We wanted to give Amelia quality time this week, ensure she felt safe. Both of us knew it would be a considerable change for the little girl, I doubted Amelia had stability in her life. A father Amelia didn't know existed, and a new mom would possibly upset our little girl.

I lifted Amelia into her highchair and began making the batter for pancakes, I turned the hob on so the pan and heated the oil thoroughly. I'd learned to cook in England, and most of my cooking was the English style. I grabbed whipped cream and syrup out of the fridge and peeked at Amelia as I poured the batter into my pancake pan. Beginning to cut up a banana into small pieces, I heard a noise and turned to see Jett crouching by the highchair and smiling at Amelia.

"What's Mommy doing princess?" Jett whispered, and my heart leapt, okay, it leapt for two reasons. My husband wore low slung jeans and was barefoot and tousled haired. Water pooled in my mouth looking at him, forcing me to swallow hard. The second reason was because Jett called me Amelia's mommy! Amelia looked at me, confused.

"That's your new Mommy princess, she's going to look after you. Mommy's gonna treat you like the little princess you are," Jett reassured Amelia, his voice soft and gentle.

"Mommy is making pancakes with whipped cream, syrup and banana's, Daddy. Amelia decided she wanted them this morning." Jett winked at Amelia. She tilted her head to study us, and I wondered what Amelia was thinking.

"That sounds messy princess, you want Daddy to help you eat them?" Jett asked her, and now Amelia studied him. Jett took that as a yes and rose to his feet and hooked his foot around and chair and dragged it over to sit with Amelia. He sat down and began clapping his hands together and then clapping hers.

"Let's cheer, Mommy and the pancakes!" Jett whispered to Amelia, and then they both faced me. God, they looked so alike it was uncanny, my heart leapt again as Amelia clapped her hands once on her own. Progress! I flipped the first pancake and then carried on with the bananas. A few minutes more and I put the pancake on a plate and made a banana smile, eyes and nose and syrup and whipped cream beard and hair.

Amelia's eyes opened wide as she stared at what I placed in front of her. Before either Jett or I moved to help, Amelia grabbed hold and tried to shovel the pancake into her mouth. Within seconds her face and hair were covered in cream and sticky syrup, uh oh, that hadn't been a good idea. Jett's eyes narrowed on our daughter, and then he got up and fetched a damp cloth and wiped Amelia clean.

"Why don't we get Daddy cut it up for you?" I asked Amelia, and she gathered the plate close to her. Hell, Amelia thought we would take her food, tears gathered in my eyes and Jett visibly struggled to control his temper. Amelia looked at Jett and shoved more pancake into her mouth. I made a second and Jett whipped the mess of the first one away, and before Amelia reached for it, Jett held up his hand.

"Amelia, you know Mommy and Daddy have given you a new princess name?" Jett asked. Amelia's little sticky head tilted towards him, she blinked and dropped her eyes. An awful sensation hit me straight in my gut when I realised Amelia had learnt it was bad to hold eye contact. If Dina had been anywhere near, I'd have throttled her.

"Hey," I whispered approaching, and Amelia looked alarmed. "Don't be afraid of your Daddy, he loves you very much. I love you very much, if you want pancakes every morning, we'll give you them little angel."

"Your name is now Amelia because it's a princess name," Jett spoke softly. My heart melted at this badass biker being so gentle with a child. "And you're mine and

Mommy's princess, so you need a princess name, but princesses don't eat with their hands, little one. They use a knife and fork. Want Daddy to show you how?" Amelia looked at us for a few minutes, and then I saw Jett's eyes light up as she nodded once. He began cutting up her pancake and feeding it to her. Amelia opened her mouth, mimicking a baby bird.

"Chew," Jett told her. Amelia granted Jett another nod and began chewing her food. I carried on flipping pancakes as Jett fed his daughter for the first time ever.

After breakfast, we decided Amelia needed a bath. While I ran the water testing the temperature continuously, Jett stripped her sticky clothes off. I closed my eyes to keep the image of Jett carrying Amelia gently and protectively in his arms, into the bathroom. I'd made a bubble bath for her and Amelia's eyes widened at the magic in front of her. I stripped off her diaper, which was luckily only wet and placed her into the water. Amelia looked startled, and I realised she'd never experienced a bath. Amelia didn't fuss as I put her in the warm water. Honestly, I wanted to throttle Dina right now, but Amelia took priority.

"If I ever get my hands on Dina I'll kill her," Jett muttered, "bitch abused my daughter. Neglected her at every turn." I placed my hand in Jett's as we watched our daughter play in her first bath. I had a sense we'd be seeing many of Amelia's firsts.

Reid came in with bottles and crouching down Reid showed Amelia how to fill them and then squirt them at people. We were soaked by the time she'd finished, and my heart broke because while she'd clearly enjoyed herself, Amelia hadn't laughed or giggled once.

Getting her out of the bath, the three of us worked out

how to get a diaper on her. I wasn't sure if Amelia should be toilet trained or not and made a mental note to check with Phoe. Between the three of us, we got her dressed, and then Jett carried Amelia downstairs while I showered.

When I came down, I found Jett lying on his back while Amelia sat on top of him. Reid sat next to Jett and played peekaboo with her. Every time Reid covered his eyes, Amelia pointed at him, and when Reid uncovered them, she dropped her arm. I took her while Jett showered, Reid had already showered, he was planning on coming shopping with us today.

In the last week, Reid scored some big sales on our rare books and papers, and we were comfortably in the black again. Of course, the sale of the Downing papers had put us into it, but the last few sales put us well and truly into a large comfort zone. This meant that we could splash out today. Jett had been making rumblings about a pick-up or truck as obviously, Amelia couldn't go on the back of his bike.

We'd had a little argument when he realised I intended to spend money, so we'd come to an agreement. I'd buy Amelia's clothes and baby toiletries. Jett would buy the big stuff she needed and the toys, it was an agreement that worked for both of us. We piled into Reid's car, and he drove us into town, where I literally went to town buying her clothes. The guys had to do two car runs, and I hadn't even started on the toiletries!

Jett carried Amelia on his hip while we were shopping, ignoring the pushchair we had at the house. It was panty meltingly hot, and Jett was oblivious to looks he received. His aviator covered gaze remained firmly fixed on either Amelia or me, totally boosting my ego. There was more than one snide look aimed in my direction, as Jett tugged me around by my hand. Many incredulous looks were aimed in our direction, asking, what the hell is he doing with me? Ha! My husband is hot!

I had a fit of giggles when Jett first dragged me to one of the most exclusive jewellery shops in Rapid City and picked out an engagement ring. The woman who had been drooling over Jett looked confused when she saw my wedding ring. Jett raised an eyebrow at her when she double-checked.

Bluntly Jett told her, he'd been so eager to make me his wife, he'd dragged me to the altar and screw the engagement. I buried my head in his shoulder giggling as the woman looked at us both head to toe.

Jett paid for a stunning emerald and diamond ring and then proceeded to look for an eternity ring along the same lines. By the time we'd left Jett had dropped ten thousand dollars on my rings to my horror, and he'd stopped any argument with one glare. Glaring back at Jett, I bought Amelia a cross in rose gold, and his lips twitched. God, I loved this man.

Only then did Jett let me loose in a clothes store for Amelia, he held her while I pushed the cart around and threw in clothes. Tiny little jeans and dungarees, tee's, skirts and dresses all got inspected before being put into the cart. I spent far too much on hair accessories, and Jett found me cooing over tights and tiny socks. Jett rolled his eyes when I filled a cart and pushed me to the cashier before I bought more. I snuck in three more dresses on the way to pay for our purchases.

Jett didn't blink when I paid for them and then we hit a toy store. I was surprised Jett didn't go as mad as I had, but Jett bought a few items. When I tried to get him to buy outdoor toys, Jett just shook his head at me, I pouted while he paid his far cheaper bill. Jett did, however, spend a fortune ordering furniture for Amelia's bedroom in the new house.

We met Reid outside the Reading Nook where he had his own arms full of bags. Reid had bought Amelia books and toys of his own. Which Reid dumped into the boot of his car and then drove it the short distance to the Rage forecourt.

I was teasing both of them when we entered the clubhouse, and a loud roar greeted us. Amelia instantly hid her face in Jett's neck visibly jumping in his arms. Jett held her tight and then pried her little face free, to see all his brothers and old ladies waiting for us. We'd had the hog roast last night, but this was different.

To one side of the clubhouse was several tables laden with food and a huge stack of presents stood next to it. Some were wrapped, and some weren't, I gave Jett a sideways glance as I realised there was a heck of a lot of toys there.

"My brother's babe," Jett muttered. Tears rose in my eyes when I realised the Rage brothers had been out buying presents for a little girl who'd probably never even had one. Phoe's kids ran screaming past led by Eddie, who was waving her arms above her head and hollering something. Ezra bent down and scooped the little girl in his arms before she wrecked the clubhouse. The others stopped, and Eddie pointed in our direction.

"A new biker babe!" Eddie screeched, and I saw Phoe give her a look that I wouldn't argue with. The child ignored her mother and wriggled free and dashed over to Jett and I. "Down Jett," Eddie demanded. Jett bent down and allowed Eddie to check out Amelia.

"This is Amelia," Jett told Eddie who was still appraising Amelia. Although Eddie had met her last night, Amelia had been asleep. To my surprise, Amelia was no less curious about Eddie. Jett put her feet on the floor, and Eddie gently reached out a hand.

"We got you presents, Amelia, lots and lots'a presents. Wanna come open them?" Eddie asked Amelia who nodded after glancing at Jett and me for approval. I snuck my hand into Jett's as he stood up and I choked back tears as Amelia was led away. She sent several wary glances over her shoulder to check Jett, and I remained, and then Amelia sat down in front of the pile.

"You gotta wait, our Uncles will bring their presents," Tony told Amelia as he sat down next to her. Phoe and Drake's cute little boy patted Amelia's hand. "This is from Eddie and me," Tony said, giving her a strangely wrapped present. Amelia looked at it, not knowing what to do, and my tears rose again almost choking me.

Before Jett or I could move to show Amelia what to do, Texas was there, sinking his massive body next to Amelia. Her eyes grew huge at the sight of the gigantic man next to her, Texas lifted his hands slowly, and Amelia watched him looking ready to bolt.

"I'm your Uncle Texas. I'm every kid's Uncle, but for biker babes as yourself, I'm a special Uncle." Amelia looked at Texas, her eyes still huge, but she gave him a small nod. Amelia moved towards his hands, and Texas lifted her gently on his lap. Jett's hands snuck around my waist, and Jett tilted my head into his shoulder as I realised suddenly my tears were falling. I sniffed and rubbed the back of my hand over my face drying them up.

"This is how you open a present sweetheart," Texas

boomed softly peering into the little face gazing up at his. Amelia snuggled into his lap as Texas's big hands grasped the present and ripped the paper flinging it in every direction. Amelia gazed up at Texas in wonder as he made a mess of the wrapping and then her hands reached out for the pink teddy bear in front of her.

"I got you that. Daddy says every little girl should have a pink teddy," Eddie said her eyes finding Drake immediately. Drake grinned at his hellion daughter and gave her a nod.

"You got a lotta Uncles little lady, these men here gonna be your Uncles and your Uncles been spending like hells gonna freeze over tomorrow. So why don't we see what they got ya?" Texas asked as he reached for another wrapped present. Amelia clung to her pink teddy, but as Texas encouraged her, Amelia tore into a gift from Gunner. It was a hand-carved wooden carved horse, and Amelia's little hands run over it in wonder.

"Uncle Gunner," Gunner said, crouching down near her. Amelia's eyes tracked his movement, and she gave Gunner another nod.

"Gunner made that," Jett whispered in my ear. Wow, Gunner had talent wood carving.

"We got a meetin' Sunday. You and family need to be at the clubhouse at three, prospect," Apache said from behind us. Jett looked over his shoulder and gave him a nod. Jett didn't ask what type of thing it was, he just nodded. It rankled a little, but Jett had explained to me that until he earned his patch, Jett was at the club's beck and call. But they stayed as legal as they could.

As long as Jett loved me and came home, I didn't care. The woman who'd have fretted herself sick with worry six months ago had long gone. The club was clean, sure

I'd seen a couple of them smoking pot, but nothing harder came into the clubhouse. Jett had explained that was respect. Drake wanted a club built around four things, freedom, riding, family and respect. Rage had that and would fight to protect it.

Yeah, I'd seen the women hanging around and didn't like it. At the end of the day, I could either hang with the old ladies and ignore the skanky bitches trying it on with the men or I could stay away. I'd learnt early on, that blazing fight we'd had, that the MC was Jett's world. Jett trusted me by bringing me into his world, and I wouldn't break that trust.

Gazing around, surrounded by Jett's brothers and their old ladies, I knew this was a good world. Sure they might blur the line at times, in Artemis's case she was more than slightly grey, but they had good hearts. Drake only let a certain man into the club, Phoenix had explained. Men that thought and acted like Drake, men who put family and their brothers first.

One night we, the old ladies, had sat down and they'd each given me their stories. I'd been wide-eyed and shocked by the end of the night. Marsha gave me the background behind Rage and their history, and I was glad Jett had missed most of the struggle they'd been through. It explained the edge the older brothers had.

The prospects did a two-year stint, Drake determining he let the right man into their brotherhood. I'd guessed that somewhere in the past blood had been spilt although that was the one thing Phoe hadn't told me. Phoe just said they'd had a hard and dangerous fight getting the club clean. Jett was nearing the end of his two years, he'd only got four months left before he became a full brother.

So yeah, this Sin, was more confident, more settled and

definitely loved, Jett's eyes told me that every time he looked at me. I'd friends, a business that was succeeding, and I now had a daughter and husband. I'd come a long way, and I believed I was the wife Jett deserved. Jett made me believe in myself and given the confidence to be braver and not so afraid. In truth it wasn't just Jett, the club had too.

I was a nerd, there was no getting away from it, I'd always be a nerd. Not one of Rage had ever judged me for it. Apache and Texas and I had long-winded conversations about what I was working on. Texas was interested in the Hellfire Club, and I'd often find him wanting a chat about our latest discovery.

Slick was often in my store, often racing to buy a new series I had in before Emily or Phoe beat him. Drake was warm and welcoming, but he held the old ladies at arms-length. Drake didn't pry into our lives, he took an interest but didn't pry, but if we needed him, Drake would be the first on the scene. Fish was often around with Marsha, Marsha had told me the club was their whole life. They couldn't have children, and so they channelled their love into the club. My heart wept for them because if anyone deserved a child, it was them.

I'd become tight with Manny, and if I'd questions, I couldn't ask Jett I knew Manny would be there. Manny became my second husband in a non-sexual way. I'd noticed that Phoe was incredibly close to Ace, considering the man had taken bullets for her, it was no surprise. Artemis was close to Drake who she seemed to idolise slightly less than Ace. So the old ladies had an alternative sexy biker guy. Manny took the role of mine.

The exception was Silvie. She was called an old lady which was strange enough as she wasn't claimed. Silvie was clearly in love with Apache, but the man kept her at a distance and Silvie accepted her lot in the club.

I'd seen the guys treat her as an old lady, but I couldn't understand why. When I'd asked Jett, he told me that is how it was and no one messed with Silvie. Drake would put them in their place. I couldn't pinpoint anyone, in particular, she was close to. Silvie treated them all the same although I saw Silvie's eyes drift to Gunner a couple of times, so I wondered if there was a little something there. Although it was clear, she had feelings for Apache.

I made the fifth old lady of the club. The women had been ravenous in their overtures of friendliness. At first, I had been disconcerted, and then I realised that these were genuinely warm women. Even Artemis with her mad skills and her episodes, as they were referred to, was friendly. I didn't want to know what Artemis's episodes were, I was just thankful Artemis accepted me into her circle.

The old ladies never mixed with the women who hung around, hoping to either get laid or score an old lady position. They kept to themselves, above those who whored themselves with whoever took their fancy. I'd learned that hierarchy quickly. Old ladies, then next were women who were friends, but not in the inner circle. People like Phoe's insane PA Emily, Susan and Diana, who both worked for Phoe, the friend circle was small and kept small for a reason. Finally, the skanks at the bottom of the ladder.

Jett jogged me out of my thoughts as he jostled me and walked me over to where Amelia was emulating Texas and ripping into the paper. Amelia held a gift from Silvie, a beautiful rag doll. Silvie reached out a hand and touched Amelia's newly cut hair with a gentle hand. Amelia tilted her head into it and then backed back up against Texas.

It was a beautiful day. The club had gone out of their way to welcome the newest member of their family. Last night I realised, had been about us winning custody, today was welcome and celebration. I caught Drake in conversation several times with Ace, Texas, Fish, Gunner and Apache, their eyes on Jett. Jett didn't seem bothered by it, so I let it go.

Jett ducked out at one point with Reid, and when he came back, he was sporting a new Dodge Ram 1500. He'd bought a black one, and my jaw dropped open, it had all the bells and whistles on and heated leather seats. Jett was pleased with himself and Reid was wondering whether he should get himself one. When asked, Jett told me, he'd paid cash for it and that he had a kid now and a wife and we needed to be safe. At my pout, Jett informed me I'd still be on the back of his bike. I grinned.

With Jett's purchase in mind, he approached Phoe and Drake and discussed how to pay back the house. Jett had lied to me. He'd said he'd had a fair bit but away, it may have been a fair bit to Jett, but to me, it was a small fortune. In the end, we only ended up owing Phoe thirty thousand dollars, Drake had insisted on leaving Jett a ten thousand fall back. I blinked realising that I hadn't discussed our finances.

Jett earned a lot more than I did, I'd forgotten he'd once told me he never brought home less than five thousand dollars a month. Jett had sunk ten thousand on my rings. Bought a new truck which cost lord knows how much and managed to pay off a massive chunk of the loan Phoe had given us. I guessed Phoe's eyes she'd make it a gift, but I knew from Jett's burning gaze he wouldn't take it. He'd provide for his family, and that was that.

Drake agreed to take ten percent off what Jett earned each month and pay it to Phoe until it was cleared. If Drake thought we'd be short one month, he'd let the payment fly. When I'd begun to argue, Drake put a finger to my mouth, shutting me up. Drake's eyes narrowed on me, and I fought against taking a step back.

"Family," Drake said to me and at that one word I gave up fighting and nodded my head.

Warmth shone in Drake's eyes, and I saw approval which made me feel cosy and warm. This man was amazing, no wonder Drake was the club president. The disagreement over and the repayment plans made I settled in to watch big badass bikers welcome their latest niece. Drake spent the night carting around either Dante, his baby son or Eddie or a few times both of them. His little son was the image of his father, and I could see a badass biker in Dante's gaze as he regarded his future kingdom.

When we went to bed that evening with Amelia fast asleep in her cot safe with us, Jett found another way to prove his love to me. The only problem was keeping our noise down.

Drake picked up his phone late that night and saw Ace's number there. He frowned before hitting answer and snapped a 'what' into it.

"Hospital now. Gunner's down," Ace snapped down the phone before hanging up. Drake's stomach sank. Gunner, his brother, one who stood by his side through the shit, Gunner was *down*. Drake turned on his heel and bellowed for his brothers as he jogged from the clubhouse. He slung a leg over his bike, and the bike roared as Drake pulled out fast, Apache on his heels.

"What the fuck happened?" Drake snarled into Ace's face.

"Dunno, found Gunner behind the bar. He was unconscious and beat to shit, had to have been jumped. Gunner ain't easy to take down," Ace muttered his eyes searching for someone.

"Anything from the street?" Drake snapped, turning to Hawthorne who had just entered. The fact Hawthorne was here so fast, meant the man had received intel that Rage had taken a hit. Hawthorne shook his head.

Rage had arrived five minutes ago and was told Gunner was in surgery while they battled to save his life from the three bullets Gunner had taken. One hitting his thigh, the second going through and through his shoulder. Someone then beat the shit out of Gunner before shooting him a third time. In the heart. Gunner was barely alive when Ace found him.

Drake tasted ice-cold fear. Fear of losing his brother. Drake called Hawthorne, was told he was on his way, he'd called Artemis, she was out hunting. Ramirez stood by Drake's side a silent presence, Ben was out chasing leads. Drake saw the doors open, and Silvie came running towards him wearing pyjama's and of all things pink fuckin' fluffy rabbit slippers. Tears streamed down Silvie's face as she paused and found Drake, her legs moving rapidly she flew towards him.

"Nothing, no one knows shit about a hit on Rage," Hawthorne replied, running his hand through his hair.

Drake had a feeling, bad shit was going down.

"Find me something," Drake said before turning to face Silvie. She was paler than he'd ever seen her.

"He'll live?" Silvie whispered. Drake couldn't find much to give in himself at the moment, anger blurring lines but that scared face burrowed deep into him. Drake reached out and roughly yanked her to him and held Silvie tight as her slender arms crept around him.

"Gunner will fight. He'll fight," Drake whispered. Hours crept by as brothers, old ladies and friends arrived. Artemis arrived informing him that her team was out. Hawthorne confirmed his was too. That buzzing sensation of something wrong got worse, and Drake looked around. They were all there, the prospects, the old ladies, Hawthorne, Ramirez, except…

"Where's Jett?" Drake asked realisation cold in his stomach, one of his prospects was missing.

"What?" Texas asked, looking around.

"No one call him?" Apache growled and pulled his phone out. Drake listened into the silence as it rang out.

"I'll call the house and store," Phoe said, pulling her phone out and dialling. Zoe answered at the shop and said no, Jett, Sin and Amelia wasn't there. Zoe was worried because Reid hadn't shown for work either. Penny had opened the shop, Drake rang their house phone, which rang out.

"Hunter, Lex, get your ass to their house now, still at their old one," Drake demanded. "Rock, Mac, go with." Drake sent his hounds after the prospect. Lowrider ran his hand through his hair and looked down at the floor.

"Got a bad feeling about this."

"Someone declaring war on the club," Ramirez replied. Drake shot him a look. "I stood with you when Phoe got snatched, when Ace got shot to shit, protecting her. I stood with you when shit went south fucking fast with Artemis, don't fucking give me that look. I'm a cop, I'm clean, but I'll stand with you," Ramirez hissed. Drake nodded.

"See if your snitches can find shit," he muttered.

"Already done. Someone declaring war on the club. Who?"

"Not heard anything, this is beyond silent," Hawthorne said, tapping something into his phone. "My guys got nothing, finding nothing." Hawthorne shook his head.

"Ben return to the scene, double-check everything. Go back over it, find me something," Ramirez said, turning to his partner who was approaching.

"Will do. Any news." Head shakes met Ben's question. Silence fell, and Ben sent Drake a sympathetic look and left.

"Fuck," Drake thundered and slammed his fist into the wall. Who the fuck was it? Drake's phone rang half an hour later, he answered on the second ring.

"Reid's on his way to emergency, beat to shit and tied up. Signs of a struggle. No sign of Jett, Sin and Amelia," Mac said. Drake's bad feeling intensified and his gut clenched. Another one missing, his prospect. His prospects family, no one touched family. It was the rule, one on one but innocents stayed out of it. Someone broke that rule, and he'd rain hellfire down on them. Drake hung up.

"Phoe, take the women, stay together, stay in hospital and get coffee," Drake said. Phoe's eyes filled with fear.

"Drake…"

"Gave you an order, do it!" Drake snapped at her, and Phoe took a step back before gathering the women and leaving.

"Reid is beat to shit and on his way here, Jett and family missing. Hit the streets, find me something or someone. Now!" Drake roared the last word and his brothers scattered.

"Gotta call this in Drake," Ramirez said, keeping eye contact with Drake.

"The fuck you do," Drake snarled.

"I don't call in a child kidnapping, my jobs on the line, we need to get this out there. Extensive coverage. Whoever has them will think twice."

"Or make them panic," Hawthorne chipped in.

"Got to call it in. We get her image out there, get out Amelia's people going to be looking for her. Someone might have seen something and not called in, have to get Amelia on an Amber alert now, Drake. Before it's too late," Ramirez insisted. Drake met Hawthorne's gaze, the man knew what Drake was thinking. Rage would find them, Rage would deal with them. Cops get brought in, it had to be done legally.

"Call it in," Hawthorne growled taking the decision away from Drake. Drake howled wordlessly and punched his fist into the wall breaking through the drywall. Not satisfied he punched a second and then a third time. Drake heard footsteps and looked up as Doc Gibbons approached.

"Drake," the man said softly. Drake's eyes closed, and he looked down at his feet. A hand grasped his shoulder and knew Ramirez had stepped closer.

"Tell me," Drake said. Fuck not Gunner, not now, not when they'd earned cleanliness. Drake's knees went weak, and he locked them.

"Gunner's alive but still in surgery, his leg and shoulder

are patched but the bullet," Doc Gibbons swallowed. "The bullet lodged in his heart. This will take hours. The repair needs to be so delicate. We got Gunner on bypass for now, but we need to act slowly and carefully. Gunner's body is in shock, and he's crashed twice. He's fighting." Drake rubbed a hand across the back of his neck. Doc looked around frowning when he saw no one else from the club.

"Jett's missing," Ramirez said. Drake heard the sharp breath that Doc sucked in. "Reid, a friend of Jett's wife, is on his way into the emergency room. Can you keep us in touch over his condition? My partner will be here soon to take a statement. I'll be with Drake," Drake felt gratitude for Ramirez. Another hand hit his other shoulder.

"You won't be alone," Hawthorne said. Who'd have thought it, a biker, a cop and a fuckin' whatever Hawthorne wanted to call himself.

"Gratitude," Drake finally muttered.

I looked around, but all I could see is darkness, my hands and feet were tied, and I was laid down on a stone floor. I shuffled into a sitting position and moaned at my sore shoulders.

"Baby," Jett said from the darkness.

"Jett?" I coughed on my word, my mouth dry as a dessert.

"I'm here, it's gonna be okay," Jett said back.

"Now why lie to her?" A third voice said, and I peered into the darkness before closing my eyes to the bright light that suddenly streamed into the darkness. When I could finally open them, my heart froze at the sight of

Jett, bruised and bloody and tied to a chair. Jett's hands were bound behind him.

There was blood dripping from a stab wound in his shoulder, and his stomach had been stabbed and sliced. Next to Jett stood a tall, lean but muscled man. His head was shaved and had a tattoo of a spider's web covering it, I flinched.

"Who are you, what do you want with us? Where's my daughter?" I croaked out. Jett's eyes blazed into mine, fury tensing his whole body.

"My daughter," a voice mumbled from behind them, and I saw Dina stagger into view. If she looked rough before, Dina looked half-dead now. Whacked out on something, Dina wore even dirtier and skankier clothes than before if at all possible.

"What the fuck?" Jett roared his muscles straining against the ropes that bound him.

"My fucking daughter, you cunts stole from me," Dina slurred and fear clenched my stomach. What had Dina done with Amelia?

"Where is she?" I bit out.

"Safe and sound with her Mommy. But, ah, not for long," Dina sung, waving her hand about.

"Who are you?" I asked, ignoring Dina and studying at the stranger.

"A friend of Dina's."

"Bullshit, you're her dealer. What the fuck do you want with us?" Jett cut in.

"Yeah okay, I'm her dealer. Hello everyone! Thank you for attending today. As for what I want with you, well I didn't want you, I wanted the brat. Dina promised me extra if I grabbed you as well. So here we all are," he said, scrutinizing me.

"See, I owe Diego money. Not a teeny bit but a big bit," Dina said, staring at me through blurred eyes. "What he see in you? You got nothing compared to me." Dina leant forward and ripped my blouse open. I heard Jett suck in a breath as Diego suddenly found me more attractive.

"Sin ain't a drugged-out ho," Jett bit out. Dina screeched and slapped me before staggering over to Jett and straddling him. Bile rushed into my mouth as Dina began dry humping my husband. Jett's eyes held mine with that burning fury.

"Why ain't you getting hard baby?" Dina slurred. Dina tried to kiss Jett, and he spat in her face. She screeched and slapped Jett across his face this time.

"Hard? How the hell can you make anyone hard? You're disgusting, a ho, tramp, scum," Jett spat blood into her face. Dina screeched again and jammed herself harder into his lap. I couldn't help it and turned my head as I vomited. Diego made a sound of disgust and dragged me away from it, he held a bottle of water to my mouth and then forced me to eat a mint. Was he joking? Asshole was worried about my breath?

"Jett won't get hard. Come on baby you used to enjoy fucking my cunt."

"Yeah well, I got some fuckin' taste finally and chose a classy one. Instead of your well used up cunt," Jett snarled at her. Dina rose to her feet and screamed in his face. Screw this, I decided.

"Where's my daughter?" I yelled.

"My baby? Ursula's safe and sound and needs to stay that way," Dina muttered, "I owed Diego a lot of money. Now Ursula will get him that money." Dina wandered out of the room. My fear-filled eyes met Jett's just as it all went dark again.

Chapter Ten.

"We have intel on Amelia, you need to get to the office, boss, asap," Leila Gibson said down the phone to Hawthorne.

"What ya got?"

"Nigel and I found something, Rage will go fucking apeshit. If I tell you over the phone, I'm unsure a hospital is the best place for Drake to learn this. Davies has sent Niko and Max and two of the Rage prospects back." Hawthorne looked over at the pacing Rage President, it had been four hours. Four fucking long hours since the discovery of Jett's missing family. Rage came and went, but there was nothing, no leads, nothing. Artemis had sent her hacker Nigel to Hawthorne's offices to help Leila. Looked like they finally had something.

"We need to hit my offices now," Hawthorne told Ramirez, "blue's and two's will help."

"On it," Ramirez moved out to bring his car to the front. Hawthorne approached the slow simmering bomb that was Drake.

"Leila and Nigel found intel on Amelia, we need to

leave," Drake gazed toward the doors which led to Gunner and glanced at the exit. Shit.

"Davies has sent Niko and Max and corralled two of your prospects to get their asses back here. Ordered Jase and Hernando to provide back-up here Drake. Gunner will be protected, and the prospects will stay for Gunner," Hawthorne said. As the words left his mouth, Blaze and Hunter walked in followed by Apache.

"Go, I'll wait, bring Jett and girls back alive, hear me?" Apache said clasping Drake's arm. Drake nodded and took off after Ramirez and Hawthorne.

"What you got?" Hawthorne asked, pushing into the crowded conference room at his offices, it was full of Rage and his own men. Ramirez had kept the siren lit all the way to the offices and Drake had followed on his bike.

"We couldn't find anything. Then we checked the dark web, discovered this," Leila frowned and switched a screen on. Drake sucked in air as he stared at the picture on the screen. It was Amelia, she was sat staring at a camera, eyes wide and fearful. Amelia wore a new dress that he recognised Phoe had bought, and she clutched her pink teddy.

Next to her picture was a countdown and then a figure underneath. Drake sucked in his breath at the number. Drake's mind made an immediate connection, his eyes snapped back to the countdown.

"Got less than an hour, can you track her?" Drake roared.

"I'm trying, but this bastard is bouncing all over the place. I'm getting there but slowly," Nigel said, not raising his eyes.

"I'm bidding on her, but there are some determined fuckers out there. There's one that bids every time I get top," Leila said. "I'm countering every bid but…" Leila broke off and leant close to the screen, the breath hissed from her mouth.

"Back off now. The child belongs to Rage MC. Taking your life in your hands," Leila read a message out loud that popped up on her screen.

"What the fuck?" Hawthorne asked, pushing closer.

"What do I do boss?"

"Answer him."

"I'm aware she's a Rage child, I suggest you take a running jump. No one's getting her apart from me," Leila spoke as she typed back. A series of dots flickered, and then another message popped up.

"The infamous LG or NM. Keep bidding, one of us should win. JW," Leila read out loud.

"JW? James Washington? What's his stake in this?" Ramirez asked, spinning to Drake. Drake shrugged.

"Rage don't have dealings with Washington."

"So why the fuck is he throwing his hat in the ring? Leverage?" Ramirez asked puzzled.

"Nah, not Washington's style," Drake replied. He had an inkling why James Washington was involved, but he couldn't discuss it.

"Getting close," Nigel piped up, and the air snapped as Drake's temper flared again.

"Find, Amelia, now," Drake yelled as he saw Amelia cringe and realised it was a live feed. Fuckers were watching the little girl live! Ace locked his arms around Drake.

"Hold it in Drake!" Ramirez said, slamming a hand into

Drake's chest. "What's the plan? If Washington's involved that means his men are working on this too, I'd rather get to Amelia before he does."

"We need to take sectors so as soon as we get a location, we have to have someone near the location. One of Rage and one of ours, get our asses out there, we can have someone to Amelia within ten minutes," Davies said. Davies shifted the screen, and a large map of Rapid City appeared in quadrants.

"No need, I got a lock. They're at this address," Nigel said, springing to his feet, "let's go."

"You can't go," Ramirez said.

"Officer, I'm licensed and armed. If you think I'm sitting here when that little girl is about to become a paedophile's plaything, you got another thing coming matey." Nigel pushed past Ramirez. Footsteps thundered behind Nigel, Ramirez was calling it in, but they were closest to the address.

"What is Diego going to do, Jett? Where's Amelia?"

"Don't know baby," Jett replied, sorrowfully, that tone alarmed me more than being tied up.

"You do!" I screamed.

"Think they gonna sell Amelia, and as for us, I don't need to tell ya, babe," Jett sighed. "Sorry I dragged you into this, never meant for this to happen."

"Fuck that, fuck Dina, fuck all of this. I love you, and that whacked out bitch does not understand what that means," I yelled at Jett. He needed to get angry, angry Jett made things happen.

"How sweet," Diego said from the shadows. Diego switched the lights back on, and I blinked furiously against them. I was still sat in the position he'd left me. Diego put a laptop down and dragged me over to the wall near Jett.

"Bastard," I spat, he laughed.

"Shall we see how much money our little sweetie pie is raising to pay off Mommy's debt?" Diego grinned as Dina staggered in, appearing even more whacked out. He opened the laptop, and my eyes flew to it. A picture of my baby girl looked terrified hit me, and I gagged when I saw the amounts being placed on Amelia and the time left. Jett threw his head back and roared soundlessly. Ten minutes, that's all Amelia had, ten minutes.

"How can you do this?" I shrieked at Dina, she smiled drunkenly.

"The money she's making should keep me stocked for a year at least."

"You're whacked," I shrieked at her. I suddenly saw a comment pop up on the screen.

"This kid is on the amber list. Police searching all over for her, I'm withdrawing," I laughed. I nodded my head as three bidders pulled out. Diego turned to look his face blackening, and another message popped up.

"Kid belongs to Rage MC. Ain't messing with an MC."

"Kid is too hot. Not worth this, police, Rage MC and Juno Group all over this."

"Just got word Hawthorne's is hunting for the kid. Forget it." One by one lights popped off as people withdrew and several of them the high bidders. I laughed as Diego went mad and began slapping Dina.

"Not gonna get Amelia sold now are you?" Diego turned to me fury in his gaze, he eyed my torn blouse, and a chill spiralled through me. Not again! I couldn't handle this again, Diego's eye's promised pain and humiliation. Jett's angry roar caught me, and I gazed at him, Jett strained against his bonds. I had to get a grip, handle this, Jett would get free, just had to wait.

"Highest bid is still thirty k. Wonder what I'd get for a Rage cunt, Rage got enemies out there," Diego said and dragged me in front of Jett. He crouched down and forced me to face Jett. I shivered in fear as his hand reached down and grabbed my breast squeezing hard. A whimper escaped me.

"Gonna fuck her, then I'm gonna sell what's left of your wife," Diego sneered. His face came close to mine from behind, and I snapped my teeth at him. Diego laughed as he ripped my blouse off completely. I tried to cower, but Diego threw me down to the ground, and I cried out, my head turned, and I found Jett's horrified and enraged gaze.

"Don't watch, please don't watch," I begged Jett. Hands groped beneath my skirt, and then it began ripping. Fear began choking me memories of Rouse's grasping hands drifted to the surface. Dina stepped up behind Jett, grabbing him by his hair and forcing Jett to watch. Dina was whispering things in his ear as she held a knife to his throat. A thin line of blood appeared, she held it that tight to him.

Jett's horrified eyes kept a lock on mine. Diego ripped my skirt entirely off, and I was in my underwear in front of him. I couldn't fight back, I had to be brave, I couldn't let this destroy Jett and myself. Jett roared and slammed his head back into Dina's face.

Blood squirted, and Dina screamed, letting go of his head. Dina covered her face with her hands and tried to stem the bleeding from her nose. Unable to stop, I laughed hysterically. Jett slammed back a second time, and I kept my eyes on my husband even as Diego cut my bra and panties from me. Diego fumbled at his belt, and then he crouched behind me.

Jett was a roaring mess of anger, he slammed backwards a third time, and his chair fell to the side. His weight smashed it, and I saw Jett struggling with his ropes. Diego rose to his feet just as Jett got a hand free and grabbed the knife Dina held. Dina shrieking like a banshee tried to grab his arm and as I watched Jett twisted the knife and slammed it upwards.

I didn't look away as the knife rammed through the underside of Dina's chin and up into her head. Blood spurted everywhere, and Jett continued to try and get free. Diego kicked me to one side and moved on Jett. Jett still had one arm tied, and I screamed as Diego grabbed my man's head and pulled a knife. Diego was cursing and spitting manically, and I screamed Jett's name.

The door burst open, and a figure came flying down the stairs. I gasped as I caught a flash of red hair and then a knife hit Diego in his hand. Diego screamed and dropped his weapon. A second knife hit him in his arm, and a third hit Diego straight in the chest. Artemis flew towards Diego and grabbed the knife from his chest and stabbed it straight into his groin.

Diego went down, screaming. Artemis was silent as she fell backwards to the floor and kicked upwards with her feet embedding the knife to the hilt in Diego's groin. Artemis spun around and flipped back to her feet. Moving fast, she used a knife to cut Jett free, and I screamed as Diego rose to his knees with a gun pointed at her. She shoved Jett to one side and dived the other way.

The sound of the gun firing echoed, and I screamed again, not knowing if Jett or Artemis was hit. Jett was moving at the same time as Artemis, he ripped the knife from Dina's skull and slammed it into Diego's throat. Artemis was launching throwing stars straight at Diego's heart, and four landed millimetres apart from each other. Jett leaned forward and grabbed the dying man's head.

"Suck it up fucker, you're gonna be our message to anyone who thinks to fuck with Rage." Diego tried saying something and blood fell from his lips. Jett calmly grabbed the end of the knife hanging from Diego's throat and slammed it home. I watched as the light died from his eyes.

Drake, Ramirez, Hawthorne, Lowrider and Mac, came barrelling down the stairs. Seconds later, the rest of Rage came behind them. Drake stopped at the bottom, taking in the scene. Drake turned back to Ramirez.

"Get out of here, brother," Drake said. Ramirez shook his head.

"Need a shirt," Jett snarled. His own ripped beyond repair and his body covering my naked one. Drake ripped his tee off, and Artemis was at my back, cutting my bonds, and Jett jammed Drake's tee over my head. I didn't give a shit that most of Rage and their friends had seen me naked. The moment I was covered, I launched upwards, my legs weak and slammed into Jett. I grabbed Jett in a stranglehold, and he pulled me in tight.

"Killed her too quick," I snarled in his ear. I'd never known hate, dislike, disgust, yeah but never hate. I'd learned hate now, Dina had taught me to hate and I hated her with passion. Jett's body tensed and then relaxed, Artemis sent me a surprised but approving look.

"What happened?" Ramirez asked, Jett and Artemis began to tell their stories. Ramirez made a motion with his hand. "Suspect had a knife to Jett's throat as you entered Artemis?" Ramirez said his eyes blazing into hers, she nodded at once. Jett agreed.

"It was self-defence," Artemis said, finally.

"Self-defence I can work with," Ramirez intoned. His partner Ben came down the stairs and looked around.

"What a fucking shit storm," Ben cursed.

"Where's my daughter? Where's Amelia?" I asked panic clawing at my throat, my baby wasn't here. I spun in Jett's arms and looked around frantically.

"Got her," a boom echoed down the stairs. At the top of them was Texas with my little girl curled into his arms, and Amelia's head buried in his neck. Texas's big handheld her head tight so Amelia didn't see the horrific scene below her. I flew from Jett's arms and pushed through everyone and ran up the stairs. I made a grab for Amelia and Texas pulled me out of the room and then handed her to me.

"Four more bodies upstairs," Texas said, "just stay here, Sin." I nodded clinging tightly. Jett's arms encircled us, and I fell back into them, it was over. We were safe. I was terrified that the police may arrest Jett, but with his own wounds, it was apparent it was self-defence, surely?

"Let's get you out of here," someone said, and I peered up into a stranger's eyes. "I'm Davies, Hawthorne's second in command." I nodded and allowed Davies to lead me away with Jett. To my surprise, another man was waiting outside, holding a medical bag.

"Doc," Jett said just as his legs gave out from under him. Davies caught Jett with a grunt, and another man helped Davies lay Jett down on the ground. Texas came up from behind and moved me forward towards an SUV. I began arguing but Texas tilted his head at Amelia and awareness sank in that Amelia shouldn't see her Daddy like this. I got into the SUV, and Texas stood guard.

Sirens wailed in the distance, and I watched as an ambulance screeched up followed by several police cars. Rage and Hawthorne men filed out and hovered around Jett. Artemis strolled out, looking calm and collected, and I found it hard to rationalise this new Artemis to the one I knew at the clubhouse. She strolled over to the SUV.

"Let's get you to the hospital, the ambulance will meet us there. Jett's stable," Artemis said, swinging into the driver's seat. I gave her a head tilt, unable to say anything as the day's events finally caught up with me.

"Say nothing until our lawyer gets to you. Nothing honey, you understand?" Artemis asked gently, and I nodded. She said nothing else but carried on driving to the hospital, after that, everything became a blur.

I'd been checked over and so had Amelia and we'd both been given the all-clear. We sat in the waiting room with members of Rage and Hawthorne's. I'd been brought up to speed on Gunner's condition and Reid's. Both men were stable for now although Gunner remained in ICU. Silvie hadn't left the hospital since the phone call and looked devastated.

Jett was having his shoulder and stomach stitched up, and we were waiting on word from him. Turned out Dina had been the one to slice his stomach open and use the knife on him, that whacked out bitch died too quickly. Detectives Ramirez and Benjamin had remained at the scene, and we were expecting officers to arrive at any moment for statements. I kept worrying, and finally, Drake took me to one side and clarified that no matter what, no one would get into trouble or be arrested.

It was a clear case of self-defence, Artemis had acted to save Jett from having his throat slit. Artemis claimed she stumbled with the groin shot although we knew different. As Drake pointed out, knowing and proving were two different things. Drake didn't think the police would push too hard on this one considering that kidnapping, child trafficking and drugs were involved.

Throw in battery, attempted murder and attempted rape, Drake said we'd nothing to worry about. When Artemis had come for us, she'd arrived first at the house we'd been held in, Rage hadn't been far behind. Artemis entered first on her own, coming for us first. Drake, Lowrider and Mac had joined her search. Ace had led the others to find Amelia.

Once they had Amelia, which was quicker than Drake had found us, they came looking for Drake. I was told that the door to the basement had been well hidden, if not for my screaming, Artemis may have been too late. Hawthorne's men had stayed to protect Texas and Amelia, while Rage came after us. I looked across to Artemis and a weight lifted from my shoulders. Hands touched my shoulders, and I twisted and curled into Manny's muscular silent strength.

"You okay?" Manny asked, I shook my head. I was still dressed in Drake's tee, which hung halfway down my thighs.

"I'm a bad person," I told Manny, clutching his shoulders.

"Honey?"

"I told Jett he killed Dina too quick, I wanted her to suffer." I bit my lip as Manny stared at me in disbelief.

"You said what?" Manny asked as if he'd misheard me.

"I told Jett he killed Dina too quick, I really wanted her

to suffer like Amelia had." Manny kept staring at me and then suddenly threw his head back and laughed loudly. Everyone looked in our direction.

"Fuck me, who'd have thought it?" Manny finally chuckled. Manny twisted his head and told a perplexed Lex what I'd said. Lex laughed and turned and told the others. Laughter joined Lex's, a very definite look of approval from Artemis, smiles and a few chuckles. A mother's hatred remained in my heart, hatred towards the one person who should have protected Amelia against all danger.

"Jett got a good'un," Texas approved. He was still smiling when a doctor came and told us Jett would be free to go soon.

Detectives Ramirez and Benjamin found Jett and me in Reid's room. Reid had regained consciousness during our kidnapping, and while he was beaten black and blue, he'd be okay. The detectives wanted our statements which were near enough identical.

We'd been eating breakfast when there'd been a knock at the door. Reid answered it and had been attacked. Jett and I had been alerted by yelling, and Jett tried to help when the back door was kicked in, and a masked man held a gun to my head. Jett and Reid stopped fighting at once as another man grabbed Amelia with a gun to her head.

Two of the men had carried on beating Reid while I could only watch helplessly. In front of me, they'd stabbed Jett in his shoulder. Jett hadn't been able to fight back not with guns aimed at mine and Amelia's heads. They'd knocked Jett unconscious and left Reid for dead, they had bundled us into a van and driven us away. The rest you know.

It had been agreed that Gunner's attack had been separate to ours, completely unrelated. Sheer bad luck both attacks happened on the same day. Ramirez informed Jett there was nothing on the streets concerning the attack on Gunner, it was a complete puzzle. Gunner had yet to regain consciousness, and we were anxious.

Drake and Hawthorne had been on the phone ever since arriving at the hospital, and their countenances became blacker and blacker. Neither men seemed to get the answers they wanted. Ben kept throwing worried looks over his shoulder at them.

Artemis had gone hunting when we came up to sit with Reid, I didn't understand what it meant. But I'd overheard a woman called Dana, who worked as Hawthorne's secretary, tell him they'd leads on those who bid on Amelia. On hearing that Artemis had 'gone hunting', Ramirez turned a blind eye to it, and Ben seemed frustrated.

Seemed everyone understood what 'gone hunting' meant apart from me, but I could guess. Oh yes, I could most certainly guess, and I hope Artemis got a damn good catch. In fact, reading the newspapers several months in the future, Artemis got more than a damn good score.

Artemis and the Juno Group brought down an entire paedophile ring. Powerful perverted men and provided irreversible evidence of their guilt. She'd been lauded a hero by the media and Rage had been under siege for a few weeks by the press, but soon enough they moved on. Artemis was my hero!

Reid insisted that we go home that night and wearily I climbed into Jett's pick-up tired out. Amelia was asleep in her car seat. Jett was uncomfortable on the way home, and I guessed something was eating him. Something other than Gunner's attack which had rocked Jett to his core. I let Jett boss me around when we got home, and we got Amelia to bed.

Jett seemed to be avoiding something. I kept seeing flashes of guilt and shame when Jett looked at me, and I decided to beard him when Jett came out of the shower. I waited for him to get into bed and then before Jett could roll over or anything else, I straddled him naked. Jett's eyes grew wide.

"Talk to me!" I demanded.

"Sin, honey, don't think this is a great idea."

"Why not?" I asked tilting my head to one side.

"You almost got raped today!" The words burst from Jett's lips angrily, and I saw that guilt again.

"But I didn't, you saved me," I told him simply. His eyes burned into mine, I could see just how furious Jett was with himself. This wouldn't do at all.

"Was tied and wounded, couldn't stop him stripping you bare baby. Was fuckin' useless," Jett ground out through clenched teeth.

"I didn't get raped because you got free and saved me. Now you might have nightmares, but I can damn well tell you I won't be. I knew you'd get free, knew you'd protect me, I didn't doubt you."

"You told me to look away."

"Of course, I did. You think I want the image in your head of another man stripping me naked? I wasn't telling you to look away because I was ashamed, I just didn't want you to do this to yourself." A shadow crossed his eyes.

"Failed you."

"Fuck that," I slapped Jett's chest, and his eyes widened,

surprise in them now. "I didn't get raped because you saved me. Our daughter didn't get sold and hurt because you got free. We had people looking for us because you joined Rage, one of the best fucking MCs' in the world." Jett's mouth dropped open, and then he closed it.

"You saw me kill Dina." I narrowed my eyes at that.

"Only thing that will keep me awake is the fact it was over so quick. You should have made that whacked out bitch suffer! What woman puts her daughter up for sale for paedophiles to buy and rape? What mother is that?" My voice began rising, and Jett glanced at Amelia's cot and then surged upwards and covered my mouth with his. When Jett had kissed me into silence, he looked into my eyes.

"It's not there," Jett muttered.

"What's not?" I asked puzzled.

"Fear of me, killed a woman like that, where's your fear?" Jett asked, as if he couldn't work it out.

"Why on earth would I fear you? You saved me, you saved Amelia, you love us. I have nothing to fear from you, silly." Jett's eyes searched mine, and finally, he slammed back into the bed, eyes still locked on my face.

"You mean it, you ain't afraid of me." I twisted my hips and slammed down beside him.

"Stupid man. Now shut up and make love to me." Jett chuckled.

"You're gonna have to do most of the work, tonight."

"Perfectly happy with that," I told my husband. I rolled back over and began kissing my way down his chest. Yeah, I was perfectly happy with that.

Drake rubbed his eyes wearily. Over the last forty-eight hours he'd hardly slept. Drake looked across to the bed where Gunner lay perfectly still. He'd still not woken up yet, but the doctors gave him a far better chance than twenty-four hours ago. The door opened, and Drake looked surprised as James Washington entered. James looked at Gunner and took a chair near to Gunner's bed.

Drake's thoughts raced as he studied a man he knew was dirtier than dirt. He'd only crossed paths with Washington in passing, but it was enough. The man's illegal activities rivalled Santos and Washington was a man that even Santos avoided. The fact James was here in Gunner's room meant shit was about to hit the fan, again.

"Why?" Drake wondered out loud, rubbing a hand over his face.

"Rage nearly destroyed Rapid City years ago in your war with Bulldog. I don't want to see my home ripped apart again. Plus I loathe child traffickers," James said simply. Drake nodded, and they sat there in silence.

"You have a problem," James said to Drake. Drake lent forward his elbows resting on his thighs, and his hands dangling loosely.

"I do?" Drake asked.

"Santos," James said. Drake rocked back in his chair, he hadn't expected that name as the one who put a hit on Gunner.

"Santos is comin' after the club?" Drake asked.

"Yup," James continued to look at Gunner. Worry creased his brow, and Drake sat back watching. "You know, don't you?" James asked Drake finally.

"Think you'll find there ain't much I don't know," Drake muttered still watching.

"Santos signed his death certificate when he came after

my brother." James rose to his feet and looked down at the bed. Then James looked Drake in the eyes. "Gunner's the better of us. The one who took the shit he was dealt and honed it. He's the better man, my little brother." Drake nodded as James turned on his heel. James stopped by the door.

"When he wakes, I'll tell Gunner, you were here," Drake muttered.

"No, don't, you understand how things are with us. Putting a hit on Gunner was a message to you, and I. Santos is a dead man walking," James left the room. Drake turned to see Gunner's silver-grey eyes focused on him. Gunner glanced towards the door where his brother had left and stared at Drake.

"War is comin' brother," Drake said, leaning forward. Gunner stared at Drake and then nodded.

Epilogue.

I sat on the bar stool wearing a cream dress Phoe had insisted I wear. We'd been shopping the day before, and Phoe had made me buy an entire outfit for today. All I knew is this was the meeting that should have happened three weeks ago but had been postponed until Gunner came home and everyone's injuries had healed.

Phoe and Artemis had their heads thrown back howling with laughter next to me. Opposite me, Mac, Ezra, Lowrider, Manny and Jett looked horrified. Jett's eyes kept searching my face as if to see if I was serious.

"You want Artemis to do what?" Manny finally asked.

"Teach me to fight like her, she's a supreme badass," I replied calmly and took a sip of my margarita. Manny and Mac shook their heads in disbelief.

"One Artemis running around is enough. Fuck we have Phoe can kick the shit out of anyone and Marsha is a crack shot. Don't need another badass," Lowrider was shaking his head, I nodded mine.

"I want to be Artemis," I disagreed, pointing at my hero.

"No, you don't," Ezra shook his head at me, trying to make me change my mind. Jett chuckled and wrapped a hand around the back of my neck.

"Prefer you not train like Artemis does," Jett told me. Humour lit his eyes, I bit my lip for a few seconds.

"Can Artemis teach me a few self-defence moves and how to shoot?" I asked, Jett nodded, and I shrieked and leapt off my stool and wrapped my arms around his neck. I kissed Jett madly, and he chuckled and kissed me back.

"Fuck me, we don't need another badass woman," Ezra said, shaking his head.

"They're all badass in their own way," Lowrider said.

"Prez wants everyone's attention," Ace bellowed as we looked up. Drake stood near the clubhouse doors, and people turned to face him. All the brothers, the old ladies and kids were present. Blaze, Slate and Hunter were behind the bar serving but came around to flank Jett. Ace, Gunner, Apache, Axel, Fish and Texas all took positions up next to Drake.

"Had a shit few weeks, but in those weeks, we'd sheer beauty too. Nineteen months ago, Alexander Cutter walked into our clubhouse looking for a place to call home. Sure we looked at the skills he'd bring to our garage," Drake paused, and chuckles met him, "but we also looked at what Cutter might bring to our club.

To be a brother in our club we've a few basic requirements. Loyalty, knowing what it is and what it means. Honour, to live your life the way it should be lived. Strength, not just in body but in force of character and beliefs. Protection, to protect your brothers, the old ladies and those weaker than us. Respect, for the life we live and the way we live it, and for those around us who earn it. Family, knowin' the meaning of what real family is, blood, club or extended family.

You know these values, you get a chance at prospect,

even so, knowin' these doesn't automatically make you one. Going balls to the wall for our beliefs and keeping true to your own convictions is a fuckin' hard thing to do. It's why we turn down so many applications to the club. Recognising Alexander Cutter had those values meant we called him prospect and named him Jett. Jett stand up in front," Drake ordered. He looked to Ace who stepped forward to speak.

"It takes a man, a Rage man to survive and thrive these last few months. Didn't make it easy on yourself or anyone else, brother," Ace chided and laughter rose. Jett looked sheepish. "I never doubted you had it in you brother, I did doubt that you could and would recognise beauty when it walked into your life. Took Manny a few lessons to knock that into you." More laughter and Drake continued.

"These last few weeks, I seen a prospect become a brother, a man grow into a hero, a loner become a lover, brother, father and husband. Saw a prospect go balls to the wall to protect what was his. His club, his family, his woman, his child. Never been prouder of you son, as I am today, standing here looking at what you earned. Knew you'd be unique, special enough for this club and I wasn't wrong.

Got a lot of love for you Jett, fuck load of love for you. Got so much feelin' for you I could burst. As of today Jett, know we the inner circle voted, and you are no longer welcome as a prospect here." Drake paused, and my heart thudded crazily. Oh my god, what was happening? Jett met Drake's eyes square on. Ace stepped up and to my bewildered eyes cut the prospect from Jett's cut, I gave a muted cry as Ace stepped back.

"Today Jett you became a brother, a full brother in Rage

MC. Welcome, brother!" Drake roared and slammed arms around Jett, lifting him off the floor. Jett threw back his head and howled with happiness. Drake put him down and handed Jett a new patch, Jett turned to the room and held it above his head and yelled again. I ran forward, and Jett swung me into his arms and kissed me soundly. Proudly Jett showed me his patch as everyone crowded round to offer congrats.

A wolf whistle cut through the room, and everyone looked up at Drake who was standing with Phoenix who had her arms behind her back. Jett grinning turned to look at her.

"He had his say," Phoe grumbled, "so mine's quick. Not every old lady has to marry her old man, it's nice when they do." Phoe glared at me and guilt welled that Phoe hadn't been able to see us get married. "When a brother finds his old lady, we get to welcome her into the sisterhood." Phoe brought her arms out from behind, and I saw she was carrying a leather cut. It had the Rage patch on the front with the words Rage MC. When Phoe turned it around, it had a large Rage patch in the middle of the back. Around it was the words. 'Sin, Jett's Old Lady.' I squealed, and Phoe walked forward so I could shrug it on.

Jett grabbed me for another breath-stealing kiss and tugged me closer, he ran his hands over my cut and whistled approvingly.

"Everyone outside," Drake hollered ten minutes later as people finally stopped offering their congratulations. Manny stopped by my side, but Drake dragged Jett out by his arm. I heard laughter from outside and looked at Manny, wondering why I couldn't go outside.

"Remember never to cross Phoe again," Manny teased

as he handed me a bouquet of roses. I frowned at my hands and looked up at him, Manny took my arm and linked it through his. As we stepped outside and Manny led me around to the back of the clubhouse, I gazed bemusedly at the streamers and ribbons decorating the place. They were in pinks, lilacs and pale blues. As we stepped around the corner, I gasped.

"What's going on?" I asked. Looking up at the grassed area, I saw a gazebo covered in flowers and ribbons. In the middle of it stood Axel, I'd only met the colossal mountain of a man a few days ago.

Axel had been away on family business and just returned. To his left was Jett standing with Drake and Ace. A little behind them and to the right was Mac playing a set of drums, Hunter on bass guitar, Texas on keyboards and Slick was singing 'Sweet child o' mine.' My mouth opened in shock. As I looked around, the rest of Rage, their old ladies and families stood at the front.

I clapped eyes on my shop staff and Reid, who appeared at my other side and took my other arm. Mr Kenna was there along with his cold case club and my old ladies book reading club. All of Hawthorne's were there, including Dana and Leila. I saw Detectives Ramirez and Ben, and some of Phoe's office staff were there, who were customers at the Reading Nook. Phoe approached me with a grin and Amelia in a frilly bridesmaid dress.

"Phoe?" I asked, having a good sense of what was now happening.

"You don't run away to get married. Next brother that thinks he can, be warned!" Phoe said loudly into a lull in the singing. I laughed along with everyone else, and Slick broke into the chorus. Phoe took her place in front of me with Amelia, who suddenly discovered she could throw flower petals down. My daughter cheerfully threw handfuls everywhere until she clapped eyes on her Daddy.

With a muted shriek Amelia wrenched free from Phoe's hand and launched herself down the aisle to her father. Jett swung her up, laughing. Amelia had been quiet for a week after the kidnapping, but she began to blossom under the attention she received. Not just from Jett, Reid and I, but Rage and the children of Rage. Amelia clapped her hands to Jett's face, and then I was there in front of Axel.

"Which badass brother gives this woman away?" Axel boomed.

"I do," Reid said loudly.

"Which badass biker gives this woman away?" Axel boomed looking at Manny, I laughed as Manny replied.

"I do."

"Woman you're being given to our brother Jett by two badasses, you got an issue with that?" By the look on Axel's face, I better not have.

"No," I laughed. Axel turned to Jett.

"Jett, brother of Rage MC, father of Amelia, father of my countless un-named grandchildren yet to come, do you take this woman to be your old lady? To have and to hold, to love and to sex up, to hold her hair back when she pukes. And to fall over her high heels for the rest of your life?" I was laughing with everyone else as Jett shouted loudly that he did. Axel turned to me as I wiped tears from my eyes.

"Sin of the beautiful eyes and face and the body made for lovin' and children. Do you take this poor excuse of a brother to be your old man? To have and to hold? To nag and bitch, to pick up dirty clothes and odd socks for the rest of your life, to be sexed up like mad whenever the feeling takes?" I was laughing so hard I couldn't reply. Axel glared at me.

"I do, I do!" I shrieked, gasping for breath I was laughing so much, and Axel nodded firmly.

"I as Chaplin of Rage MC declare you to be Old Man and Old Lady, ball and chain, beauty and the beast, Badass biker dude and Badass biker babe. Everyone, I give you Mr and Mrs Alexander Cutter, known as Jett and Sin," Axel boomed at the top of his lungs. Jett kissed me hard with Amelia between us.

"Mama, Papa," Amelia squealed, and we looked at her. Oh my god, did she just speak?

"Amelia?" Drake asked crowding round.

"Mama and Papa! Unca Dray, Aun' Nix!" Amelia squealed and threw her head back and laughed. "Grandpapa Al," Amelia squealed again, and Jett gathered me in his arms and kissed me harder. Axel swooped and grabbed Amelia and tossed her in the air. Mac began a beat on the drums and Texas, and Hunter came in a few seconds later, and Slick began belting out Take Me Home, Country Road.

Life was good, life was great. That shy, socially awkward woman had finally found a home. It had just taken a while.

The Rage of Reading Characters.

There are a lot of characters in the Rage books so I thought I'd give everyone a helping hand with who is who. As more of the Rage brothers find their girls, we'll add them to this page! Keep an eye out for Lindsey and Lowrider, next up! This book takes place at the end of March when Dante is three weeks old. (For those who like a timeline!)

Rage MC
Rage Patch. The patch is a barbed wire circular design, with flames interwoven. A Harley Davidson with Charon sat on the bike. Charon holds flaming scythe in one hand that curves around the back of him. On the front of the bike in place of a light, is a blue and purple flaming skull. On the back of the bike is a blue flaming eagle.

Drake Michaelson. DOB 1975. His father started Rage MC and died before Drake was old enough to become President. He became V.P. and then in a hostile takeover became President. Phoenix thinks he looks like Tim McGraw with longer hair, Drake has a lanky leanness to him but has well-defined muscles. Drake sports dark brown eyes with laughter lines, he's six foot 4. March

2015 his son Dante Chance Michaelson was born. Drake considers Detective Antonio Ramirez and PI Dylan Hawthorne close friends.

Apache. DOB 1967. He is one of Drakes enforcers. Ace is his only son. Apache was widowed when Ace was young. He has bright green eyes and is six foot two. He is Native American. Apache's described as absolutely stunning with gorgeous, high cheekbones, raven black hair that hangs past his shoulders. He was born in 1969. Silvie Stanton has been in love with him for many years.

Ace. DOB 1983. Ace is Drake's VP. He's described as looking like a young Lou Diamond Philips. Like his father, he is Native American. Ace has bright green eyes, six foot two. He is described much the same as his father, absolutely stunning with gorgeous, high cheekbones and raven black hair that hangs past his shoulders. Ace was in love with Kayleigh Mitchell and thought she'd left him. Ace discovers out that Kayleigh hadn't left him but instead had been tortured and left for dead. He has two children Nova and Falcon.

Fish. DOB 1978. Fish is Drake's sergeant at arms. He's been married to Marsha for many years, they can't have children.

Marsha. DOB 1979. Fish's old lady and the only old lady until Phoe meets Drake. She's known to be kind and caring.

Texas. DOB 1970. Texas is an older man, he is the MC's secretary. He was born in 1970. Does bike design and specialised paintwork. Has a daughter. Texas has a strong moral code, but he is aware of what the MC is capable of. He once alludes to cleaning up after their messes.

Axel. DOB 1951. Axel was one of the founders of the club. He is the Chaplin of the MC. He has blue eyes, and he is heavily bearded and very loud. He's built like a mountain. Axel has wild hair which hangs to his shoulders. Axel disappears in The Hunters Rage. There is mention of his messed-up kids, and Axel has gone to resolve an issue with them. He returns at the end of this book to marry Sin and Jett.

Gunner. DOB 1976. Gunner is one of Drakes Enforcers at the MC. Gunner is described as having silver-grey eyes. He was shot three times, in the Rage of Reading, resulting in heart surgery. He is the younger brother of James Washington.

Slick. DOB 1978. Slick loves books and is happy reading quietly. He has soft brown eyes and is heavily muscled. Slick loves reading and is singlehandedly keeping the Reading Nook open!

Manny. DOB 1983. Manny takes an interest in Sin, and threatens to make a move on her if Jett doesn't pull his head out of his ass! He's described as tall, sexy as in the cute boy next door way, tousled blond hair, light amber coloured eyes. Manny is firm in teaching Jett how to treat a woman like Sin.

Lowrider. DOB 1984.
Ezra. DOB 1979.
Mac. DOB 1970.
Rock. DOB 1985.

Lex. DOB 1984.
Blaze. Prospect.
Slate. Prospect.

Jett. DOB. 1990. Prospect Alexander Cutter. Jett is described as having black hair, dark brown eyes, high cheekbones, a square jawline and firm, soft lips. He was slightly taller than Reid and broader, but he was lean hipped, long-legged and as tightly muscled as Reid. Mechanic, engine designer, and paintwork designer. Jett finds out he has a daughter Amelia, who he gains custody of with Sin. Jett is estranged from his family after his brother Martin slept with Jett's fiancée, and then everyone took Martin's side.
Hunter. Prospect. Hunter is also a designer for paintwork on bikes.

Rage Old Ladies.

Phoenix Michaelson. DOB 1979. Drake's old lady/wife. She's English and left England to escape an abusive relationship. She has six children she gave birth to and adopted eleven. Phoe is exceedingly well off and runs three National Charities. The Phoenix Trust, the Rebirth Trust and the Eternal Trust. She has been married three times, the first husband died and her second was a bigamist. Drake is her third husband. Phoe is blond and green-eyed and is five foot tall. She met Hellfire MC first and is loyal to them, Chance Michaelson is her closest friend. Ace is Phoe's alternative guy in Rage.

Artemis aka Kayleigh Mitchell. She has red curly hair, green eyes, she's small, dainty and muscled. She was born in 1987. Heart-shaped pixie face full lips. Kayleigh was taken in by Master Hoshi, and out of her alleged death, Artemis arose. She's a famous bounty hunter and runs a team who operate under the name Artemis. She was part of a group called Revenge before she left and became Artemis group. The Artemis Group became the Juno group when she went legal with her efforts. She has combat skills and has killed many times. Artemis's alternative guy is Drake.

Sinclair Montgomery. DOB 1993. Sin takes over her father's shop the Reading Nook when he dies, and with Reid, they turn it into something special. Sin was an only child, and Reid became her surrogate brother. She is socially awkward and inept and feels out of place in crowds. She's described as dainty with brown hair and big blue eyes. She doesn't think she's pretty, but people describe her as beautiful. Sin has low self-esteem created by attending college and university when she was fifteen. Manny is Sin's alternative guy.

Silvie Stanton. She's looked at as an old lady even though she doesn't have an old man. She's kind and generous. The MC has a lot of respect for her. She has blond, curly hair and is close to Gunner.

HQ Staff in this book.

Emily. Emily is Phoe's personal assistant. She is young and wild and likes colour.
North. Director of Public Relations.

Phoenix's kids in this book.

Eddie and Tony 2010 African American, adopted 2012. Eddie is a hellion and Tony is her quieter shadow.
Dante Michaelson. March 2015.

The Artemis Group, aka the Juno Group, in this book.

Akemi. Akemi is Japanese. He is tall and slender with well-defined muscles. Master Hoshi calls him his son and Artemis thinks of him as a brother. There are no lengths they will not go to for each other.
Nigel. Nigel is a hacker, he has a wiry and slender build. He's often mistaken for being a geek but is as deadly as the others. Nigel's known to have hacked into government databases.

RCPD.

Antonio Ramirez. He is over six-foot-tall and has black wavy hair, olive tanned skin. He is Mexican and has brown soft, gentle eyes, Tonio is lean hipped and long-legged and broad-shouldered. He is a good cop, and

Drake thinks a lot of him.

Eric Benjamin. Known as Ben. Partner of Ramirez. He's a clean cop and thinks Ramirez sometimes turns a blind eye to Rage, but he'll always back his partner up.

Hawthorne's Investigations.

Dylan Hawthorne. Owner of Hawthorne investigations. He is extremely intelligent and will bend and break the rules as he sees fit. He thinks of Drake as a brother.
Davies. Hawthorne investigator.
Dana. The Hawthorne receptionist, she's 28 years old.
Leila Gibson. She is Hawthorne's computer genius. She managed to get a trace on Artemis which led Rage to Artemis, Stacy Conway identity.
Niko. Hawthorne Investigator. Protects the Vault in the Rage of Reading.
Max. Hawthorne's Investigator. He followed Ace when Ace went to rescue Phoe in the Rage of the Phoenix.
Jase. Hawthorne's investigator.
Hernando. Hawthorne's investigator.

The Reading Nook

Amos Montgomery. An Englishman who had lived in Rapid City for forty years. He has a daughter Sinclair. He died when he was fifty, which brought Sin to his shop to run it. His shop is called Reading Nook. Amos wasn't very sociable, and Sin is the same as her Dad. They were very close, Amos wanting the best for Sin and his surrogate son Reid.

Penny. Is a cook and server at Reading Nook. She loves cooking and makes everything from scratch. She has a warm and caring attitude to her.

Andy. Andy is a computer wiz hired by Reid to set up the networking and laptops in the Reading Nook. Andy also developed the website and for the data packages for the shop. Andy runs the computer side of the business. Andy also runs the StudentZone.

Reid Hershley. Reid went to Oxford with Sin and studied literacy and archaeology. He has beautifully chiselled features. Shaggy blond hair, he's lean and rangy and works out at a gym so has well-defined muscles. Wears round glasses. He was loosely adopted by Amos Montgomery and thinks of Sin as a sister. He is well known in his field and quit England to move to Rapid City with Sin. He was disowned by his family for going to University.

Celine. Shop-girl.

Zoe. Has large blue eyes and is a shop-girl.

Henry. Short for Henrietta. Henry is a barista.

Mr Rouse. A pushy buyer for the Lady Downing papers, he attacks Sin over them.

Mr Earl Kenna. Runs' a cold case club and interrupts the attack on Sin.

Finally…

James Washington. We find out James is Gunner's older brother. He appears when Gunner is shot. He claims Santos is going to war with rage and himself. James skirts the illegal side of life and is someone Santos is afraid of.

Byword.

Thank you for reading the Rage of Reading. Do check out the other titles in this series, and also take a gander at the Love Beyond Death Series, book one of which, Oakwood Manor is out now! If you enjoyed this book, please leave a review at,

Goodreads.com and Amazon. Your reviews are so important to me!

Check out the Rage original wild man, Texas in Rage's Heat in the next book of Rage MC.

Thank you!

Elizabeth.

Printed in Poland
by Amazon Fulfillment
Poland Sp. z o.o., Wrocław